Greek Island Mys

(Stand-alone thriller)

THE OLYMPUS KILLER

By Luke Christodoulou

Cover design: Maria Nicolaou (Mj.Vass)

Edited by: Tamarind Hill Press

Published by: G.I.M.

Praise for THE OLYMPUS KILLER

(Greek Island Mystery #1 – Stand-alone Thriller)

BOOK OF THE MONTH (May 2014) - Psychological Thrillers (GOODREADS)
BOOK OF THE MONTH (June 2014) - Nothing better than reading (GOODREADS)
BOOK OF THE MONTH (October 2014) - Ebook Miner (GOODREADS)

'...unlike many crime thrillers I have read before--which tend to be heavy and depressing by their very nature and the crimes and events upon which the plots are constructed--I did not find that to be the case with this novel. Quite the contrary. Mr. Christodoulou adeptly weaves anecdotal humor into the novel, along with Greek mythology, history, rich and flavorful Greek culture and food--all without detracting from the seriousness of the events--while bringing the story to brilliant life. For life is what continues to happen despite tragedy striking and heinous crimes ripping people's worlds apart.'
AuthorM.J.

'A journey of fast paced kills and sharp turns through the exotic Greek islands. The location descriptions were wonderful, descriptive and accurate. It is well written with intense action and superb characterization (foul mouth Ioli Cara and a couple of very Greek grandmothers were highly enjoyable). As seductive as a Sudoku puzzle, the writer has crafted an ingenious plot with nothing less than stunning revelations at the conclusion. In short, if you want a book that will shock and thrill you, read this one.'
Author J.Salisbury

'Truly a mystery to rival Patterson.' Ruth Rowley, USA

'An excellent, spellbinding psychological thriller.' Jimmy Andrea, UK

'The Olympus Killer is one amazing book...' Raghavendra. India

'I highly recommend this book to everyone...' Kristin T, Canada

'An interesting twist on the usual psychological thrillers, I found it well-written and also quite interesting in terms of the Greek mythological elements to it.' MrsG, UK

Books by Luke Christodoulou:

The Olympus Killer (Greek Island Mystery #1) - 2014

The Church Murders (Greek Island Mystery #2) - 2015

24 Modernized Aesop Fables - 2015

Death of A Bride (Greek Island Mystery #3) - 2016

Murder on Display (Greek Island Mystery #4) - 2017

Hotel Murder (Greek Island Mystery #5) - 2018

Twelve Months of Murder (Greek Island Mystery #6) - 2019

Beware of Greek Bearing Gifts - 2020

Don't forget to follow me on **BOOKBUB** for more future deals: https://www.bookbub.com/profile/luke-christodoulou?list=about

Sign up to my newsletter and receive a short story for free: https://greekislandmysteries.webs.com/

To my wife Polina for her love, support and patience.

Thank you for reminding me to live life to the fullest.

THE OLYMPUS KILLER

"As Dawn prepared to spread her saffron mantle over the land, Zeus the Thunderer gathered the gods to the highest peak of many-ridged Olympus, and spoke to them while all listened: 'Hear me, gods and goddesses, while I say what my heart prompts. Let none of you try to defy me..."

HOMER, The Iliad, Book VIII

Chapter 1

The bright Greek sun had just sunk into the ocean.

It had been a beautiful sunset. The way the light jumped upon the waves, en-flaming the waters of Vathy Bay, was spectacular.

''Eye candy,'' Stacy thought as she ambled past the colorful, little fishing boats, all lined up, waiting for their masters to arrive, before setting off for the night's late catch.

Stacy realized that this was the first time she had truly been alone since her divorce was finalized last week, back home in L.A. Her socialite friends had persuaded her to get away from it all and the very next day, they were on their way to the Greek island of Rhodes.

It was so quiet and peaceful by the rock where she had sat and stared at the full moon. She gazed upon the shadowy still ships sleeping on the dark horizon, before taking off her red Manolo Blahnik heels and carefully climbing down to lie on the golden sandy beach, isolated by the rocks from the rest of the world. All the aloneness felt a tad weird after being surrounded by crowds of every age and color imaginable, just a few days ago at Faliraki, Rhodes main club scene. After Rhodes, the gang headed to the island of Ko, where they continued to party hard. She smiled as she remembered them all lined up on the bar counter at Jackson's Beach Bar dancing the night away. Now, she was enjoying the serenity offered by the island of Samos. Jennifer, Ginger and the rest of the girls had done a terrific job taking her around the Greek islands – island-hopping as

Ginger liked to call it - to help her forget him. Him. She wondered what 'The God' was up to at the moment. That's what everyone called him at the company.

''Hmm... to everyone but me,'' she thought out loud. Deep down, certain feelings lingered in her, but she could no longer bear the pain of staying with him.

''Cheating bastard,'' she said and closed her eyes.

''Beautiful night.'' A voice from behind her interrupted her reverie.

Startled, she let out a brief scream as she leaped to her feet and turned towards the direction of the voice.

''I'm so sorry. I didn't mean to scare you,'' the handsome, black-haired man rushed to say, the moonlight revealing his sparkling green eyes as it danced across his face.

''I don't scare that easily,'' she replied, trying to catch her breath. ''You surprised me, that's all. How long have you been there?''

''Oh, I'm not a stalker,'' he joked, mocking her with his smooth, relaxing voice. ''I come here to write.'' His whole face lit up as he produced a silver Parker pen and a thin red notebook out of his backpack as evidence.

''So, you live here?''

''No, only been here a couple weeks. I'm on holiday too. Alone,'' he pointed out. ''Tom Smith,'' he said, stretching out his right hand.

''Stacy Anderson,'' she replied. Her hand fitted perfectly into his. It felt strange using her maiden name again. Even stranger was the fact that she felt comfortable with this man she had just met. Ginger would have been so proud to see them sitting side by side in the sand, making small talk as the warm Aegean Sea caressed their feet.

''So, what are you writing about?'' Stacy inquired.

''It's a *thriller!*'' he announced, deepening his voice and taking on a scary tone. They both laughed. It had been a while since she had laughed and meant it.

''I love thrillers,'' she said with flirtatious excitement.

It was the last thing Stacy Anderson ever said. As the knife hit her chest and penetrated her heart, Stacy tried to catch a breath and scream out, but Tom's left hand quickly covered her mouth. His right hand lifted the knife again and the blade flashed silver in the moonlight. Blood was dripping from its sharp end as he stabbed her again with more passion this time and with obvious exhilaration in his devilish green eyes. All seven hits were to her heart. Tom leaned in close and slowly unbuttoned her bloody shirt, taking his time before turning his attention to the button of her jeans.

He gazed upon her beautiful, naked body and gently touched her fake breasts. They were perfect; probably the best money could buy.

Then, with savage fury, he plunged the knife between Stacy's legs, burying it deep inside her, before slicing viciously upward. Tom stopped, pleased that the pomegranate in his bag would fit. He stood up, admiring his work. He then walked into the water and with a smile of satisfaction upon his face, Tom swam away.

*****

Chapter 2

8:47 and as always, here in Greece, I was early. I laughed at the thought that New York made me quick. Apparently, the years of being a homicide detective in the Big Apple had left their marks on me. Athens was a jungle too, but a smaller jungle than my previous one. Just an hour ago, I had received a phone call from one of the many charming secretaries down at Headquarters.

''Captain Costa Papacosta?''

''Yes?''

''Good morning,'' she said with a dull tone and proceeded to inform me that the chief had requested to see me. My office down Athinon Avenue, where the crime investigations department was housed, would not be seeing me today. I had to be at Headquarters at nine o'clock sharp.

''What is this about?'' I said as I managed to interrupt her fast flow of words. *We Greeks talk fast, but boy, this girl took the cake.*

''Be there at nine. Have a nice day, Captain,'' she said, and the phone went silent.

Captain. I still haven't gotten used to being called Captain. Since I quit the NYPD two years ago, came back to my homeland and joined the force here, I had been Police Lieutenant Costa Papacosta.

It was still a step back from being a N.Y. detective and the money, believe it or not, was even lousier, but I did not care. I wanted to get away. Besides, life here is cheaper than back in the States and you actually get to see the sun every day.

9:12, the clock said, and I was still sitting in the badly-lit hallway on the top floor of the huge, grey building with the hundred little windows that was the headquarters of the Hellenic Police.

A few minutes later, a tall girl with huge brown eyes hidden behind strict, black, reading glasses, wearing a tight 'woman's suit' and a fake smile, informed me that the chief was ready to see me now.

''Was he preparing himself all this time?'' I said and earned myself a semi-confused, semi-angry look as she did not register my attempt at a joke. Maybe the tight suit squeezed all the humour out of her body, leaving nothing behind but the perfect police secretary.

''Enter,'' she said coldly and showed me the slightly opened door with her right palm.

The office was huge compared to my own and just a little smaller than my filthy, rented apartment down at Ampelokipous. It was fitted with outdated, worn-out, Persian designed carpets. On the surrounding walls were portraits of past presidents, prime-ministers, retired chiefs, maps of Greece and various police symbols. The desk was made out of thick, dark Acacia wood and everything upon it was tidied in military fashion. The only thing that looked remotely homey in the whole place was a colorful, handmade frame with a photo of the chief at a younger age playing with his two boys.

“Sit down, Costa. We need to talk.”

I sensed a level of anxiety in his voice that I had never heard before. This was, after all, a man capable of scaring away Charo, the ferryman of the underworld himself! Well, at least that was what police officers joked about during very long coffee breaks.

“Good morning. What’s this about, chief?” I asked as I slowly placed myself in the maroon armchair opposite his desk.

“Do you watch the news, Costa?”

“Most times... yes,” I replied, slightly puzzled while picturing myself in my boxers sitting on my black leather couch with a kebab in one hand and a cold Mythos beer in the other, killing lonely nights in front of the TV.

“What do you know about the murder in Chania 5 days ago?” he asked.

“American tourist. In his late forties. Multimillionaire CEO of a major pharmaceutical company in Chicago. On holiday in Crete with a young, hotter-than-the-weather twenty-year-old. Also American. He was found dead a few kilometers away from his hotel in the outskirts of Chania. He was completely naked, tied to a tree, stabbed...”

“Stabbed? Now there’s an understatement! His whole stomach and head were cut open with his guts hanging out all over the place,” the chief interrupted. He then asked in a slightly calmer tone, ‘‘and what do you know about the murder in Samos 3 days ago?’’

‘‘Again, an American tourist. Early thirties. Rich, and if I may add, beautiful blonde woman. Police found her, naked on the beach, also stabbed.’’ As I answered, I realized the similarities, so the chief's next words did not shock me.

‘‘It was the same killer, Costa.’’

‘‘And what facts do we have to base this on?’’ I asked.

‘‘Always the Yankee detective,’’ the chief said, smiling at me. ‘‘The two were married until a week ago. A young lieutenant down in Crete made the connection. You see, the woman was using her maiden name. Got the lab results too, this morning and it confirmed that the two were struck by the same blade. The lieutenant’s name is Ioli Cara; she will be waiting for you in Crete tomorrow.’’

Now his words shocked me.

‘‘What? What do I have to do with all this?’’

The chief looked straight at me and spoke with the tone of a father explaining to his son that some things in life we have to do whether we like them or not.

‘‘You were a homicide detective in New York. You have seen freaky shit before.”

“Freaky shit? Sir, I don’t...”

"We kept the gruesome details out of the media," he admitted and took a deep breath that ended with a long sigh.

"The man's head was cut wide open and his brains were carved in half."

He gazed at me to check that he had my full attention and added, "the sick bastard even tore open the woman's vagina and placed a pomegranate inside her."

"A what?"

"You heard me, Papacosta! It's July. There are more tourists on the islands than locals. The victims were American, and any potential witnesses will most likely be tourists. I want you on this. End of discussion. Get your flight details from Helen outside and keep me informed."

Before I could say anything more, I was in my car, plane ticket and case files on the back seat of my second-hand, black Audi A3, on my way home to pack.

*****

Chapter 3

Olympic Airlines flight 308 landed at nine in the morning at the small airport of Crete's second largest town, Chania. I dislike flying as I am quite a tall guy at 6'foot or 1.84 meters as we would say here in Greece and I have broad shoulders, so the tiny space these airplanes call seats are a nightmare to me. Thankfully, this was no transatlantic flight, but a fifty-five minute 'up-have a drink-here are some stale nuts-down' kind of flight.

I picked up my black Samsonite bag and rolling it behind me, I exited the building.

Ioli Cara was not what I was expecting. Don't get me wrong, Greece has some of the most beautiful women I have ever seen in my life, it's just that you don't find many lookers working homicide cases.

She was tall, nearly as tall as I was and that perfect kind of slim. It was not the 'not-too-slim' that turned me off, but that healthy, athletic slim. Her name definitely did her justice. Ioli was a mythological princess and Cara meant black in Turkish. She had long, shampoo advert, shiny, black hair, dark, seductive eyes and sun-kissed skin. She must have been at least fifteen years younger than me, in her early thirties. As she walked over confidently in her tight blue jeans, I could see the men around us turn and look, probably thinking *τι μανάρι είναι αυτό,* loosely translated into a common *what a babe.*

"Captain Papacosta?"

I nodded with a smile.

‘‘Ioli Cara. I’ve been waiting for you. My car is over there,’’ she said and turned towards her car.

‘‘*No handshake?*’’ I thought as I whispered a ‘‘nice to meet you too’’ and followed her, trying not to stare at her figure and come off like some dirty old man. Having tucked my luggage in the back, I sat in the passenger seat of her navy-blue Opel Corsa. Ioli placed her hands firmly on the wheel and asked, ‘‘do you want to go straight to the police department or do you first want to pass by the B&B we have booked for you to... freshen up?’’ as she looked at my unshaven face, my messed up hair, my deprived of sleep eyes and my scruffy looking grey suit.

‘‘Take me to where the body was found.’’

‘‘Straight to business. My kind of guy,’’ she said, smiling and put on her black shades from Madonna’s D&G collection.

Chania was a fifteen-minute drive away. We drove through town and headed towards the beach and the luxurious, five-star hotel of Antlantica Kalliston Resort and Spa.

‘‘This is where Eric Blair stayed. The body was found five minutes away, over those hills.”

‘‘Let’s go to our crime scene then.”

Just a few moments later, we were in front of an enormous, thick-trunk oak tree. There were no buildings in sight. A hardly used dirt road led to the spot and as the murder occurred at night, the killer must have had Eric to himself.

I ducked under the police tape, took a few short steps forward and stopped to process the scene. My eyes started to scan the area. Stains of blood were scattered all over the ground and spatter from the blow to the head had painted part of the oak dark red. Besides the blood, there was nothing really else to imply that some wrongdoing took place here. Ioli stood patiently, a few steps to my side, examining my method or so I hoped. I closed my eyes, rebuilding the area in my head as I tried to picture the killer's movements. He must have been quite strong to have lifted Blair's body and then carried it up to the oak tree. Did he give a sedative to the victim or did he make him walk up to the tree and then tied him up?

I turned towards Ioli. ''So, Lieutenant Cara, you were the first officer to arrive at the scene, walk me through everything that you saw. Leave no details behind. There were no insignificant details when it comes to murder." I did not intend on sounding so uptight.

''The body was found early Thursday morning by an elderly couple passing by on the way to their farm. The poor old woman broke down in shock and had to be hospitalized for the day. Thankfully, the old man had a cell phone and found the courage to call it in. I arrived ten minutes later. It was like nothing I had ever seen before...'' She paused as to gather herself emotionally and then started to describe what she had seen. I just stood there, taking everything in and scribbling down the main facts in my small black notepad. I did not want to interrupt her at the moment with questions. I needed her to be my eyes to something that I did not witness.

"... the man was completely naked and tied to the oak by two pieces of thick rope. One piece was around his legs at knee height and the other piece was around his chest."

She stepped up close to me and placed her index finger on my stomach. "He was cut wide open from here to here," she said as she ran her finger all the way across my beer belly. "It was revolting. His guts were hanging out. Pieces from his insides had fallen to the dirt and were already filled with flies and a few worms. But the worst was the head. It looked like it had taken a blow from an axe. It was cut right open and you could clearly see that the brain had been carved in half. This is one sick fuck of a killer if you ask me."

She stopped and looked at me to catch a reaction and as I did not move a facial muscle, she took in a small, soundless breath and continued.

"We found nothing else. And I mean nothing. It was so fucking frustrating. Not a single hair, not a single fingerprint, not even a goddamned footprint in the dirt."

I looked down and noticed many footprints around the scene. Ioli quickly remarked that when she arrived, the whole area from the road to the tree had been raked to perfection. The footsteps belonged to fellow officers and the paramedics that took away the body.

"I obviously took pictures of everything and checked the grounds for evidence before allowing them near," she continued and went on to state that she had a fellow officer working on a list with tourist rental cars, but so far nothing suspicious had come up.

"Good job, Cara. Did you personally speak to the girlfriend?" I asked.

"Yeah, I questioned the *girlfriend,*" she said.

"Girlfriend?" I repeated, imitating her tone and rolling of the eyes.

"Well, I wouldn't call her that, to be honest!"

"And what would you call her then?"

"His poutana! She was a slutty, young, would-have-been-a-whore if not so gorgeous, woman. Clearly with him for his money. I mean, the guy wasn't that great looking, he was married until last week and was old enough to be her father."

This girl sure did have a tongue on her. I realized that even though I had just met her, I liked this girl's attitude. We Greeks do swear a lot, but I never really did. Mama's training had worked well. Whenever a "gamoto" used to slip from my adolescent mouth, a firm strike from mama's right hand would find me on the back of my head, followed by the line "no need for language, young man." I remember sitting on the stairwell of our apartment block in Astoria, telling my mate Jimmy about mama's views on swearing. Jimmy looked at me like I was from another planet. "Fuck. It's just a fucking word. It's even in the fucking dictionary, if you don't fucking like it, then fuck off,'' he said and we both burst out laughing. Quite the character that Jimmy. He was also, like most kids in our neighborhood, the proud offspring of Greek immigrants. We grew up together and both of us joined law enforcement. Jimmy was now an FBI agent; ''just like in the movies,'' as his mother Toula proudly announced to everyone she met.

''His escort, one Lizzie McAdam, aged 21, reported that Eric had gotten out of bed after sex, had a shower, got dressed and said that he was going for a walk down at the beach to smoke a cigar. That was the last time she saw him. She woke up the next morning and realized that he had never returned."

I flicked through the crime scene photographs that Ioli had given me as we exited her car. I looked at the close up of Eric's hand and noticed the faint yellow color on his fingers and nails. Clearly a smoker. ''Is she still here?'' I asked.

''No, we let her go after questioning. The security cameras from the hotel showed them both entering their room and only Eric was recorded leaving a couple of hours later. The suite was on the top floor, so she could not have left the room from the room's balcony. Anyway, she hardly knew the guy, was too petite to have carried him and to be honest, we all found her irritatingly dumb. She could not have planned this. As nothing, though, is unlikely in this world, we kept all her contact details and checked that she arrived in New York after leaving Greece. Eric's sister is coming today to escort the body back to the states tomorrow. Hopefully, she will be more helpful."

"Let's get going to the body then, before questioning the sister."

*****

Chapter 4

Alicia Robinson could not believe her luck. Winning Miss England two years ago was still her greatest success, but this came as a close second. She was in Cyprus soaking up the hot, sizzling Mediterranean sun, browning up her pale white skin with the rest of the youthful and glamorous models by the pool of the prestigious Columbia Beach Resort in the small, coastal village of Pissouri. They deserved a good bake in the sun after a morning-long swimwear photo shoot down at the beach of Pissouri Bay.

Columbia Resort was located upon the slope of a verdant hill that headed down to the clear waters. Tall palm trees and green gardens surrounded it and the view was breathtaking. The resort offered every luxury imaginable and the girls, all young and most never having left their home country before, were enjoying the feeling of royalty. At night, all the girls came down together after spending hours on make-up applying, combing their hair and picking out dresses. They gathered around the pool area and were faced with a mile-long buffet dinner. All tables were set perfectly with expensive porcelain plates and exquisite silverware. The tables were spread out under the night sky; a sky filled with countless stars that seemed to shine so much brighter in Cyprus. The buffet had everything your heart –or stomach- could desire.

Alicia mostly wanted to try the Greek-Cypriot cuisine she had heard so much about. Delicious, steamy kleftiko, wine-marinated pieces of pork called afelia, mousakka, golden oven-cooked potatoes and the freshest salad she had ever seen, soon filled her plate. Even Londis grocery store back home in Canterbury did not have tomatoes this red. As she walked over to their table, her plate drew a few looks from the rest of the models who had mostly placed a few olive oil marinated croutons and some lettuce on their plates. She could sense the envy building up.

‘‘What? I have a good metabolism. Anyway, I’m not going to keep it all in!’’ she joked, in an attempt to break the tension. Most girls smiled and the drop-dead-gorgeous, crazy Italian girl laughed out loud as they all sat down to enjoy their salad feast.

Pissouri was a quiet village and it literally stood up to its name. Pissouri in Greek meant pitch black and after ten o’clock, it was exactly that. Visitors soon realized that the tranquil village had no nightlife. Most models did not care as they needed their beauty sleep. After many air-kisses and wishes for sweet dreams, they scattered to their rooms.

‘‘Living clichés,’’ Alicia thought. She did not feel like sleeping.

‘‘I am young, on top of the world, with so much energy from my youth or is it perhaps from the kleftiko?’’ she joked to herself.

She decided to take a walk down to the beach but thought to buy a triple-chocolate Galaxy ice-cream before heading down to the bay for a moonlit stroll in the sand.

Just a few minutes later, she was walking into Pepi’s mini-market, ice-cream in hand. No one was seen behind the scratched wooden counter and she then heard a screeching noise coming from the rear end of the shop. The owner was busy with his closing up of the shop for the night duties.

''Excuse me?'' she called out discreetly.

''Well, hello there,'' the owner said and quickly walked towards the counter, dusting off his hands upon his blue shirt. He offered Alicia a generous smile that lifted his heavy moustache.

''Just this, please,'' Alicia said and placed her ice-cream on the counter.

''That will be 1.95, thank you,'' he said, with his thick Cypriot accent.

''*Oh, what an idiot I am,*'' she automatically thought to herself as she realized she had left the hotel without any money.

''I'm so sorry. I seem to have forgotten my money at the hotel. I'll be right back,'' she apologized.

''It's ok. I'll pay. These too,'' said the gentleman behind her as he placed his bottle of Evian water and a Mars ice-cream on the counter.

''No, no. No need for that. I'll just pop back to the...'' Alicia rushed to say.

''I insist! Come on... Can't a guy buy a beautiful girl an ice-cream anymore?'' he interrupted as his right hand pushed through his shiny black hair and awkwardly scratched the back of his neck.

He had amazing green eyes and that voice, *"oh that voice, so smooth yet so masculine,"* Alicia thought.

"Thank you," she whispered gently as they exited the shop together and stood on the bricked road that led down to the beach.

"Sam Newton," he said, and offered his hand.

"Alicia Robinson." Her hand entered his.

"Care for a walk, Alicia? Before these melt?" he asked, ice-creams in hand.

Alicia nodded and smiled in reply. They walked downhill along the path, side by side, with the silver moon serving as their only light. Soon, they had reached the narrow stairs that led down to the sandy beach.

"Ladies first," Sam said. He stepped aside and with his hand stretched out he showed her the way. Alicia smiled and thought, *"does chivalry still exist or does he just want to check out my ass?"*

They slowly strolled further down and having finished their delectable and refreshing ice-creams, they sat down on a wooden bench and gazed at the sea. The waves were the only sound breaking through the silence and the darkness.

"Are you here on holiday with family, friends? Boyfriend?" he asked with a cheeky smile and a double raise of his eyebrows.

"Co-workers. I work for a London-based modelling agency," she replied, trying not to sound pompous.

‘‘That’s fantastic! I should have guessed,’’ he said, and his eyes scrolled down her face and started to scan her body.

‘‘You?’’ she quickly asked as to retrieve his eyes back to eye level.

‘‘Oh, I’m a writer. I’m writing a book at the moment,’’ he stated and pulled out of his backpack a red notebook with a silver pen clipped to it.

‘‘It’s a thriller,’’ he proudly announced, with a mischievous grin.

‘‘Here, let me read you a passage.’’

*****

Chapter 5

I stood outside the coroner's lavatory, having a much-needed smoke. I had seen my fair share of bodies during my career, but this was atrocious. Atrocious. *I always liked the ring of that word,* and with that thought, I walked outside to avoid disapproving looks by medical examiners passing by.

Official cause of death was *bled out after a strike to the lower abdomen by a sharp object, most likely a knife*. The cutting of the skull and the carving of the brain into two happened postmortem. The small carved lightning bolt on his forehead puzzled me the most. I gave the demure coroner a good laugh when I first gazed upon the marking and asked her, ''what's this? Are we looking for some freaky Harry Potter maniac or what?''

Ioli, on the other hand, was not amused. It bothered her that we were stuck at square one. She had, so far, a perfect record. Solved every single case she had ever worked on. No wonder she became a lieutenant so young.

''Didn't know you smoked,'' she commented as she pushed open the beige aluminium door and strolled out to the small parking lot.

''I don't,'' I replied as I dropped the cigarette I had gotten from the coroner and stepped on it. ''Well, I used to, but I quit years ago," I admitted.

I'll never forget the day when Gaby came back from school -she must have been six at the time- with a sad look upon her face. I asked her if something was wrong, to which she firmly replied, ''you are going to die."

It took a while to get the whole story about how little Andrew's uncle died of a heart attack and Andrew repeated to his fellow pupils that his mama said that smoking killed him. The kids then asked their teacher about smoking and she described as PG as she could about all the terrible effects smoking could have on your health.

''And if you are going to die, I don't want to play with you anymore,'' Gaby continued, and just like that, I had been blackmailed into quitting.

''Good for you, 'cancer in a box' my grandma used to say,'' Ioli remarked as her phone rang.

''Ioli Cara... hmm... yeah... ok, we'll be there in five."

''Sister's here,'' she said, and started to stride towards her parked car.

As we drove down Irakliou Street, where Chania's police station was located, Ioli pointed to an old building on our left with tiny little balconies that made you wonder if they could fit two chairs on them.

''That's your hotel, Captain.''

''Lovely,'' I answered sarcastically and won myself one of her Julia Roberts' smiles.

The police station was quite small with just one floor and a few police cars and motorcycles parked outside. Above the white door, the proud symbol of the Hellenic Police was hanging and all windows were shut.

"*Air-conditioning,*" I thought with a smile as I wiped the sweat away from my forehead. Sometimes I wondered what made the first settlers to these islands stay. Did they not complain as often as I about the heat?

As we entered the building, all eyes turned to see the New York detective turned Greek Police Captain who was with Ioli. The curiosity was not fed though, as Ioli did not bother with any form of introduction and instead led me straight to the questioning room.

Jenny Blair was in a terrible state sitting there with tears gathered in her eyes, ready to fall, and with an untouched coffee in her hands. She could not have been over forty, ladylike manners, dressed in a plain black dress that could not hide her stunning figure. Blonde and with beautiful characteristics, she had a warmth about her that made you relate to her pain. As I introduced Ioli and myself, I could see that she was glad to hear an American accent, but she made no comment of any sorts.

"I want to see my brother," she said, with a crackling voice.

"All in good time, ma'am. I understand this is a very stressful time for you and your loved ones, but you have to understand that this is a murder case. It has been days since your brother's murder and to be honest, we need your help to catch the person responsible."

"I... I don't know what it is you think I could help you with. What do you want me to say?" she answered, slightly confused.

"Ms. Blair, as you were informed, your brother's ex-wife was also murdered by the same killer and this cannot be a coincidence. Do you know anyone who would want to hurt them? Any known enemies? Any disagreements that they may have had?"

"My brother is... was... the CEO of a major pharmaceutical company, PharmaBlair if you've heard of it."

I nodded with a slight smile, even though I had never heard such a name before. I wanted her to feel comfortable and open up to us. Ioli had caught on to how Jenny Blair relaxed with hearing my accent and sat back listening to us, while her eyes revealed that her brain was processing everything being said.

"Of course, he had enemies and jealous foes, but I doubt anyone would go as far as this. And poor Stacy? She was truly the most loving person and had nothing to do with my brother's business. They were a great couple with many friends and if it wasn't for my brother's erotic... escapades, they'd still be together. He loved Stacy and she was crazy for him. You see, my brother had a thing for beautiful, young, twenty-year-olds and cheated on Stacy a few times too many. He had agreed to enroll in a sex therapy program, but the trust between them was long lost. I still can't believe they are both gone,'' she cried, and the tears started to fall.

My hand reached out and gently touched hers. ''Mrs. Blair, we are doing everything in our power to bring the person responsible to justice. At the moment, I need you to be strong and concentrate. Here you go,'' I said and passed her a block of papers and a pen. ''Please list anyone you can think who for whatever reason had any disagreements with your brother or Stacy and why. Anything you can remember. Deals gone bad, arguments over money, the business... everything. We'll leave you alone for a while and when we come back, we'll get an officer to take you to your brother,'' I said, feeling sorry for the distressed woman and for what she was going to face at the coroner.

''Thank you,'' she responded and started to write.

Ioli got up first, smiled at Ms. Blair and exited the small, dimly lit room. She was eager to check up with her team. She had officers checking up on everything. Rental car agencies, flights to Crete, ship departures from Crete to Samos in the time between the two murders, and interviews with locals and tourists around the murder area. Samo's police department was doing the same, but nothing had yet come up. All dead ends. I could not shake the awful feeling that with no suspect, no evidence besides two naked bodies without DNA left on them, and no sign of fingerprints, our killer was eluding us. We had to be missing something here. There is no such thing as a perfect murder.

*****

Chapter 6

Greek History and Mythology professor, Michael D. Johnson, woke up at six in the morning like he always did and got out of bed having enjoyed a good night's sleep. He never had time to relax back home with all his ongoing work at UCLA, where he taught. Now, exams had been marked, his latest book about the outcome and aftermath of the Trojan War had finally been completed and he had been invited to speak the day before at a history conference, here in Cyprus. He flew to Cyprus through Athens and was glad his transit flight had been delayed due to union strikes. He spent the day visiting the Acropolis and the famous temple of Athena, the Parthenon. He stood there, still between the herds of tourists; eyes closed and picturing how life was back then. The professor wished that one day he would receive enough grant money to visit important Hellenic sites, like the Acropolis, with his post-graduate students. He desired them to love Greece and its enthralling history as much as he did.

Michael went over to the large window on his right, pulled the blue silk curtain wide open and stared into the tiny fraction of the sun that was sneaking up from the horizon, being born out of the sea.

"*Just like Aphrodite, the goddess of beauty herself,*" he thought and at that moment he knew how he would be spending his morning. Petra tou Romiou or Aphrodite's Rock as it is commonly known was only a five-minute-drive away. This is the sea, where, according to myth the goddess of beauty, Aphrodite was born. As blood from the god Uranus –or his testicles, according to more hardcore myths- fell into the ocean, the most exquisite and beautiful woman ever to walk this earth came out of the thrashing waves.

After a quick visit to the delicious 'what-to-eat-first' breakfast buffet at the Aphrodite Hill Resort, where he was staying, the professor was ready to go down to the rock for a swim.

"Perhaps I'll swim around the rock three times backwards," he joked to himself as he turned the key and brought to life the engine of his rental Mazda 3. Legend has it that if you swam around the rock backwards three times, then the goddess herself would grant you with beauty beyond words. Not that the professor needed much help in that department. An athletic, young-looking, forty-year old with careless blond hair and turquoise eyes: he was quite the handsome man. Not that he ever had much time for the ladies who, with great disappointment, discovered that he was married to his career.

At ten minutes to seven, he was the first one to the beach. He walked down to the shore, laid down his Scooby-Doo towel, and sat there enjoying the endless blue sea, the sounds of the waves hitting the tiny beach pebbles and the cool morning breeze. He rarely felt this carefree as he looked upon the rock imagining Aphrodite being born. As he stood up, sun in his eyes, he thought he was going crazy.

"My mind must be playing tricks on me," he said as he saw Aphrodite herself standing there upon her rock. He placed his hand above his eyes and tried to focus as he moved closer to the sea.

He never knew he could scream so loud. A wild cry came out of his lips as he stumbled backwards and fell into the sand. He looked around, desperately searching for someone in sight. He was alone.

The professor ran to his car and picked up his cell phone.

"Shit, what's the number to 911 in this country?" he yelled to himself. He scrolled down his contact list and with relief, he found the hotel's phone number.

"Aphrodite Hills Resort, how may I help you?" the receptionist asked in a formal voice.

"The number to the police, what is it?" he said in a panic.

"Is something wrong, sir?" she inquired dropping her formal tone.

"Just give me the goddamned number... now!" he yelled.

"It is 112 sir, but if I..." she replied and the professor hung up to dial the police.

"Astynomia, parakalw?"

"English. Do you speak English?" he asked hysterically.

"Yes, sir. What is your emergency?"

"I'm at Petra tou Romiou. Come as fast as you can. There's a girl here and... and her arms have been cut off."

*****

Chapter 7

Since we were not catching any leads investigating Eric Blair's murder, we decided to go over the case files from the murder of the ex-wife. We had both already gone over the coroner's report and photos from the crime scene, however, we were hoping that maybe by reading it together, something new would pop up.

''You might see or notice something and spark my little grey cells,'' I said.

''Whatever, Poirot,'' she replied and rolled her eyes.

''Yes, I read Agatha Christie. I doubt you will find a true investigator who doesn't enjoy some Hercule Poirot or some Sherlock Holmes every now and then,'' I remarked.

We had also received files sent over by our labs in Athens and we were eager to find out what the lab rats had come up with. We had everything set in front of us on the small white table in the same interrogation room we had sat with Ms. Blair. Just as I was about to suggest we start with the lab results, Ioli grabbed all the files, stood up and said, ''I'm suffocating in here and I cannot concentrate at all when I'm hungry. Want to go to an amazing tavern I know, grab a bite and go over the case there? Maybe the waiter will be too scared to bring us the bill,'' she laughed away as she held up the case photos.

"Who am I to argue when food is offered?" I replied, and soon we were back on the road.

Ela Taverna was situated in a quiet, little back street in downtown Chania. It was an idyllic place to sit back, relax and discuss the case. The shade from the pink bougainvilleas covered the tavern's mahogany tables and was an oasis away from the burning Cretan sun. Moments later, we were joined by an amiable and agile waitress. The dowdy blonde with rosy cheeks took our order with a wide, sincere, Greek island smile. We ordered Greek salad, pita bread with taramosalata, octopus, calamari, some home grown, home cooked French fries and a couple of bottles of ice-cold beers. This truly was a step up from my takeaway *meals* back in Athens.

I hadn't really opened up to Ioli yet and had not shared my views about our case. Not that I am not a team player. On the contrary, I'm a firm believer that it takes teamwork to bring in a suspect, especially one who obviously had carefully planned and executed his murders. I like to be sure before I speak; to let things swirl around in my brain before connecting and finally settling down.

''I believe we are looking for one murderer: a tall and quite strong male, most likely a foreigner with knowledge of the Greek seas — someone who owns their own boat for sure. As for age, I do not know. Anything from eighteen to fit-enough to sail around and to carry Eric Blair. Probably someone who knew the two victims as this seems to be a revenge plan against them,'' I said as Ioli was ready to dip her pita bread in the taramosalata. She paused, looked at me and I could nearly hear her fastidious brain processing everything I had just said.

“I’m not saying that I disagree with you, but can you elaborate on how you reached these conclusions?” she asked and finally dipped the round end of her pita bread in the pink tarama.

“One murderer. This is obviously the work of a maniac. He killed and he killed viciously. Maniacs tend to work alone. Male. I base this on the needed strength to carry and tie Eric Blair. Also, the force used to stab and cut open a head and a woman’s lower body. If we had two non-connected victims, I would say we were looking for a Greek, but as it seems, the killer knew the victims. He must be a foreigner, most likely American like the victims. However, to sail from Crete to Samos, he must have knowledge of the area and good sailing skills. His own boat. Your team checked everyone on the ferry that left after the first murder and arrived before the second and there aren’t any direct flights between Crete and Samos. He wouldn’t have enough time to fly to Athens and wait until the next day to fly out to Samos. I don’t think he would have had the patience either. After the thrill of the first kill, this guy needed to kill again.”

“Foreigner with knowledge of the area? Might be Greek-American,” she said, and gave me a suspicious look before smiling and giving me a gentle nudge with her left fist. She then picked up the file from the labs in Athens. We were both eager to see if any light would shine on our in-the-dark case. Before opening the large, brown envelope, she asked, “what do you think the pomegranate stands for?”

“Well, it is a known symbol of fertility.”

“I was wondering if we checked if the victim was pregnant or had any problems having kids.”

“The coroner in Samos would have written it in his report if she was pregnant, though we should give him a call and make sure. As for any pregnancy problems, we could get in touch with Eric’s sister before she leaves.”

“I need a reason, you know. I mean, you don’t place a pomegranate in a woman’s vagina for no reason.”

“Or cut open somebody’s head,” I added.

“If we find the meaning in his symbols, maybe we will find a connection to the killer who as we agree, most likely, knew the victims.”

She did not wait for a reply. She pulled out the papers from the envelope and looked down at them. Her eyes scrolled up and down the documents for a few seconds and then she said, ‘‘they have identified our murder weapon. It’s an Imperial Bowie knife and listen to this; it’s vintage. Most likely from the late sixties, early seventies. Thousands were made and sold in most western countries. Not much help there,’’ she said and paused to check my reaction. I nodded with a slight smile. ‘‘Ah, this is interesting. Eric Blair was drugged,’’ she continued.

‘‘Drugged?’’ I asked.

‘‘In Eric Blair’s body, we found remains from powerful sedatives called Alpha-2 drugs and Acepromazine (ACP) used mostly on horses during operations,'' she read from the report. ''It says that the combination of the two drugs, in the right amount, would sedate the victim within less than a minute. No such sedatives were found in the body of the second victim, Stacy Anderson Blair."

''So that's how he got Eric to the oak and as Stacy was not drugged, she was most likely already down on that isolated beach.''

"We need to call the coroner and ask him to check for a needle entry on Eric's body. Does it mention if the sedative could have been inhaled?" I asked.

Her eyes moved rapidly across the document.

''No. Just that traces were found in the body. Maybe we should call the lab and make sure."

She paused for a second and continued, "the rest is known to us. It goes on about pre and post trauma stabs. What the victims had eaten etc., etc. Here have a read,'' she said and passed me the papers.

As I was reading, Ioli kept herself busy with her well-cooked meal. Suddenly, she looked up, and out of the blue she asked, ''why did you leave New York?''

The question caught me off guard. ''Well... I...'' I said, trying to take my focus off the document and focus on an answer.

''None of my fucking business, right, sorry, too personal,'' she rushed to say. ''It's just...''

''It's just been bothering you and you could not get the thought out of your head,'' I replied. ''You would not be an investigator Cara if you didn't ponder upon it. Anyway, to satisfy your curiosity, my wife left me and I needed to get away."

''And you gave up your life and your career for a woman?'' she instantly said in obvious shock. ''Sorry,'' she added hastily as she realized that she had crossed the line. Her indiscretion provoked an answer I had not uttered before in Greece.

''She left me because she blamed me for the death of our daughter... I blamed me too,'' I said dryly.

Ioli sat up, all of a sudden feeling uncomfortable in her chair, hoping that the earth below her would open up and swallow her whole.

''I'm really sorry. I did not mean to stir the past. I was just trying to make small talk and get to know you. I did not know you were married,'' she said in a hurry as she noticed the white circle round my index finger and thought to herself, ''yeah, I'm a great investigator, did not even notice that he used to wear a wedding ring."

''It's ok, ancient history, don't stress about it. Let's enjoy our meal,'' I said and looked away.

Cold silence filled the air as our eyes focused on our octopus and calamari which we consumed without talking or making any sort of eye contact. The Greek singer Anna Vissi finally broke the silence as Ioli's phone started to *sing*.

"Hey mum," she answered. "Yes, mum, I have eaten! I'm not five you know."

This is where I would have made a joke about overprotective Greek mothers whose main worry is to feed their children until the day they die; however, I was not in the mood to be funny. My mind was travelling over oceans and back in time to my apartment, back in N.Y., where my love for Tracy was housed. I could see her, elegant as always, cooking an amazing roast dinner in our small kitchen while my angel, Gaby, was drawing on the kitchen table. She would have been eleven now. My baby girl, my life, gunned down in the street by the drug gang whose ringleader, Jesus Sanchez, I had shot dead during a bust... an eye for an eye!

*****

Chapter 8

New York – Two years earlier

It had been the perfect family day out.

The Bronx River Festival took place on a warm July Saturday. My beautiful wife Tracy and I were with our little nine-year-old angel, Gabriella, riding upon 2Train heading to Burke Avenue, west of Bronx Park where the festival was in full swing. Gabriella looked stunningly beautiful for a young girl, in her white Benetton dress and her hair tied up into two ponytails.

''She is as excited as a porcupine meeting a pineapple,'' Tracy joked, and we all laughed. Gabriella always laughed at her mother's sayings, even though most of the time she had no idea what she was talking about. Why would a porcupine be so happy to meet a pineapple anyway?

The Bronx River Festival is a celebration of the Bronx River with loads of activities on deck for the entire family. Gabriella was eagerly looking forward to the nature scavenger hunt where she had high hopes of proving to daddy what a good little investigator she was. Tracy was going to take part in all calorie-burning activities like capoeira and power yoga while I would stand by a tree smoking in secret so Gabriella would not see me. I would stand there all day if Tracy let me, admiring the two of them and occasionally waving and giving a thumbs-up to every, ''daddy, daddy look."

The festival did justice to the saying, *time flies when you're having fun* and four hours went by without any of us noticing. Soon, it was time to head back home.

The party of three came out from the underground holding hands, letting the love flow through us. Little Gaby was ecstatically happy, having played all sorts of games, eaten a bunch of junk food mama would not have allowed on a normal day and she had her face painted as a fairy princess.

The tires of the car racing around the corner and down the street made us jump, and as I turned, I saw the barrels of their guns sticking out from behind the slightly opened tinted windows of a black Lincoln MKS.

''Get down,'' I yelled as I pushed Tracy to the ground behind a parked yellow Chevrolet and fell upon my daughter to roll with her behind a rusty dumpster. The sound of multiple and constant firing penetrated the air and it only took one bullet, out of the one hundred and sixteen shots fired, to penetrate young Gabriella's left lung. Blood started oozing out pretty quick, and soon her white dress had turned dark red.

''Long live Sanchez, asshole,'' a shrill voice was heard, and the car sped away to oblivion.

I knelt next to my baby girl, held her close in my arms and that's where little Gabriella 'Gaby' Papacosta took her last breath.

Tracy was screaming erratically for help and an ambulance, but I knew that it was too late. I closed my baby's eyes and kissed her gently on the forehead. As her heart stopped beating, I could feel mine break and all I could do was to cry. I held on to Gaby until the paramedics pulled me off, having already given a strong sedative to Tracy who was curled up behind the Chevrolet's wheel, repeating, "no, no... Costa, say it isn't so."

We did not speak to each other again, not even at the funeral and one fine, sizzling N.Y. August evening, Tracy came out of the master bedroom, suitcases in hand. She walked over to me as I was on the couch, *no*t watching the news on TV.

"I always hated your job. I told you to accept a desk job now that we had a child. This is all your fault," she cried with no more tears left in her eyes.

"I know."

"Bye, Costa."

I found the strength to look up and watched Tracy as she walked out the door and out of my life. As the door slammed behind her, I whispered a silent "goodbye, Tracy." Over the next few days, my phone never stopped ringing, so I threw it right out the apartment's window. I really hate stupid cell phones. I had no intention to accept condolences and life-goes-on speeches from relatives and co-workers. My mother Maria came twice a day, knocking on the door, begging me to answer her and leaving food outside the door. One day, without her needing to yell, I opened the rusty hinged door and calmly said, ‘‘Mama, I’m leaving for Greece... today. For good.”

*****

Chapter 9

The grass was so green. The sky was so clear. Everything was so vivid.

The sun was sending down its bright rays, making Gaby's hair glow as we both ran through the park before falling down to the ground and laughing out loud. She was in her white dress with her face painted like a fairy princess and she looked magical.

''I love you, daddy,'' she yelled happily and kissed me on my shaved cheek.

The air was filled with children laughing, dogs barking, birds flying above and squeaking and the telephone ringing... *the telephone ringing?*

I sat up in my hotel room bed and tried to open both eyes. So far, only my left eye obeyed and I watched as the alarm clock changed to 07:52. The pale-grey hotel telephone was still ringing. That was when I realized I had turned my cell phone off last night after reporting back to the chief and receiving a ''get me results'' in that threatening, charming way of his. I stretched and reached out to pick up the telephone and put an end to that awful, uproarious noise.

''Hello?'' I said in my hoarse morning voice.

''Costa, good morning,'' Ioli said.

''I'm down at the reception. Get down here quick. There has been another murder."

My thoughts were all over the place as I rushed to get dressed. '*Another murder related to Mr. and Mrs. Blair?*' The killer had now killed three people. That's the magic number to be admitted to the hall of fame for serial killers. I hoped for clues. Any clues. Not another clean murder scene. '*Another victim. Where? How?*'

I could not wait for time to pass in the hotel's ancient elevator that you could feel dying with every screech as it lowered me from the 5th floor to the reception area. '*I should have taken the stairs.*' My palms started to sweat and when the elevator doors opened, more sweat formed at the top of my forehead. Another hot Greek summer day combined with my anxiety to solve this case.

"Good morning, boss..."

"Morning. Where you parked?" I asked as I walked in a hurry right pass her and headed to the hotel's glass front door.

"Breakfast?" she asked as I exited the building.

"Screw it," I shouted back and gained myself a disapproving stare from a forty-something woman that was passing by carrying groceries in her hand. I bet at this time and hour, she must have bought the freshest vegetables and fruit. I missed my wife's cooking. I missed watching her prepare it. I missed her. '*Concentrate, Costa!*'

"Find me a good coffee on the way and tell me where we are going." I wanted to know as I placed myself in the passenger's seat.

‘‘To the airport,’’ she said with no emotion in her voice and gave no further details, prolonging the revelation of our destination, possibly amused by my anxiety.

‘‘The airport? Where was the murder?’’ I asked in no mood for guessing games.

‘‘Cyprus,’’ she replied monolectically.

‘‘Cyprus? That’s another country! How did this come to our attention? Are we sure it is the same killer?’’ I said, trying to control my confused thoughts.

‘‘Well, the first officer on site called our labs in Athens as soon as he saw the naked body with its arms cut off. You see, our case was quite the news and was familiar to him. He photographed the cuttings and the stabbings and emailed them to our lab guy who confirmed the similar markings. To cut a long story short, no pun intended, the chief arranged for us to work with the Greek-Cypriot police. They will be picking us up from the airport. Paphos airport is only twenty minutes away from the scene. The body is still there, having only been found an hour ago.”

The one-hour-something flight went by quickly as Ioli and I never stopped talking about the new direction of our case.

The fact that our newest victim -suspected to be one Alicia Robinson from the UK- had as it seemed no connection to the previous victims was puzzling. As the first two victims were married, we had both thought that the murderer knew them and for his own reasons, wanted them dead.

"Maybe she was one of Eric's *girlfriends,*" Ioli suggested.

"Could be," I replied bluntly. It annoyed me that my theory of the murderer knowing the victims and moving around by boat was blown out of the water. There was no way he could have sailed all this distance through international waters on a one-man crew boat and entered Cyprus without anyone noticing.

"So what's your story, Cara?" I asked, trying to tear my mind away from all the unanswered questions that surrounded our case.

"Nothing special really," she said and went silent.

I gave her the anything-better-to-do look and with my hand, urged her to go on. "Come on, family, brothers and sisters? Where did you grow up?" I asked.

She took on a movie narrator kind of voice and said, "our story today begins in Epanochori. It's a small, traditional village, southwest of Chania town if you have never heard of it. 1980. Twenty-year-old farmer Giannis Cara first laid eyes upon a seventeen year old farm girl from the nearby village of Prases, named Anna Tzanoulaki. Love was in the air and soon wedding bells were ringing at Saint George's church. As they didn't have a TV in the beginning at their farmhouse, Anna was pregnant within the month."

“You?” I asked, enjoying her semi comedic, semi soap opera tone.

“Yep! But, you see, little Ioli did not want to come out to the world and caused many complications to her poor mother. She was in surgery for hours and Gianni nearly lost his beloved Anna that day. A healthy baby was finally born; however, something overshadowed their joy. Anna was told that due to extensive damage to her uterus, she would not be able to bear any more children. Anna's dreams of having a large family were shattered, as was Gianni's dream of having a son. They got over it quickly though, as they realized what a beautiful and talented kid they had,” Ioli said laughing.

“That's true,” I responded.

“Hey, I wasn't fishing for compliments,” she said while giving me a nudge on the shoulder.

“I always worked hard to make them proud and helped mama in the kitchen and papa with the land. I guess I did not want them to ever feel the lack of more children. Dad always used to joke that I was twice the man any son could have been.”

“Do you want kids of your own one day?” I asked as she was being this honest with me. It felt nice to get to know my partner a bit better and I had not been interested in getting to know anyone since arriving in Greece two years ago.

“I say I do, mostly to save poor Gianni and Anna from a stroke and a couple of heart attacks, but marriage and kids just doesn’t seem to ring a bell with me,” she replied.

“Yet,” I added. “Never say never, Cara.”

“Please fasten your seat belts and remain seated...” the air stewardess started announcing over the speakers, interrupting our conversation. Soon we would be landing in Cyprus. I always wanted to come to Cyprus, but not as Captain Papacosta, just plain American short trouser, flower shirt, cheap sandals tourist Costa. Cyprus, I had heard, was an amazing vacation destination. An exotic island with luxurious hotels, great food, sandy beaches, sunny nearly all year round and the clearest waters you could wish to swim in.

As the plane touched down, Ioli turned and said, “I always wonder what fucked up shit happened to these people during their lives and they turn out so... so wrong, you know?”

I nodded and thought “Ok, no more chit chat, focus back on the killer and heads back in the game.”

*****

Chapter 10

Dayton, Ohio 1972

''Boys are bad. Boys are bad,'' seventeen year old Katie kept repeating inside her head as she hastily walked down her school corridor, trying hard to keep her eyes away from all the boys' crotches. The devil was sending her images of her touching them up while they kissed her passionately and roughly up and down her neck, unbuttoning her blouse. Not that such a thing was likely to happen anytime soon. Katie was a devout Catholic, raised to know that before marriage, no unholy boy should touch her.

''Anyway, who would want to touch me?'' she thought as she looked at her reflection in her locker's glued-on oval mirror. She had nice green eyes, but they were hidden behind her thick, brown, granny reading glasses. No sinful make-up touched her pale skin and her dull black hair was pulled right back in a tight ponytail. Katie knew that she looked like a spinster librarian and was used to being an outcast. She had grown used to her fellow pupils calling her a freak and all the other cliché, unoriginal names the deprived-of-an-imagination teens of Dayton High whispered behind her back and sometimes even uttered right to her face.

High school was hell. Home was worse.

Her only joy came late at night when, after an inner fight of good and evil, she would masturbate. Katie longed to feel someone deep inside her.

After biology class and a C- on the latest test, Katie headed to the toilets, entered one of the many white cubicles, sat down on the toilet seat, pulled up her old-fashioned, hand-me-down, plain blue dress and lowered her white underwear to her ankles. ''Daddy is gonna be so mad with this C,'' she thought as she licked her fingers and started to caress herself down below. Soon her fingers were inside her and she tried hard to keep quiet as her much-needed release was near.

Suddenly, the door opened.

''Oh... my... God! She's masturbating!''

Katie looked up to see a stunned Gillian White staring at her in disgust.

''*Shit, I didn't lock the door,*'' Katie thought and rushed to pull up her underwear.

More girls gathered behind Gillian whispering to each other as they all gave her dirty, disapproving looks.

''At school?''

''Horny bitch!''

''Get a room.''

''Get a life, more like it.''

Their laughter only got louder and louder as Katie rushed by them, opened the bathroom's ruby red door and ran down the long hallway. Red-faced, she felt sheepish as she ran and sobbed to herself. ‘‘I’m so embarrassed, I could die. What if mother and father found out?’’

Her heart was about to burst and the girls’ laughter kept on echoing in her head.

She finally reached her sanctuary. The school’s west wing had been closed off the entire school year as it was being renovated. She ducked under the do-not-enter yellow tape, skilfully climbed over some sand barrels, raced down the long corridor and turned left. She quickly entered one of the small rooms that used to be offices and closed the door behind her.

‘‘What the fuck?’’ Chris shouted as all four boys stood up at once. The room stunk of marijuana.

‘‘Sorry,’’ she said quickly and turned to leave.

Jonathan, the captain of the basketball team, at 6”2 had no problem slamming the door shut with his left hand as she tried to leave. With his right hand, he vigorously yanked Katie back into the center of the room.

The boys surrounded her.

‘‘This geek is going to rat on us,’’ Andrew yelled in a paranoid state.

‘‘Not if she stays and has a smoke with us,’’ John said, stepping closer to her, joint in hand.

‘‘Please let me go. I won’t say anything, trust me,’’ Katie said in a panic.

‘‘If you want us to trust you, come sit down with us,’’ Jonathan said and pushed her down to the line of pillows that the boys had placed on the floor to chill back on.

‘‘I’ll have a smoke and then I’ll go,’’ Katie said scared. As she released the smoke and coughed hard, she felt Jonathan’s hand journey on her thigh and go up her dress.

‘‘Dude, she is soaking wet!’’ he declared enthusiastically, and all the boys smiled in union.

‘‘Bitch fancies us,’’ Chris proudly announced.

‘‘Wanna fuck us, cunt?’’ John said and *gracelessly* placed his hand on her right breast.

Katie instinctively slapped his hand away and John slapped her back, hard on her face. So hard, her whole body turned.

Before she knew it, two boys were holding her arms, forcefully keeping her down. She could feel another lifting up her dress and pulling down her underwear. She saw a belt fall to the ground as Jonathan pulled down his jeans and laid on top of her. Seconds later, he slowly entered her, and all Katie could do was to scream. That was when she felt the cold blade on her neck.

‘‘Listen, bitch,’’ Chris said, holding a knife to her throat.

‘‘You are going to be very, very quiet while my boy Jonathan has his way with you. You should feel grateful; he is doing you a favour. He has fucked half the cheerleaders in this school, and none has ever complained.”

Jonathan started to pound away even harder, encouraged by his friend’s pep talk.

‘‘And now,’’ Chris continued in his creepy, calm voice ‘‘you are going to open your mouth and suck my cock. You are going to suck me real good. If you are a bad girl, you will be punished,’’ he hissed and pressed the knife harder up against her skin. ‘‘This is an Imperial Bowie knife and it can cut you up real good. Understand, whore?’’ he demanded to know.

Katie shook her head in agreement as they pulled her up on all fours. Jonathan let out a small groan, asked ‘‘who’s next?’’ and switched places with a delighted-looking John. After a few minutes, Chris and Andrew switched places too. As the boys took turns with her, they thought they must have scared her real good as Katie co-operated well in pleasing them. What they could not have guessed, is that Katie was enjoying herself. Her insides down below were going wild and those four, long, hard penises were driving her crazy. Just looking at them turned her on. She had no idea they could be so big. The only penises Katie had ever seen were on Greek/Roman statues in the park and they were nothing like these.

After all of them exploded with joy –Katie included- they quickly started to get dressed. Lessons had started a good twenty minutes ago. That's when Chris suddenly grabbed Katie by the throat and pushed her with force up against the musty wall.

''Now listen here, whore...'' he started to yell, not realising that Katie was holding his knife.

''Go call your mama a whore, you fucking prick,'' Katie yelled back and slightly cut him on his arm, forcing him to release her. Chris pulled back in evident pain while Katie waved the knife in front of all four boys.

''Now you listen here you fuckers, we had a good time and that's it. I won't be telling on you so let's all just forget this ever happened."

The boys stood there stunned and amazed that she would not be giving them any trouble. The thrill of the moment, along with the marijuana's effect was wearing off, so guilt, along with a fear of being reported to the school and the police were kicking in.

''Oh, and I'm keeping the knife,'' she said, closing the door behind her.

Katie never went home that day or any other day for that matter. After school and with a smile upon her face, Katie boarded the white and blue bus that was headed from Dayton to New York. A brand new chapter was starting for her.

Two days later, her parents received a letter in the post. It was short but to the punch.

Mother, please quit your drama-crying

and your worthless prayers, I am fine.

Better than fine actually, I am great.

Father, I hope you die painfully, you son of a bitch.

Now that your favorite punching bag is gone,

I hope you don't beat mama twice as often.

DO NOT LOOK FOR ME.

I AM DEAD TO YOU!

Katie.

*****

Chapter 11

The International Airport of Paphos was located in the rural village of Timi, which, as it turned out, was only a fifteen-minute drive to our crime scene. I was glad it was just a stone's throw away as I was eager to get there. The crime scene in Samos I *saw* only through photographs, testimonies and mortuary shots, while the crime scene in Crete I saw days after the murder actually happened. Now was my chance. Now, I could really get close. It was only twelve past ten and the body, the coroner, the police officers and the witness were all there.

Two young officers were expecting us and greeted us very formally. We had officers Andrea Charalampous and Giorgo Georgiou as our escorts. They looked so young. Neither looked older than twenty-five and were probably still cadets or new to the force. It seems that in every country, the same rule applies. ''The lower you are in ranking, the jobs you get suck,'' to put it rather bluntly. An amazing crime scene by a serial killer and these kids were stuck with the vastly important chore of picking us up from the airport. Both looked alike. Average height, black hair, green eyes, muscular and clean-shaven. After introductions were made, they led us to their police car. It felt weird having to sit in the back of a police car. I did not think much of it and went to sit in the passenger's seat up front. However, I entered the driver's seat, making a fool out of myself in front of the officers and Ioli who laughed out loud. In Cyprus, as I should have known, they drove on the other side following the driving code of the British who colonised the island not so many decades ago.

As we drove along the scenic route to our crime scene, Ioli made small talk with the two cordial Greek-Cypriot officers that were sent to pick us up. I was more focused on the endless, deep, blue sea that filled my view, all the way to the horizon where the sea caressed the light blue cloudless sky. "*If there is such a thing as a paradise and my girls are there, I wish they have views like this*," I thought. My thoughts did not distract my attention from the conversation ongoing in the police car.

"It is nothing like we have ever laid eyes on before," Andrea admitted.

It was amusing to see these youngsters discuss the case, while obviously trying to flirt with Ioli. Ioli, though, remained professional and I could tell that every question she made was aiming to gain clues to the case. This girl truly had a way of getting others to open up.

"Where did you live in the US, Captain?" Giorgo asked.

"I see your reputation precedes you," Ioli commented.

"Astoria," I answered.

"My grandmother was American. I think she lived in the Bronx."

"You never visited?"

"My father left us when I was young. He didn't keep in touch. I would love to visit America one of these days," he said with a slight complaint in his voice.

"There's Petra tou Romiou. On your right, down there," Andrea pointed out.

We looked down and saw the long winding road leading to the beach where a great rock and many smaller ones around it stood out of the water. We parked right next to the beach just behind the police tape that kept back the curious tourists and the noisy reporters. We ducked under the tape and walked over to who seemed to be the person in charge.

"Captain Filippou, this is Captain Papacosta and Lieutenant Cara of the Hellenic Police," Giorgo said introducing us.

Captain Filippou shook both our hands firmly and with a slight smile said, "welcome to our island. Sorry it is not under better circumstances."

We took turns in shaking his hand and slightly smiling that awkward murder scene smile. We both nodded in agreement that the circumstances were not the greatest.

Captain Filippou was a short, square-looking man with scattered grey hair and tired eyes. A man that looked well past his prime, but probably was not even in his late fifties. The job sure did get the best of him.

He looked up to us every time he spoke, and I wondered if he would have a neck-ache by the time he was through with the two tall Greek police officers.

We followed him as he led us down to the beach. Law enforcement officers and the crew of the forensic team were scattered all over the beach looking for evidence. It was at that moment when I noticed how quiet it was for a crime scene. The sound of the waves crashing upon the pebble beach overlapped all other noises. In all the organized chaos happening around us, one image stood out above all — the dark-blue body bag. A blonde lady in her early fifties, wearing the smallest reading glasses imaginable, stood beside the body. From her posture and her manner, my brain identified her as the coroner.

"Notice how nobody is smoking?" Ioli murmured.

"Or holding a cup of take away coffee," I replied.

"No one is striding up and down barking orders," she continued, pointing out the differences between this crime scene and crime scenes back in Greece.

''There,'' the captain said, pointing at the rock in the sea as he stopped just a few steps from the water. ''The body was found there, standing up...''

''Standing up?'' Ioli asked, with evident curiosity written in her voice.

The captain looked down and quietly said, "the killer passed a whole metal bar through her back tissue. You know, the thin ones used at construction sites. Like a fence spike it was. That's how he got her to stand up. He cut off her arms too. Mrs. Angelidou, the coroner, will tell you more."

"Who found the body?" I inquired.

"An American professor staying at a hotel nearby. He came for a morning swim. He was in a right state. Still is kind of. I cannot say I blame him, to be honest. This is not something you get to see on any given day. He is over there with the paramedics if you wish to speak with him after the coroner."

"Did you find anything else on the body, the rock...?" Ioli asked next.

"Nothing on the body. She was completely naked. However, there was a red rose with a hand mirror placed on the rock in front of the body. We did not find any fingerprints."

"This is a very careful murderer," I remarked. "Have you managed to identify the body?"

"An Alicia Robinson was reported missing from her hotel in a nearby village an hour ago. She went for a walk last night and no one has seen her since. A model from the UK. Judging on the victim's looks and age, I believe it's her, but of course, we have arranged for someone from the modelling agency to come down to the hospital's morgue and identify her officially."

“Excuse me? Captain?” a decorous cadet interrupted us. “Excuse me for interrupting you sir, but the coroner said she has to leave, so if the Greek police want to talk to her...”

“Ok, ok, we are coming,” the captain said and rolled his eyes.

I don’t know why, but every time I walk towards a body bag time seems to slow down, noises fade away and everything around turns to grey. The only thing I see in color is the body bag. I do not know why. Maybe I am just weird that way. Maybe I just watch way too many crime shows.

As we approached, the coroner, not caring about pointless introductions, knelt down and unzipped the bag all the way down to the waist of the victim. The young girl was stunningly beautiful. She looked peaceful for a victim of such a violent crime. There was a tranquillity you did not often observe with murder victims. She looked asleep as the crime was fresh and no decomposition had taken place.

“Sleeping beauty...” Ioli whispered as if she was reading my mind.

“Yeah, if sleeping beauty was missing a pair of arms,” the coroner remarked sarcastically and further peeled the body bag to reveal how the girl’s arms were chopped off just below her shoulders. They were violent and messy cuts and you could clearly see how the killer struggled to cut through the bone. Pieces from arteries and skin were dangling from the remaining part of the arms.

"The arms?" Ioli asked.

"Haven't found them yet. He has either taken them with him or most likely he threw them into the sea. Quite deep waters we've got here, just a few meters in. I've called for the coast guards' scuba diving team to search the area. I'll keep you informed," the captain replied.

Coroners in New York and Greece had no differences when it came to how detached they had become due to the nature of what they witness daily and the Greek-Cypriot coroner was just the same. She showed no signs of emotion as she ordered the cadet to help her roll over the body.

Both mine and Ioli's eyes widened at the sight of the girl's back. It was badly bruised and swollen. Two bloody circles stood out: One precisely under her back spine and one just below her neck.

"She was already dead when the arms were cut off. She died due to extensive loss of blood from repeated stabs to her lumbar vertebrae, here around her waist. After the stabbing and while the victim was still alive and bleeding out, the killer dug his knife deep into her and cut open a cavity around three centimeters wide by twisting around the blade. He... or she ...proceeded to puncture her body with the sharp end of a long metal bar -two centimeters in diameter- which we removed and was collected by the evidence grew. The pointed end bar ripped through her body along her spine and exited here, at the top point of the interscapular. Time of death? Roughly six to eight hours ago."

“Any defensive wounds? One of our victims was drugged, the other was not,” I said during her short pause for breath.

“None I can see at the moment, though most defensive wounds are found on the hands and arms. She had no other bruises other than the ones on her back and these faint ones here around the neck. The killer must have stabbed her from behind and locked her close to him by putting his arm around her throat here,” she said as she pointed to the girl’s throat.

“As for being drugged, you will have to wait for blood testing to be completed.”

“Any needle entry marks?”

“No. Not anything visible at the time. I’ll check again thoroughly during the autopsy.”

“No other bruises you say? So she wasn’t raped?” Ioli asked as she gazed upon the girl’s beauty.

“No, no marks indicate rape. I’ll check for any signs of sexual intercourse. I will know more after the autopsy and I will send in my detailed report ASAP. The captain has my number if you need any clarifications. Still got my number, Andrea?’’ she threw the question at Captain Filippou accompanied with a wink that caught him off guard. Some history there for sure.

‘‘Erm, yeah, Helen.’’ He awkwardly smiled back.

"Use it one of these days, will you?" she said as she stood up and without saying goodbye, she walked towards her car.

As Captain Andrea Filippou watched Helen walk away, Ioli and I knelt next to the body.

"And the plot thickens," she whispered.

I knew exactly what she was thinking, as it was on my mind as well. We had no clue on how this victim connected to our two previous victims. We had another murder scene, again without any fingerprints and in another country.

"We need to have our team check all flights to Cyprus from Greece over the last four days, see if anything suspicious comes up. Especially flights from the islands. Also, I want people working on Alicia. I want to know where she went, who she saw, what she ate... everything."

Ioli nodded and added, "I'll call our team now and then check with the local police that they are working on Alicia's timeline since her arrival on the island. Maybe get some men to check out local construction sites, see if anyone saw anyone suspicious. I mean, the killer must have picked up the metal bar from somewhere, right?"

"That's a great idea, Cara."

As she stood up and wandered off with her phone in hand, ready to dial, I remained next to the body. I gazed upon the area and then closed my eyes, recreating the scene in my head. No blood was found on the beach so the stabbing must have taken place in the shallow waters. '*Could she have been drugged like Eric Blair or was she attacked like Stacy?*' The toxicology report would take a while, but my gut told me she was lured here and attacked. The killer must have the ability to act normal. This was no creep. This was a handsome, sociable guy capable of flirting with a girl and persuading her to follow him for a late night's swim.

''Captain, do you wish to interview the eye witness before we dismiss him? We've got him over there, on one of the picnic tables. My men have taken his statement, but I thought you would like to hear from him too."

''Yeah, for sure,'' I replied to Captain Filippou.

''See you when you're done. We have arranged a hotel for the both of you. I'll take you there afterwards." He shook my hand in a hurry and left me to go check up on his men.

''Thanks,'' I quickly managed to say and stood up. I was dusting off my knees when Ioli came up to me.

''Next stop the witness?'' she smiled.

''Clever girl. He's over there."

The professor sat in the middle of the left side of an old, worn-out by time, wooden bench. He did not look like a university professor with his white, tight, square cuts and a cobalt blue T-shirt on top. He was a tall and masculine man sitting there like a scared school boy, looking anxiously around him, mechanically playing with his thumbs by rubbing them together. Every now and then, he would stop playing with his thumbs and would scratch the back of his head. It was obvious he did not want to be there. He probably was wishing he chosen another beach for his swim. But life does not work that way and as it turned out, luck was in our corner. Who would have guessed that the professor would reveal what was right in front of our eyes all this time?

''Professor?'' I said politely with my good cop smile.

''I am Captain Papacosta and this is Lieutenant Ioli Cara. May we have a word with you?''

''Erm, yeah... sure. Are you American?'' he asked.

''I'm of Greek origin. Born and raised in New York. You?''

''Los Angeles... I already told everything to the other Captain, though his English wasn't the greatest...''

His voice had money written all over it. Obviously grew up rich with some beach mansion along Paradise Cove in Malibu. The type of guy Jimmy called posh.

''If you don't mind answering a few more questions for us...'' Ioli commented.

The professor turned and looked at her with his teary, red, sore eyes and it was the first time he relaxed his facial muscles and sat up straight. He smiled at her and answered, ''sure, of course, anything to help."

The effect of a pretty lady always amazed me.

‘‘What time did you arrive at the beach, professor?’’ Ioli started the questions as we both sat down on the picnic bench opposite the witness.

‘‘Call me Michael, please. Around ten to seven. I’m sure about the time because according to my phone I called the police at 06:58.”

‘‘Can you describe what you saw? Did you see anyone else? Any cars leaving the scene?’’ I asked.

‘‘No, the place was deserted. As I drove down, I saw no other cars. Guess most tourists were still in bed or having breakfast. I parked up there, next to the road and walked down. As I laid down my towel, I looked up and there she was. Aphrodite herself standing right there on her rock. Obviously, someone copied the pose from the sculpture of Aphrodite of Mylos that is exhibited in the Louvre. And the roses and the mirror that the police found next to her? All symbols of beauty and Aphrodite herself.”

That moment I had a flash in my head of Eric’s body and the bizarre lightning scar the murderer had left on his forehead. Lightning was the symbol of the god of gods, Zeus.

‘‘Where was Zeus born, Professor?’’ I asked, knowing the answer that was about to find me. I noticed Ioli’s eyes open wide as she immediately understood where I was going with this.

‘‘Erm...’’ The professor began to say unsure why I was asking him a job-related question. ‘‘In Crete, at Mount Ida,’’ he replied.

‘‘And Hera?’’ Ioli added.

''Well, no myth tells of a specific birthplace; however, Hera's sacred island was considered to be Samos.''

That moment we knew. We had a pattern.

''As you say the hands being cut off, the roses and the mirror were based on Aphrodite. Could you enlighten us as to what a cut open head and stomach would mean to Zeus?'' I said with my curiosity running wild.

''There have been more such murders?'' the professor said, obviously nervous and with terror painted in his baby-blue eyes.

''I am not at liberty to discuss murder cases with you, but I would really appreciate your discretion and I could use your knowledge. We are looking for a very dangerous killer and anything you may say could help us catch him,'' I answered and sat back to hear his answer.

The professor took on a lecturing tone, habit of the profession I guess, and said, ''they are two different stories –the opening of the stomach and the opening of the head- concerning Zeus. Zeus along with Poseidon, Hades, Demetra, Estia and Hera were all children of the titans Cronos and Rea. Cronos though, feared that one of his offspring would one day kill him and take his place as king of the gods. So, Cronos decided, to Rea's dismay, to eat his children. He actually swallowed them whole. Rea was desperate and when Cronos asked to eat their last child –Zeus- Rea gave him a large stone wrapped in cloth to swallow. Zeus remained hidden and grew up in Crete until he felt strong enough to challenge his father. Zeus managed to defeat Cronos and he proceeded to cut his stomach wide open as to release his five siblings with whom they would form the Olympian Gods.''

''I thought the Olympian Gods were twelve,'' Ioli said.

''Yes, they are. Aphrodite, daughter of Uranus and offspring of Zeus with various women, were added to the original group of gods. Athena was one of his daughters and our second legend. You see, the Oracle told Zeus that his mistress, who was bearing a child, was going to give birth to his murderer. Zeus, having taken a lesson or two from his father, but not willing to kill his unborn, decided to swallow his mistress so he himself would give birth to his child, therefore, changing the prophecy. I know these myths are weird to us today, but they were a reality to the ancient Greeks,'' he added, most likely having read our expressions. Our ''what the fuck?'' looks as Ioli so elegantly put it later on.

''Believe me, Professor,'' I said, ''this is the most interesting lesson I have ever attended. Please go on."

''Well, when it was time for Athena to be born, Zeus had terrible migraines. Migraines so bad he asked the god Hephaestus to cut his head wide open. Myth tells how a full grown Athena was born out of his brain. Thus, she is considered to be the goddess of wisdom."

''What can you tell us about Hera and her symbols?'' I asked.

"Hera!" he said with fascination. "Hera was the wife of Zeus. She was also his sister, but such details did not matter back then," he said with a smile and Ioli smiled back at him. He was quite the good looking guy and I could sense some chemistry filling the air between the two.

"She had various symbols, mostly animals like the cow and the lion. Her most known symbol, though, was the pomegranate which symbolised fertility. Hera was the goddess believed to bless the woman's genitals as to be fertile and bear many strong and healthy children. Hera, we could say, was the queen of the gods. However, she was not envied. Alas, Hera was cheated on, on way too many occasions. Perhaps that was the price she had to pay as she was married to The God. Zeus could do and act as he pleased and he often broke her heart," the professor added.

Ioli and I exchange a look and it was obvious that we were thinking the same thing. Not only did we have a killer who killed based on Greek mythology, but we also had an intelligent and erudite killer. A killer who did his research, conceive their sick, twisted plans and then execute them to the point of perfection, leaving little for the police to go on. The worst kind. He had managed to find a couple who were Zeus and Hera. A powerful man who often cheated on his wife and gave her a broken heart. He had managed to find a model to create his Aphrodite. He did his homework, but now we had a way to catch him.

‘‘Professor, I will need you to provide me with a list of the Greek Gods, their birthplaces or special islands, their symbols and anything else that could help us on this investigation,’’ I said.

‘‘Ok. Of course, I will. Just answer me something, Captain. Were other people murdered like this poor girl?’’ he asked.

‘‘Yes,’’ Ioli answered and extended her hand and laid it above his.

‘‘That is why we need your help. Maybe if we understood where he might strike next, we could save a person’s life.”

The professor smiled back at Ioli and their eyes met.

‘‘Pen and paper, please,’’ he said with a certainty in his voice and Ioli got up to ask Giorgo for some paper. I pulled out my blue Bic pen from the right pocket of my unironed, wrinkled, plain Beige shirt and placed it on the table next to the professor’s soft looking hands. We remained silent during the two minutes it took Ioli to return with a bunch of white A4 papers.

We left the professor alone to consider the task which we had provided him with and walked over to the much-needed shade of an old olive tree to discuss our case. Believe it or not, it was even hotter here than back in Crete. I could feel the sweat on my back and my shirt began sticking to my body. I was not made to be a Greek. The heat and I rarely got along. Maybe I would have been more successful as a Swede or a Russian.

‘‘I could have googled the Gods and printed the info out, you know,’’ she said with a smile and gave me one of her not-so-annoying-anymore nudges.

‘‘Why? To free the professor’s time, so you could flirt with him?’’ I joked back.

‘‘I do not know what you are referring to, Captain,’’ she said all formal and we both laughed.

‘‘Sick bastard killing by mythology, huh?’’ she said when my laughter died down.

‘‘Everybody needs a plan, right?’’

‘‘To be honest, I never had a case with so little to go on. I know what everybody says about me being some kind of top-of-my-class police star and all that, but really, I did have the luck of mostly clean-cut cases. And now this. I don’t know if I am intimidated or just so pissed off that I want to work my ass off to catch this fucker.’’

‘‘We all have such cases. You’re doing just fine Cara. And for my turn for honesty, it has been quite a while since I’ve worked with a great partner that I actually get along with.”

And yes, I earned myself another Julia smile and of course, a nudge/punch on my right shoulder.

‘‘Well, aren’t you one for compliments today. So, you had cases like this before in New York?’’

“Most serial killers plan their murders carefully and execute them to the point of perfection. If they don’t follow their rules or their pattern precisely, that’s how they end up making mistakes and get caught. I remember this one case. The New York Annihilator the papers called him. A sick ‘enter-curse-word-here’ as you would call him. He melted his victims with a blend of acid in their own bathtubs, leaving behind no evidence at all. His victims had absolutely nothing in common. He killed men and women of every age randomly. The only connection was the fact that all victims lived alone. He killed thirteen people before we finally caught him.”

“How did you finally catch him?”

“Got lucky. An old lady living across the street from the 12th victim noticed a suspicious minivan and wrote down the plates. Police went around his house to ask a few questions and he poured acid on them from the top window as they knocked on his door. Unfortunately, one cop did not make it and the other suffered severe burns on his left arm.”

“Shit!” Ioli commented as I ran my right hand all down my left arm. That was when I noticed the professor approaching us, papers in hand.

“Here you go,” the professor announced and gave me the paper in an attempt to keep me busy as he talked to Ioli. An attempt that, I must say, worked well. I looked downon the scribbling and was amazed by the knowledge he had written off by heart in such a small amount of time and had categorized it for us too.

The twelve Olympian Gods

1. Zeus – Symbols: oak, eagle, sky, thunder – Known for his erotic escapades – born in Crete, Mount Ida
2. Hera – Symbols: Cow, lion, pomegranate – Known for giving fertility and known for her jealousness – Holy Island: Samos
3. Poseidon – God of the sea and of earthquakes – Symbols: His trident, water, horses, dolphins – no particular birthplace or holy island/city
4. Demetra – Sister of Zeus – Goddess of the harvest – Symbols: various grains, wheat – known for changing the seasons
5. Athena – Daughter of Zeus – Goddess of wisdom – Symbols: owl, armor, olive tree –

Known as being against marriage - Holy City: Athens

6. Hestia – Sister of Zeus – The quiet one – Known for giving health, protector of doctors/healers – Known symbol: the fireplace – Also born in Crete

7. Apollo – Son of Zeus – God of the sun, of music and of future telling – Symbols: musical instruments, mostly the Lyra – Born on the small island of Delos

8. Artemis – Daughter of Zeus and the twin sister of Apollo – Goddess of the moon and of hunting – Most known symbols: the deer – Also born on the island of Delos

9. Ares – Son of Zeus – The God of War – Symbols: various weapons and the color red, also animals like the dog and the boar – no associated island/town though worshipped

more in the towns of Sparta and Mani

10. Aphrodite – Daughter of Uranus – Goddess of beauty – Symbols: Roses, dove, mirror, swan, shells, myrtle–Born in Cyprus.

11. Hephaestus – Son of Hera (Maybe Zeus) – God of metalworking and fire– Symbols: Hammer, anvil, tongs – Major cult following on the island of Lemnos (The island Hera threw him after giving birth to him)

12. Hermes – God of Commerce, the flying God, the messenger of the Gods, the protector of thieves – Symbol: His winged sandals – no particular island or town

If I may add: besides these 12 Gods, ancient Greeks had variations of the twelve Gods. The most found were the omission of Hestia and the adding of either

-Dionysus – God of wine and of a good time – Island of Naxos

-Hades – The oldest brother of Zeus – One of the major Gods, but he never lived on Mount Olympus – God of the Underworld

Some lists even went as far as adding Hercules.

Also, there were many other Gods and demigods and entities that the ancients believed in.

If I could be of any further assistance, do not hesitate to call me (my USA cell number is 001 718 917 646 347). I will be visiting the Greek Islands next and maybe Rome before heading back home.

A feeling of despair came over me, after the initial feeling of jubilation. We had a rough pattern, but what were we supposed to do? Protect the entire city of Athens? Police several islands with tens of thousands of locals and even more tourists? The thought that our deleterious killer was most likely planning on killing another ten people or so would not leave my mind. I read through the papers again, only smiling at the end. Don't get me wrong, I appreciated the professor's willingness to help but his phone number was an obvious "here's my number" for Ioli. I looked across at the two of them making small talk and awkwardly smiling at each other. I took out my phone and with a sigh, I opened my contact's list. A... B... C... Chief... another sigh and I pressed call.

I must have been on the phone with the chief a good twenty minutes before I noticed at the corner of my eye, Captain Filippou standing a few meters away from me. As tactically as I could, I managed to close the conversation with the chief.

"Yes, Captain Filippou?"

"My men arrested a man a few miles down the road. He was driving way over the speed limit in an old pickup truck. When he saw the police block, he turned off the main road. My men followed him and forced him to pull over. He cursed and yelled at them that he did nothing wrong. Oh, and you're going to love this. When asked where he was last night, he said at home sleeping as he just got back from Crete yesterday morning!"

I called over to Ioli that we were off, and from the tone of my voice, she knew something important had happened. She quickly said goodbye, a thanked the professor and ran to catch up with Captain Filippou and I.

''Let's go with my car,'' the captain suggested, much to my relief of not having to sit in the back of a patrol car.

''The suspect is being detained at a local station just five minutes away, get in,'' he said as he beeped open his black series 3 BMW.

''Must pay better in Cyprus,'' I whispered to Ioli and we exchanged guilty smiles like naughty school children not wanting to be heard by their teacher.

"Still love my little car."

"Yes, I have noticed," I joked as I recalled how she would walk around her Opel every time she returned to it, to check for dents or scratches. Or worse, both.

"How did it go with the chief?"

"He wants it all very hush-hush. Don't let the papers know it is the same killer and so on. As long as we have what seems to be the killing of a married couple, he is happy. It would be bad publicity for the islands if news gets out about a serial killer."

"I was hoping that now with a third victim, we would be getting a bigger team."

She was right. The two officers in Vathy had pretty much wrapped up their local investigation of the murder of Mrs. Blair and only two men from the force back in Crete were assigned full time to our case. They were mostly caught up with checking flights, rentals and interviewing people around Mr. Blair's hotel and murder site.

“We’re here,” the captain announced, interrupting my flow of thought.

The small local station of Pissouri village was literally five minutes away. A local policeman welcomed us all formally and led us to the only holding cell the old building had.

A brawny, tattooed man wearing worn-out, ripped army trousers and a tight, black T-shirt was sitting down with his fists clenched together on the table. Three chairs stood opposite him, waiting for our arrival. He looked up with obvious fury in his green eyes as we walked into the room.

‘‘I am Captain Filippou...’’

‘‘Great!’’ the suspect said angrily. ‘‘Maybe you can tell me why the hell am I here!’’

‘‘Mr. Stelio, you avoided a police roadblock and you resisted arrest by yelling and cursing officers of the law!’’ the Captain said calmly as he sat down in the middle chair opposite the suspect. This was our case, but this was his jurisdiction. As Stelio did not say anything, the captain continued by introducing us. I sat down on his right and Ioli on his left.

“Do you wish to have an attorney present?”

“Why? Are you arresting me?” the flippant forty-year old said.

“No, but you have the right to have your lawyer present during questioning.”

"I don't need that greedy bastard charging me one hundred euros just to sit here and warm the freaking chair!" he snapped in a nasal, quavering voice.

"Ok, then. Let's get this going."

"Ooh, yes, please. Let's! Nothing better to do!" he rudely said.

''Do you have a reason for your behavior, Mr. Stelio?'' the captain asked.

''No. I saw no road block. That was the turning I always take to go home, ok?''

''There are no houses nearby the exit. Where were you really going?''

''Home! Are you calling me a liar? I take that exit because I enjoy the scenery of the vine fields,'' he sarcastically remarked.

''And all the cursing towards the officers?''

''I don't like being bothered. And I don't like cops, ok? Meddling in people's businesses all the time for stupid reasons when you should be fighting real crimes, you know?''

''A murdered girl is not a real enough crime for you?'' Ioli asked.

The suspect sat up all uncomfortable. His facial muscles relaxed and his voice tone was lowered to a civilized standard.

‘‘What? A girl was murdered? Wait... and you think that... no, no... I had nothing to do with any of this... I... I thought you just picked me up for avoiding the road block. This... this is some serious shit.’’

‘‘Yes, Mr. Stelio. This is indeed some serious shit. Now, do you want to start working with us and tell us exactly why you were acting so suspicious?’’ I asked.

Stelio looked up at the cheaply painted ceiling and with a deep sigh, he slowly lowered his head.

‘‘I had been out catching ampelopoulia!’’ he admitted all guilty, to mine and Ioli’s total confusion.

‘‘You serious?’’ the captain said annoyed.

‘‘Yeah, that’s why I avoided the road block,’’ the guilty, dim-witted man admitted.

‘‘Sergeant!’’ the captain called out.

‘‘Yes, sir?’’ the interrogation room’s door opened.

‘‘Have you finished with searching the pickup truck?’’

‘‘Yes, sir. Nothing suspicious. Just some sticky sticks used for bird catching and some poor dead ampelopoulia in the back.’’

‘‘Thanks, that’ll be all,’’ the captain said disappointed.

Birds! Ampelopoulia, from what we found out later on, was a Cyprus delicacy enjoyed for many years throughout the island.

However, with the island's admission to the European Union and under pressure from wildlife protection committees, the government banned all hunting of the birds and outlawed their sell island-wide.

''How do we know this is not just a clever alibi? Where were you last night Stelio?'' I asked.

''Please, I'm sorry for my bad behaviour. I was at home sleeping. I was exhausted. Just returned from Crete, you see. I was on holiday with my girlfriend. Call her. She will tell you."

''When did you go?'' Ioli asked.

''Three days ago. Just a short-getaway trip."

Eric Blair was killed a week ago. This was not our killer. My instinct was screaming out that this guy could not have planned such complicated murders.

''Sergeant!''

''Sir?''

''Come, get his statement, check his flight details and release him.''

''Thank you for your time,'' he said dryly to our now former suspect and we exited the room.

''It has been a long day for you. Let me drop you off at your hotel and if anything new comes up, I'll be in touch,'' the captain said and disappointed with another dead end we followed him to his car.

*****

Chapter 12

New York, 1972

The travelling bus was getting closer and Katie could see the Empire State City rising up from the endless horizon.

During the entire journey, Katie's nose had never left the window glass. She wanted to see everything: Everything she had been missing for the last seventeen years of her God-fearing life. Her eyes were exploring every house, every tree, and every little town. Katie had never really left Dayton before. On the one occasion where her family ventured out of Dayton's town limits, it was to go to a religious study meeting in a nearby village. She could not even remember the name of the village as all she could recall from the tender age of seven was that she had to behave like a good little Christian girl.

As the crowded bus entered the city, Katie was ecstatically excited. She was in New York. With all its tall gleaming buildings and with all the millions of people who had the luck to not be raised by her parents back in Dayton and did not have to go to her harrowing school or her boring church. The bus turned into the station on Canal Street, entered between two other buses and came to a complete halt.

Katie stepped off the bus with eyes wide open and strangely enough with no fear. She had no money, besides the pocket money she had taken to school that day, no clothes, no home to go to, but Katie felt no fear. She had been liberated. She had been released and she had power - the greatest power of all, right there the whole time, between her legs. She saw how those boys went crazy for her. She saw how the foolish boys at her school thought of just one thing and it was that one little thing that Katie was planning on using to get ahead. No more hiding. No more suffocating. She would be who she wanted to be. This was Day One of living under Katie's rules.

She walked through the station with the many buses and the even more people. The diversity cheered her up as she whispered to herself, "Dorothy, you're surely not in Kansas anymore."

She spotted the small blue WC sign and entered the ladies room, ignoring flashbacks to what happened to her the last time she was in a ladies' lavatory. She walked through the dirty, glutinous restroom towards the once white ceramic wash basins. The odour was unpleasant and overwhelming. Katie quickly splashed some water upon her face and ran her fingers through her hair that had been finally freed from that awful ponytail. She looked at herself in the mirror and was glad to see her eyes glowing without those ugly glasses. Glasses she did not really need.

"Showtime," she said and rushed out into the station. She headed straight over to a big brown board on the side wall of the station. Papers of different sizes and colors filled up its space. NOTIFICATION BOARD, it declared at the top and the word that stuck out was FOR RENT. New York was surely more expensive than Dayton but to Katie, that was the price to pay to be in the big city.

“The City of Sin,” her father would call it as he watched the news. “You know why it is called the Big Apple, right? Because just like the apple Satan gave to Eve, so does New York lead you to sin and dismay,” he continued.

“Modern Sodom and Gomorrah,” mother would add.

Katie took out her pink Poochie pencil case from her school bag and her biology notebook which she was glad she would not be in need of anymore and started to write down all the numbers for one bedroom and two bedroom apartments. She emptied all her change into her right palm and with a never felt before confidence she walked over to the pay phone.

First number.

“Hello?”

“Woman,” she said as she hung up the phone.

Second number.

“Yes?”

“Shit,” and hung up again.

Third number.

“Hello?” came the man’s voice through the receiver.

“*Third time lucky,*” Katie thought as she arranged to meet the man at the apartment. She wrote down the address and looked for a cab. There was a whole line of yellow taxis, but Katie was searching for the right one. After a quick look, she walked over to the last one on her left, went up to the window and looked in. The indolent taxi driver was in his fifties, bald, unshaved and was wearing some old jeans with a blue and red checked shirt. ''The perfect choice,'' Katie whispered to herself.

''Excuse me,'' she said. ''I need to go to this address in Brooklyn?'' and passed the paper to the driver.

''Sure, jump in,'' he said with his rough voice.

''Erm, there's just one problem. You see, I just got back from out of town and my handbag was stolen. I haven't got any money on me. If you could just take me home, I'd be very grateful."

She saw the taxi drivers' face go dark in a heartbeat.

''Listen kid, I'm not driving all the way up to Brooklyn for free,'' he barked.

''I said, I'd be very grateful,'' Katie said, emphasizing the *very* and giving him her best shot of a seductive look.

''What?'' he asked, obviously puzzled.

''I could sit up front, next to you and my hands could help kill the boredom of driving all the way up to Brooklyn for free,'' she smiled.

The cautious cab driver looked around, not believing what his ears were hearing.

He probably thought if it was some sort of set-up with hidden cameras.

"Get in," he finally said as if being forced to.

When the scruffy and now excited cab driver drove out of the bus station and turned left down the street, Katie's left hand reached out and touched his knee. The driver looked down and smiled mischievously with pure excitement in his round brown eyes.

"*At his age and with his looks, he must not get any that often. This is going to be easy,*" Katie thought as her hand ran up his thigh. She could see him getting hard, his bulge pushing up against the zip of his dirty, tattered, blue jeans. He helped Katie unbutton him and soon he was in heaven. Katie loved it, hearing his small grunts and heavy breathing while he desperately tried to concentrate on the road.

A few minutes passed before he gasped "Fuck... I'm going to explode."

Without a second thought, Katie leaned over and began to please him orally, just in time to feel his release.

"Oh my God," she heard him repeating in a whisper as she sat back up in her seat. The satisfied driver tucked away his genitals, turned right and drove for a while in silence as Katie turned up the volume on the radio and began to sing *Gypsies, tramps and thieves* out loud.

Finally, he parked outside a tall bricked building with a couple of young Ginkgo trees planted outside on the grey cracked pavement.

''We're here,'' he said, pointing to the old looking block of apartments.

Katie opened the door, but she did not get out just yet. She turned and looked at her fifty year old and overly excited driver and asked, ''what's your name, mister?''

''Huh? Matthew,'' he replied, not expecting the question.

''Matthew, I am Katie. Can I have your number if I may require your services again?'' she asked and watched him clumsily open the glove department, take out a piece of paper and write down his work number.

''Here you go,'' he said and passed her his number. ''Just ask them to send Matthew, ok.'' he said and Katie nodded back.

''Have a nice day,'' she said with a flat smile and got out of the car. She stood there watching the cab drive off and vanish into the traffic that was flowing like a river through the endless streets of this strange big city.

''Transportation? Check!'' she whispered as she mentally ticked the list of things to do in New York. She looked around. All the buildings looked the same with the same old brown-red brick, same tree every few meters, same steps leading up to the entrance and all the little windows with the same few plants and flowers.

"How do they find their house when they come home drunk?" she joked to herself as she walked up the steps and pressed the doorbell button for flat 312.

"Hello?" the deep, manly voice answered over the speaker phone.

"Yeah, err... its Katie. I called you earlier?" she questioned as she heard the buzz and pushed upon the front wooden door.

"Come on up," he replied cheerfully.

The elevator was small and obviously outdated; however, it had a very pleasant scent of roses. She stepped out on to the third floor and looked left and then right. The walls needed a good repainting while the carpets were quite clean; probably changed recently. She looked at the little golden numbers nailed on each brown door. "306...308...310...312!" she silently said as she walked passed each door. She stayed still for a good whole minute just looking at the door of apartment 312.

"Showtime, Katie! Act 2," she finally said and gently but firmly knocked on the door. The wooden door opened to reveal a man in his late thirties, clean shaven, with short dark-brown hair and modern black reading glasses. His eyes were kind and he smiled widely at her.

"Come in, Katie. Come check out the place."

Katie smiled back and walked past him to stand in the middle of the living room. It had an old brown sofa and opposite it was a small bookshelf and a little TV stand with an outdated television upon it. There was only one picture on the wall and it was of some yellow flowers placed inside an orange clay vase.

''Well, this is the main living area and that's the kitchen. There are two bedrooms of equal size and a bathroom. Have a look around,'' he said with an unwavering smile. Katie walked into the tiny kitchen, thinking that she did not know how to cook anyway. One bedroom had a bed in it while the other was completely empty. The bathroom was one of the ugliest she had ever laid eyes upon, but at least it was clean and had all the essentials. Green and purple tiles obviously did not combine and had no place living together in a two by two bathroom.

''Staying alone?'' he asked.

''Yes.''

''Student?'' he asked, slightly bemused as colleges had already started back in September.

''Yes,'' she answered, hoping he would not ask her where.

''Where you from?'' the questions continued coming.

''Florida,'' she said as it was the first that popped into her head.

''Wow, must be lovely down in Florida this time of year."

Katie just smiled back and walked into the bedroom on the right and sat on the double bed with the red bed sheets and the two puffed up pillows.

“So, how come you are late to college, if you don’t mind me asking?” he asked, entering the room behind her.

“I was going to come in September, but financial difficulties in the family kept me away. I guess I have a lot of catching up to do.”

She hoped the mention of financial difficulties would lead him away from asking personal questions and getting down to business.

“It’s one hundred dollars per month, two rents upfront,” he said, looking at Katie.

Katie looked up at him with her big round eyes looking straight into his. She stood up, never releasing their eye lock, and walked towards him. She pushed her body up against his and with her right hand, she cupped him right between the legs. He then placed both his hands on her thighs and kissed her passionately on her neck. Katie, who was caught off guard by his spontaneous erotic response, sighed out loudly and gently bit his earlobe. His hands ran up all over her body as he kissed her with force on her youthful, rosy lips. It was Katie’s first kiss and it could not have been more perfect; she felt her whole body shiver and her knees got weak. The robust man, whose name she did not even know, picked her up and threw her on the bed. Katie sat there watching him as he rashly took off his grey shirt and pulled down his blue jeans. The bulge in his boxers was where Katie kept her eyes. He teased her, pulling them down slowly, finally revealing his erected penis. Katie’s eyes opened wide and she smiled in delight at the sight of the naked man she had opposite her.

"Take *all* your clothes off," he said, emphasising the all in his demand.

Katie, without hesitation, stripped away all her clothes and laid naked on the bed. The man then climbed up on the bed and came on all fours above her. He kissed her gently on the mouth, then on her neck and with his tongue, he journeyed down to her breasts. Katie's heartbeat was echoing in his ears. He continued his journey down and found himself between her legs. Soon, his tongue was inside her and his hands were caressing her upper body. Katie could not control herself any longer and began to breathe out loud. As he heard her screams get louder, he lifted his head and with his tongue, he journeyed back up to her mouth. Katie yelled out with joy as she felt him inside her. She thought she was in heaven as he changed positions with her. Her young body melted in his experienced arms. Soon, Katie was on top of him and he was thrashing Katie back and forth with his hands placed on her lower body, giving Katie her strongest orgasm yet. He lifted his body, hugged her and turned them round for him to be on top. He pushed deep inside her while swirling around. Then, he suddenly pulled out, and with a small grunt, he came all over her belly and breast. Panting, he fell on top of her and kissed her on her forehead.

"That... was..." he began to say breathlessly.

"Amazing!" Katie cried out with pure satisfaction.

He smiled at her as he got up and walked over to his jeans. He bent down and searched for his pack of cigarettes and his silver

Zippo lighter. Naked as he was, he stood there looking out the window, enjoying one of his Marlboros.

''I want to stay here but... I can't afford it,'' she said, sitting in the nude on the edge of the bed and quickly added, ''but I will! I promise I will pay you. I will find a job...''

''It's ok, kiddo. I knew you didn't have the money. A young and beautiful girl like you going for an older guy like me. Don't stress. Pay me when you can and... if it's ok by you, maybe I could come round and visit you now and then,'' he said as he turned and smiled at her.

''Sure,'' she rushed to answer, happy to be called beautiful for the first time.

As he got dressed, Katie remained naked. Her body was too hot for clothes. She had just made love for the first time and she did not want it to end.

''I've got to go baby girl,'' he said, winked at her with a warm, gentle smile and slowly walked out of the room. Katie walked behind him to the front door and as he opened the door, he turned and laid a tender kiss upon her lips.

''See you soon my little Katie,'' he said and turned to leave.

''Wait! I don't even know your name,'' she said with sorrow and gave him a love struck puppy eye look.

''It's Alexandros,'' he said.

‘‘Alex...an-dros?’’ Katie repeated never having heard the name before.

‘‘Yeah, it’s Greek. From the ancient general, Alexander the Great.”

Katie shook her head to say she did not know who he was talking about.

‘‘Guess I’ll have to teach you a thing or two about Greece and its history!’’ he laughed and closed the door behind him.

With the door closed, Katie ran and jumped onto the bed. Her smile was running from ear to ear.

‘‘Accommodation? Check!’’ she said and giggled out loud.

The next morning, Katie headed down the street to the phone booth and called up Matthew. She remained there waiting for him to show up. As she stood there, she wondered for a second what her mother could be doing and if they had the police looking for her.

‘‘I should send them a letter, just in case,’’ she thought.

The thought of being forced to go back terrified her. That was her old life and she had buried that horse deep in the ground.

Soon, Matthew parked up beside her and leaned over to open the passenger door. Katie sat in the cab and smiled a good morning to enthusiastic-to-see-her Matthew. He had not anticipated her to call so soon.

‘‘So, where to, my lady?’’ he asked.

‘‘Nowhere,’’ she replied and saw that same puzzled face like yesterday.

‘‘I need a job. I need cash.”

‘‘And what do I look like? An agency or something?’’ he said and chuckled.

‘‘Well, you drive around. I thought you might have seen some wanted signs.”

‘‘Now that you say, there was a wanted sign at the diner just a couple of blocks down,’’ he said.

‘‘Perfect!’’ she responded and placed her hand on his leg.

*****

Chapter 13

We both just stood there, looking at the car.

The Greek-Cypriot police had provided us with a rental car: A shiny silver Honda Civic. It was a nice car. It was just that the steering wheel was on the wrong side.

''Go on then,'' Ioli said.

''Ladies first,'' I joked and passed her the keys.

''Chivalry when needed, huh?'' she asked as she took the keys, opened the car and situated herself in the passenger's seat.

''Oh, the wheel is missing, oh, look it's over there. In *your* seat!'' she said and laughed out loud.

As I sat in the driver's seat, I knew that one of her nudges was to follow and I was not wrong.

''Pissouri village here we come,'' she said as she placed the Nat Vat on the board and gave me a nudge.

I turned the key, the engine started and we were on our way to the village where our murdered model had walked her last hours.

For the first time in a while, I had enjoyed a dreamless good night's sleep at Aphrodite Hills Resort where the good old captain had booked us two rooms. Six hours without a visit from Gaby. No waking up shouting as cold sweat fell from my face. I had enjoyed a good meal too. Late evening, Captain Filippou came back to the five star hotel and offered to buy me dinner at one of the resort's high maintenance restaurants.

"Two Captains on a date," I joked, but once again, my humor did not register well. Maybe that was why I am into homicides and not comedy. I must admit, it was a pleasant evening, which halfway through, detoured from the case and turned personal. Drinking our Cypriot brewed beers after two amazingly well-cooked, honey marinated, Godzilla size pork chops, I realized how much I had missed hanging out with friends back in the States. Especially Jimmy, who by the way I had to call and ask to check up on the list provided by Mrs. Blair. Captain Filippou, as it turned out, was the type of guy that after a few drinks opens up about everything without even being asked. Soon, I was listening to how he had started an affair with Helen, the seductive, sultry coroner, how his faithful wife finally found out and how his marriage ended badly after twenty years.

"Of course, my daughters took their mother's side and now I only hear from them on birthdays and holidays. They didn't even care to ask if I was unhappy in my marriage and what a miserable cow my ex-wife was. And Helen? She thought that after the divorce we could be something! As if I would marry again! I'm not *that* crazy," he announced laughing.

Ioli too was being entertained over dinner at a nearby restaurant. She had bumped into the helpful professor at the hotel reception and he missed no chance on asking her to accompany him to dinner. An offer she at first declined, most likely thinking of me being alone. Now it was my turn to give her a nudge. ‘‘Go, I’ll be fine. Go be young and have fun,’’ I said and then added, ‘‘be home by 10,’’ to gain an angry look with tones of ‘‘enough said, go away now.”

‘‘So how was your date?’’ I asked as I drove the wrongly-steered car.

‘‘It wasn’t a date,” she retorted and then added in a low, toneless, calm voice “and it went fine, he’s a good man that professor.’’

‘‘Never had you for the geeky type!’’

‘‘Me neither,’’ she replied and we both chuckled.

‘‘Please bear left and take the next exit on your right,’’ the mechanical voice from the device advised me.

‘‘Read me the details of our eye witness,’’ I asked Ioli, who was busy looking through her notes from the crime scene. She flipped a couple of pages in her little black agenda book and read, ‘‘an Apostolos Demetriou. Shop owner of Pepis Mini-Market. Last person to see the victim alive, according to Captain Filippou’s call this morning. The witness told the police that the victim left with a man she had just met at his shop and that he saw them walk down to the beach together.”

‘‘Let’s hope he remembers what the man looks like,’’ I remarked.

Pissouri Bay was quiet. Just the one lane with a few shops, a pizza place and many restaurant signs popping out at you every now and then. Some senior couples from northern Europe were walking by the shops, side by side, and further down was a British family obviously beach dressed and heading for the water. Soon, we both saw the sign *Pepis* and I indicated left and parked outside of the shop. It was a tall stone building. Later, I found out that it was used as a warehouse in the old days for grape storage. Now, outside, it had ice-cream fridges and fridges with every sort of ice cold drinks along with swimwear, beach toys, hats, shoes and anything you could imagine for the beach. Inside were mini-market goods, a wine and spirits cava and low-cost souvenirs. We entered the shop and introduced ourselves to the owner.

''Would it be easy for you to go talk somewhere a bit more private?'' I asked as I looked upon the few tourists that were shopping souvenirs and discussing what would look better on their grandma's bedside table.

''Yes, of course. My wife can take over here and we can go upstairs,'' he said and called over his wife, who smiled politely at us.

Upstairs was an old wooden office with three Greek coffee shop chairs where we could sit and discuss the night Alicia walked off into the night with our murderer. All kinds of stock for the shop below filled the high ceiling room.

''Would you like something to drink?'' he inquired kindly.

“Thank you, but no,” I said as I looked over to Ioli to see if she wanted something. She quickly shook her head that she did not.

“Mr Apostole, according to the report of the police officer you spoke to this morning, you were the last to see the girl before her death. You say, she left here with someone?”

“Yes. She came for an ice-cream as I was closing up the shop. Very beautiful girl. She had forgotten her money at the hotel so the man in queue behind her offered to pay. He had bought an ice-cream too.”

“Was the man Cypriot?” Ioli asked.

“No, I believe he was a foreigner. Well, he did not speak Greek,” he replied.

“Would you say he was English, like the girl?” I asked.

“They all sound the same to me. He could be. He was white like the girl but more tanned. He spoke to me and to the girl in English. I’m afraid I do not recognize the different accents of my customers. Mostly Europeans down here. British, Germans and Russians. And lately, we have been getting quite a few Israelis. Don’t get many from other countries.”

“Mr. Apostole, when I first started out in law enforcement I wanted to become a sketch artist for the police. I took most of the lessons, but field work won me over in the end. Do you think you could describe the man to me?” I asked.

“Sure, yes. I’ll go get you one of our sketch pads,” he said and got up quickly to go get them from the shop below.

“What a kind man,” I remarked to Ioli who was staring at me.

“Well, what you know, sketch artist huh?” she said and raised her eyebrows.

“Oh, shut up,” I snapped back and gave her one of the same goofy looks I used to give to Gaby when she was being a smart-ass. Which was quite often, I must add.

“I just hope you’re good!” she said, copying my look.

“Here you go,” he said coming back up the stairs. He passed me the pad and pencil and sat back down in his chair.

I pulled my chair closer to him and sat opposite him. I placed the sketch pad on my lap and took the well-sharpened pencil into my sweaty hand. Ioli got up, walked over to a camp bed in the rear of the room, sat down carefully and began to flick through her notes. Guess she thought to give us some space.

Mr. Apostolos looked anxious as he fiddled with his fingers waiting for me to say something.

“Mr. Apostole, just try to relax. Take a deep breath... exhale... I need you to close your eyes and really focus. Try to picture the man who was in your shop. Focus on his head and its features... relax... open your eyes,” I said in a calm voice as I drew some different circle and oval shapes on a piece of paper.

‘‘How would you describe the shape of his head? Was it round, did he have a long face...”

‘‘Oh, I can’t really say... he... well... he looked normal, if you get what I mean,’’ he said with complaint coloring his tone.

‘‘Take a look at these. What shape would you say suits him the most?’’

He pointed at one and said ‘‘But a bit more open at the forehead.”

People don’t realize how long these sketches can take. Especially by hand. Even with the help, nowadays, of computers and facial reconstruction software, a sketch artist will take the least a good half an hour. I sat there gently drawing the head and finally asked ‘‘Describe his hair for me.”

‘‘Like yours. Very short. But, if I may say, with more volume. More thicker if you know what I mean.”

I nodded with a half smile that I did and asked, ‘‘color?’’

‘‘Black. Dark black. They were the two things that were very distinct about him. His really black hair and his really green eyes.”

‘‘And his eyes? Can you choose a shape out of these or describe them to me?’’

Mr Apostolos was very cooperative and put in an effort to help us, though he could not recollect many specific details as I asked about the suspect’s nose, mouth, jaw, eyebrows and ears. He was just another guy in the shop. The owner had no reason to pay extra attention. The only things that stood out for him were the color of the hair and the eyes.

''You said his jaw was like mine?''

''Yes, but a bit bigger I think. It was a strong jaw, you know? If only my eldest daughter was here at the time. She never forgets a face. She is very fastidious. She is thirty years old today and she sees people on the street and remembers that they went to kindergarten together.''

''You're doing fine. You are more helpful than what you imagine," I calmed him.

"And finally, do you remember any distinctive features like a mole, a tattoo or a scar maybe?''

''No, no. Nothing like that,'' he said and sighed with relief.

''Ok, I think that just about covers it,'' I said, looking down at my sketch and realising that Ioli was standing right above me scanning the sketch too.

''I just wish I could have been more helpful. You know, it was late and I was tired. Should have paid more attention to the man,'' he remarked with sorrow in his voice.

''There was no way you could have known that he was not just another customer, Mr. Demetriou. And from what I can see, you two did an excellent job,'' Ioli kindly said and earned herself a wide smile from the caring man.

We thanked the owner and his wife and even allowed them to offer us some refreshing beverages as they would not let us leave otherwise. When we sat in the car, I gave my sketch to Ioli to hold and said ''We have to take this quickly to the police station. The bird guy they arrested does not fit this description and they should get men to go door to door or better, shop to shop down here."

''Ok,'' she said and pulled out her phone. She took a picture of the sketch, played around with the gadget for a second and said ''Ok, now what?''

She laughed at the amazed, confused look on my face.

''Who did you send it to?'' I asked.

''To Giorgo. He gave me his number this morning."

''I bet he did,'' I said and raised my eyebrows.

"Next moves?" she asked, disregarding my comment.

''Well, since we do not have to deliver the sketch, do you want to take a walk down the beach? I want to follow the victim's and the killer's last route."

''Sure. Good idea. I need a stretch,'' she said smiling.

We walked down the little stone steps that lowered you to a narrow, sandy path right next to the beach. The beach had that wild beauty feeling. Sandy but with stones and pebbles. Clear waters, but with tall waves. To the right, the path headed and ended at Columbia Beach Resort.

''They must have turned left,'' I noted.

"I agree. Someone would have seen them if they headed towards the hotel and all its lights. I doubt the killer would have risked it, especially considering that the hotel is probably fully booked this time of year."

"Is it summer time? Hadn't noticed!" I joked as I wiped, for the millionth time, the sweat off my forehead.

As we walked further down, Ioli pointed out that the street lights did not go all the way to the end of the bay.

''He could have parked in any field nearby. No one would have noticed them in the darkness of the night,'' I continued on her observation.

''She was not drugged, though," Ioli thought out loud as she scanned the area, turning round 360 degrees.

No needle entry found read the text I received early morning by the coroner.

"We'll have to wait for the lab report to be one hundred percent sure, but my gut tells me she wasn't drugged. And with no needle entry visible and no clear defensive wounds, I would assume she most likely went with him willingly. He may have offered her a ride to see Aphrodite's Rock,'' Ioli continued her thought.

''A pretty girl like that. He must have been one good looking charmer to...''

''Don't these girls watch the news? Hell, don't they watch any movies? I mean, who gets in a stranger's car so late at night?" Ioli interrupted me, aggravated.

We spent the next half hour looking through the fields up ahead for clues between the summer flowers and the water-deprived olive trees.

''Case solved! It was Colonel Mustard with the wrench in the middle of freaking nowhere!'' Ioli said angrily as she lifted up an old, broken, rusty wrench.

Just then, my phone rang.

''Grandpa ringtone!'' she chuckled at the sound.

''It's a classic. Reminds me of my house phone as a child,'' I quickly remarked before answering the call from Captain Filippou.

''Didn't know you grew up during the Great War."

The girl was on a roll in an attempt to relax her nerves, but I was dead serious listening to how a local hotel owner identified a guest of his as the man in my drawing.

‘‘The police are with him now at Hodjas Hotel Apartments just across Pepis Mini-Market. He is English just like the girl. I thought to let you interrogate him there.”

‘‘On our way now,’ I said, walking off towards the road.

“Filippou?” Ioli asked.

“Yeah. A guy was arrested opposite the mini-market. Fits the description apparently.”

As we approached Hodjas’ steps that lead up to the reception, Giorgo came towards us smiling.

‘‘Captain, room 201. It’s the one just there,’’ he said, pointing towards it.

‘‘Hey, Ioli,’’ he greeted her in a high school manner.

‘‘Hey,’’ she replied, rushing up the steps, following me and crushing Giorgo’s hopes for a conversation.

Hodjas apartments looked like every other holiday apartment block found in Greece in its price range. Nice gardens with buildings dying for a dip of paint and a cosmetic lift. The chipped wooden doors looked worn in and the furniture was bought somewhere near my entrance to this world.

Room 201 was spacious with everything a studio apartment could need. Well, everything basic that is. A bed, a sofa, a TV, AC, bathroom, small kitchen area, two armed policemen towering over you, and a view. The view that included the entrance to Pepis’ Mini-market. The balcony where he could easily have seen Alicia entering the shop and be right there behind her in a matter of a minute.

Mark Russell sat in the middle of the sofa looking guilty as hell. A tall, handsome guy in his early forties with thick, black hair and green eyes. He looked so touristy with his blue Speedos and a plain white *Just Do It* T-shirt over his athletic body.

''Indeed, he bears a striking resemblance to my sketch,'' I whispered to Ioli as I approached to introduce us.

Two shabby, wooden kitchen chairs had been placed opposite him for interrogation purposes.

When we sat down, Mark got even more nervous and tears began to run down his cheeks.

''Thank God, you speak English. No one is telling me anything. I was instructed to just sit here. What's going on?'' he cried as I introduced us.

"I am Captain Papacosta and this is Lieutenant Ioli Cara," I said, while reading a piece of paper provided to me by one of the officers with us in the room. Apparently, the senior lady in the room next door heard him opening his door at three o'clock in the morning on the night in question.

''Woke me up, he did! Old, creaking doors! And then he took a shower, waking up all these old pipes! I've been up since then, tell the stupid boy,'' the cranky Swiss lady yelled at the officer.

‘‘Mark, are you here on holiday alone?” I asked.

‘‘Yeah,’’ he said, fighting back more tears from falling.

‘‘How long have you been here?’’

‘‘A month or so.’’

‘‘Been here the whole time or did you pop over to Greece?’’ I kept the questions coming.

‘‘Greece? No, no... been here since I flew in from London...’’

‘‘Do you know how to sail a boat?’’

‘‘A what?’’

‘‘A boat,’’ I repeated calmly.

‘‘No, I... what is this about?’’ he said, looking first at me, then Ioli and proceeded to place his face in his hands.

‘‘If he’s the killer, he fucking deserves an Oscar, along with his life sentence,’’ Ioli commented in Greek.

‘‘Came back to his room at three a.m.,’’ I replied and gave her the note.

‘‘Can you please speak in English? And what’s that paper? Who is saying what about me? I have rights, you know!’’ Mark said, gathering himself out of his pitiful state.

‘‘Do you prefer we go down to the station and sit in a cell until you find a lawyer?’’ Ioli asked.

After a long pause, he quietly answered, ‘‘no’’ and exhaled heavily.

‘‘Where were you Tuesday late evening, Mr. Russell?’’ she continued.

‘‘Down at the bay.’’

‘‘Late night swim?’’ I asked.

‘‘Something like that. Listen, this is getting ridiculous. I don’t even know what it is you think I have done!”

He sounded angry, but his voice had guilty written all over it.

‘‘Met anyone?’’

His eyes dropped to the floor.

‘‘Mr. Russell?’’ Ioli asked, slightly leaning forward to follow his gaze.

‘‘I think I want an attorney now,’’ he firmly said with his eyes never leaving the dusty floor.

‘‘Why the change of heart?’’ I asked.

‘‘Listen, I didn’t mean to, ok? One thing just kind of led to the other. I didn’t know. That’s what I will say in court. You can’t harass me like this! I ain’t going to stand for it!’’

‘‘What happened on Tuesday night, Mark?’’

“I’m not telling you shit till you tell me what it is you think I’ve done! I’ve watched too many shows to know never to reveal anything that the police pretend to know!”

I was starting to get annoyed by this guy's behaviour, but I managed to remain serene.

“Pretend to know? I’ll tell you what I think I know. I think you met someone Tuesday night. I think you went for a walk together. And at three in the morning, you came home... alone. Where did the other person go, Mark? What happened?”

“I have no idea! Is he missing?”

“*He*?” we both asked simultaneously.

“Sorry, I don’t remember his name. He told me, but it was too difficult to remember. Something like Chris-o-do-los.”

“Christodoulos?” Ioli corrected him, still confused.

“Yeah, could be. Listen, I left him sound and well. Who knows what he got up to after me.”

“Where did you leave him?” I asked, not knowing who we were discussing.

“At the beach, I swear I did.”

“Here, down at the bay?”

“No, the next beach, the gay beach behind the rocks. That’s where we met. Listen, I swear to God, I did not know he was a prostitute. I thought I got lucky, then he asked for money. What was I supposed to do? I paid up. Please, I came here to relax. Broke up with my boyfriend back home after two years and thought to get away, you know? I swear, I did not know...''

''Mark, relax! We are investigating a murder case...''

''He's dead?'' he said with terror in a high-pitched, ear-splitting voice.

''A murder case of a dead girl,'' I continued raising my voice.

''I... I... Had nothing to do with that! I swear...''

''Stop swearing because I'm going to start swearing soon and boy, you are not going to like it! Please, be quiet!'' Ioli announced, annoyed as hell.

''A dead girl that went missing Tuesday night, here in the bay. You fit the description of the guy last seen with her. Did you buy a girl an ice-cream on Tuesday night from the mini-market across the road?''

''No, I surely didn't sir. I went down to the gay beach as the locals call it before dark to hook up. After my encounter with Chrisidolo, I went for a drive into Limassol for a drink. Salut was the name of the bar. I saw no girl. Please, I sw..., I did not harm.''

''Ok, we will have the police look for this Christodoulo guy. Give his description to the officers here with you and we will pick him up. Prostitution is illegal. Also, you will agree to have your picture taken so we can show it down at Salut. If both your stories turn up clean, you will find yourself off the airport's blacklist, get it?''

"And they will check your rental car with your permission and full co-operation," Ioli added.

As he nodded and repeated, "yes, of course, anything you want," a few times, we both stood up. Ioli walked off without saying anything while I just said a cliché ''Have a nice day'' before explaining to the officers how I wanted them to proceed.

After an evening of interviewing a bunch of clueless models who thought Alicia was in her room and walking around Pissouri village showing pictures of our victim, and my sketch to the locals and tourist alike, we headed back to our hotel disappointed with our fruitless labour.

The next day found us once again with no suspect and with huge, bold titles in the morning papers.

Killer on the loose!

Maniac *kills* in Cyprus!

Serial Killer Strikes in Pissouri!

Third victim DEAD!

One stood out from the rest.

How the hell did they find out? Oh, the chief is going to love this especially when the Greek papers pick it up.

THE OLYMPUS KILLER was the title and the article went on to explain how a serial killer was positioning and hurting his victims according to Greek mythology!

*****

Chapter 14

"The Olympus Killer," he read to himself with vast satisfaction and put down the newspaper on the small, round coffee table.

"I like the ring of that."

"*The* Olympus Killer!" he repeated.

"I AM THE OLYMPUS KILLER," he shouted and laughed out loud. He picked up his backpack and his camera and opened the door of his hotel room. He whistled all the way down the aging stairs and even blew a kiss to the young, pretty receptionist who slightly blushed at his gesture.

It had been four days since he had the pleasure of stabbing that beautiful girl down at the beach in Cyprus and killing yet another god. He remembered with joy how easy it was to chop off her arms. He was a bit doubtful in the beginning, but his good old knife did not fail him.

"The bone gave a good fight, but all the weight lifting at Big Tom's gym finally paid off," he laughed to himself and exited his hotel. Soon he was a part of the flow of tourists that filled the narrow stone streets between the little blue and white houses that mostly housed souvenir shops, ice-cream parlors and jewelry shops nowadays. There were thousands of tourists window shopping down the many winding paths. It was summer time and the island was at its peak. Mykonos, the island of the winds, is considered by many as the most beautiful out of the Greek islands with its picturesque white and blue painted villages; with its turquoise clean and clear waters, and the endless, exotic sandy beaches. The island had countless shops and restaurants for every taste and even more bars and clubs. In the daytime, tourists from all over the world sunbathe, dance at one of the many beach bars, enjoy the Greek cuisine, window shop and go sightseeing in Little Venice or the majestic windmills. However, it was at night when the island truly came alive, boasting one of the best club scenes this side of the Mediterranean.

Not that he was interested in all of that. He looked interested, but he was not. These were going to be his most difficult victims to find, after Zeus and Hera. The gods, Apollo and Artemis. The twins.

Opposite Mykonos was the tiny island of Delos. The twin gods' birthplace. The island where their mother finally found sanctuary from the wrath of Hera, who had pursued her during her pregnancy.

He looked up at the sky. The sun was low on the horizon just ready to dive into the blue waters while the moon had already appeared, ready to rise and shine through the dark. He thought it was the perfect time to kill the god of the sun and his sister, the goddess of the moon.

As he was standing in queue for a delicious double chocolate chip and banana ice-cream, he turned around and faced the group of young, German speaking adults laughing behind him.

"Having fun? Mykonos is great, is it not?"

He earned himself a few hesitated stares, but a young dark haired girl finally answered, ''Ya, it is amazing."

He did not even look at her as his attention was focused on the two honey blond, blue eyed, same height, same features pair next to her.

''You make a lovely couple,'' he noted.

The group of six giggled and the blond guy said in a heavy German accent ''Nein, we are not together! She is my sister."

His eyes instantaneously opened wide. ''Twins?'' he asked, hoping for a yes.

''No, I am much younger!'' the girl objected.

He replied with an unemotional flat line smile and turned back around.

After ordering and receiving his ice-cream, he walked out of the Italian ice-cream parlour and headed down to the town's main square. He looked around the area and chose a perfectly situated for spying, blue wooden bench to sit down upon. He sat there enjoying his ice-cream not bothered at all from all the commotion from the group of youths beside him. He had his reasons for sitting so close to the loud group. A very handsome, tall Italian wearing white shorts, an elegant blue shirt that was unbuttoned down to his worked out chest and funky green sun glasses turned and joyfully said ''That ice-cream looks delicious'' while his eyes looked deep into his.

He smiled back at the Italian and replied, ''yes, it is."

''Want to try some?'' he then asked.

''Sure,'' the Italian answered without hesitation and leaned over and licked the chocolate and banana ice-cream. He took his time; letting his tongue travel along the ice-cream before retrieving it back to his dry mouth and enjoying the iced dessert that now laid on the tip of his tongue. Mykonos was, after all, a very gay-friendly place. All his friends looked at them, smiling and trying with no success to be discrete.

''I'm Antonio from Italia,'' he said.

''Tom Newton,'' he answered, smiling at the thought of combining two fake names he had used in the past.

''Here with your friends, I see."

''Ah, yes, all these mad people are my friends,'' he said and they all turned around to face them. ''This is Gabriella, that is Maria and her brother Luigi... and this is Sergio."

They all exchanged smiles and then he asked ''Maria and Luigi, you look so alike. You twins?''

''No, but people tell us this all the time. We only have a year between us,'' said Luigi.

''Fuck, fuck, fuck! Give me a break,'' he thought and acted that his phone was vibrating.

‘‘I have to answer this. Scusa Antonio. See you guys later,’’ he said as he stood up and started to walk off, throwing the remaining ice-cream in the trash.

‘‘Come to Glam Club tonight. I’ll be there,’’ Antonio shouted with slight disappointment in his voice.

‘‘Dream on,’’ he thought. He had plans to go out clubbing but a gay bar was not the perfect place to find twins; twins that are male and female that is. After today’s setbacks and his failure to find Apollo and Artemis, he had decided to spend the night hunting at SpaceDance club. The biggest club on the island as its colorful leaflet had written all over it with bold pink letters.

He had a good feeling about the night as he stood in the queue with the massive crowd of people that had gathered to enter the club. He paid the girl at the door and smiled at the muscular giant that was the club’s bouncer. He pushed open the club’s heavy entrance door and in a blink of an eye, he found himself in a very different world. People were everywhere, dancing, drinking, singing, flirting, kissing. In the middle of the club was a huge, long bar and all around the club were massive screens and flashy lights. It had a very unique and colorful interior that pleased him; if he did not have an important task in mind, he would even consider having a bit of fun. The DJ was handing out the latest hits from techno and house music, and the club’s professional dancers were the sexiest he had ever seen. He might have even had a good time; he enjoyed dancing after all. However, there was work to be done and he got straight to it. He walked around looking like just another single guy enjoying all Mykonos had to offer, but he was a predator and all of his senses were enhanced and fixed on a very specific goal. To find the twin Gods. His eyes looked around for similarities whiles his ears listened in to every conversation going on around him.

Hours past by and Lady Luck kept on ignoring him. He was starting to feel tired. He sat down on the red, sparkling couch just below the VIP lounge and glared at all the people living in euphoria thanks to the alcohol and the music. It was at the moment when his eyes felt heavy that a young, giggling couple sat next to him and started kissing.

''I can't believe I did not talk to you sooner,'' said the tall guy with a distinct Greek accent.

''I was looking at you all night, waiting for you to make a move,'' the petite, red haired, Irish girl answered.

''It's not my fault!'' he laughed and kissed her again. ''I thought you were here with that guy,'' he added as he pointed to her brother who was having his fifth beer at the bar.

''Him? He's my brother! Can't you tell? Don't we look alike?'' she asked.

The Greek man looked across to the bar, gazed upon her brother for a few seconds and honestly answered ''Not really."

''Well, he is my twin brother and most say we look alike!"

They both giggled and continued kissing not noticing the glow upon his face. His green eyes were now once again wide open. He got up slowly and as cool as ice, he walked over to the brother.

''Hey, wanna drink?'' he asked, smiling, only to receive an icy look.

''Nah, I'm ok,'' the Irish man replied and looked away.

''Another cold beer maybe?'' he insisted.

''Listen mate, I don't swing that way... I'm ere for da ladies,'' he replied, clearly annoyed.

''Oh well, worth a try. It's just that I thought I had seen you before at my hotel, at Damianos."

''Nah, couldn't have been me. I'm staying at Myconos Beach Hotel."

''Sorry for the misunderstanding,'' he said and walked away with a smile of satisfaction drawn upon his face.

*****

Chapter 15

New York, 1972

Katie could not take her eyes off the clock. She had another longer-than-usual thirty-five minutes until her shift was over. The diner Matthew had taken her was a great place. Katie fell in love with the diner the moment her right foot made contact with the floor inside. From the outside, it did not look like much, but as her grandma used to say "Never judge a book by its cover."

Katie thought most diners looked like dining cars, but this place looked so ordinary. You could easily have classified it as just another coffee shop when passing by. However, the inside had a whole different story to be told. Maybe that was the point. To give you that Alice-in-Wonderland feeling. Inside, everything was so colorful and vibrant and encompassed various styles from the '50s and '60s. It had the usual, long diner counter and the many booths, but with an added twist as each counter stool was a cartoon character and each booth was painted in a different color than the next.

"A slice of carrot cake for the gentleman on Bugs Bunny" and "two chocolate sundaes for the blue table" were not unusual sentences to be heard in Reeve's Diner.

Mr. and Mrs. Reeve, the proud owners of Reeve's Diner, were two kind, hard-working, middle-age people who immediately fell for Katie's sweet, little, innocent 18 year old poor-student act. She was given the job and the pink uniform on the spot, and she started work the very next day. It had been three weeks since she first started. It was hard work and her feet were aching all over, but Katie was determined to stay in New York. It was worth it, both money-wise as the tips were a great bonus and people-wise. Katie was over the moon to be in such a multi-cultural city and enjoyed the fact that her customers were of every different race and face. No more looking at the same old boring faces of the folk back in Dayton.

As she wiped table 12 or the green booth if you prefer, she gazed up at the clock. Still twenty-five minutes to go. Time was surely taking it slow tonight. She prepared table 12 and walked over to the young couple that had just sat down at table 8.

''I love purple!'' the excited brunette said to her date while admiring the setting, unaware that he always brought his lady friends here and was used to each girl choosing where to sit based on their favorite color.

''Really? Mine too!'' he lied, as Katie approached them.

''Good evening,'' Katie said with a wide smile. ''Here are your menus. Just holler and I'll be right with you,'' she said and handed them the black and pink menus.

''That's ok,'' the vigorous, youthful man said. ''We know what we want. Two Reeve's Burgers with fries and a couple of chocolate milkshakes."

Katie smiled politely, took the menus and walked over to the counter.

''Joe, two Reeves. Mrs. Reeve, two milkshakes, please."

‘‘Coming right up,’’ smiled Mrs. Reeve as she watched Katie look up at the clock for the fiftieth time since her break. ‘‘Katie, honey, you can go now. It’s only another twenty minutes till the end of your shift and it’s not that busy,’’ she said as Katie shook her head and whispered a ‘‘No, it’s ok, I’ll...”

‘‘Go on now! I insist!’’

‘‘Really? Oh, thank you, Mrs. Reeve,’’ she said as she quickly removed her pink apron, hung it up on her personal hook and rushed out the door.

‘‘Ah, to be young,’’ Mrs. Reeve muttered to herself and started to prepare the chocolate milkshakes.

Katie put on her hot-pink coat in a hurry and rushed down the street. She turned left and sighed with relief. The flickering red light above the sign indicated that the pharmacy was still open. Katie pushed open the glass door and walked down the brightly lit aisles, looking left and right. She eventually found what she wanted and paused for a minute. There were tens of different brands.

‘‘The cheapest is always bad quality and the most expensive is always a rip off, granny used to say,’’ Katie whispered as she picked up the one which she thought was at a reasonable middle price. She walked up to the counter and stood behind a dirty-looking old man complaining about the rising prices to the drug store owner.

‘‘Trying to kill us off, that’s what they are doing. We cost too much, so Uncle Sam raises the prices of our medication to force us to stop taking them,'' the old man snapped, tapping his index finger on the white counter.

''I'm sure no one is trying to kill you, Mr. Harman,'' the friendly owner said as he passed him his arthritis pills. ''Yes, miss?'' he asked as he turned towards Katie.

''Just this, please,'' Katie said quietly.

''One pregnancy test. That will be $3.50, please.''

''Bring a kid into *this* world? You must be mad, child!'' the old man grunted.

''Mr. Harman!'' the owner told him off with a strict tone in his voice.

Mr. Harman just turned around and walked away, complaining about the weather being unusual for this time of year.

''I'm so sorry Miss, he is a funny old fellow that one,'' he said with a smile that had *I feel bad for you* written all over it.

''No problem,'' Katie said very casually, being used to verbal abuse all her life. ''Here you go,'' she said and passed him a five dollar note.

''Here's your one fifty.''

Katie took her change and her little white box and turned to leave.

‘‘Good night, Miss,’’ said the owner as he watched Katie walk out the front door just like so many young girls in trouble before her. All with the same worried look about what the future could behold for them.

It was quite a cold night outside with a chilly breeze swirling around through the streets. However, Katie was sweating. Anxiety had just kicked in.

‘‘What on earth would I do with a baby?’’ she said.

The thought of Alexandros coming round and finding her knocked up frightened her. He had visited Katie another three times since their first encounter and each time felt even more magical. Would he demand rent or worse, kick her out? The small flat had become her home. She took great pride in putting little touches around the place like the flower vase she had bought real cheap down at the Sunday market and an imitation painting of Van Gogh’s *The Starry Night* which she had Alex hung up above her bed.

She slammed the door behind her and ran to the bathroom. With trembling hands, she opened the box and carefully read through the instructions.

‘‘Bring the test pouch to room temperature... Immerse the strip into the urine with the arrow end pointing towards the urine...’’

Every word fed her panic.

"Come on Katie, get a grip and just pee on the God damned stick for crying out loud!" she scolded herself as she flicked through the little booklet to find the section *results.*

"Wait for colored bands to appear... Positive results may be observed in as short as 40 seconds. However, to confirm negative results, the complete reaction time (5 minutes) is required..."

She sat down on the toilet and looked at the stick.

"Maybe I should wait. I'm only a week or so late... Those stupid fuckers," she said angrily, thinking which of those four immature junkies could be the father. It couldn't be Alexandros. He always ejaculated outside of her. She wished he didn't as she would have loved to be able to lie to him that the child was his.

"Guess I'll just have an abortion," she whispered and paused.

"Get a grip, Katie!" she cried to herself.

"You haven't even pissed on the damn stick yet," she said with anger. She then took a deep breath and placed the stick between her legs. She had never felt so nervous in her whole life. She stood up, placed the stick on a piece of toilet paper she had previously left on the bathroom sink and sat back down. It took a couple minutes and a lot of courage before she stood back up and peeked at the stick.

"One line," she sighed with relief and exhaled deeply. She picked up the stick and stepped on the bathroom bin. As she was about to throw away all her worries, she noticed a faint second red line appear. Soon, two fully visible lines were staring back at her and

Katie felt the world disappear from under her feet. Her knees felt like jelly as she sat down on the floor in the middle of the room. Everything was spinning around her, sucking up her dreams and her planned future like a vicious, strong twister. She closed her eyes and allowed her watery eyes to shed a few lonely tears.

Katie could not figure out if it was her fear of hospitals and surgeries or something from her Catholic past, but the idea of keeping this baby was swirling inside her inner thoughts. She gently placed her hands over her tummy and rubbed it with a warm smile. A life was growing inside her. She could become the loving mother she never had.

Very slowly, she lifted herself up from the hard, cold bathroom floor, took one determined look at herself in the mirror and wiped away her tears. She had work to do.

She walked into her little colorful kitchen, opened the second drawer, took out a pencil and a piece of paper and began to write.

My dearest father,

Words cannot describe how much I have missed you.

I cannot believe I let the devil get the best of me.

I am in New York and I want to come home.

I took out a loan from a pawn shop to buy a car and if I leave N.Y. without paying them back, they will find us and hurt us.

Please send me $1500 to pay them off and we can sell the car (which is worth much more) when I get home.

Send the money ASAP to Bronx Main Post Office, locker 314.

As soon as I pay them off and with The Lord by my side, I will journey home where I belong.

Yours always,

Katie xxx

"Yep, that should do it!" she said and thought she better remember to warn Matthew that he would be receiving an envelope for her. She took one more look at her letter before folding it and placing it in a small brown envelope. She carefully licked the two stamps and placed them in the right hand corner of the envelope. She wrote down her former address back in Dayton, picked up her coat and envelope and left her apartment with the mailbox down the street as her destination.

After she had posted her letter, she walked over to the phone box and first called Matthew who as always was puzzled by this young, strange, slightly crazy girl and then Alexandros to invite him over for dinner.

"Don't bother cooking, my little Aphrodite," Alexandros joked. "I'll pick up that pizza you love and rent a movie. A good thriller, maybe? Have you seen *The Clockwork Orange* or *The Andromeda Strain*? Both new releases."

"Nope," Katie replied, thinking of the weird titles Alexandros always came up with. *Even dwarfs started small* was the last movie he had brought over for them to view.

“I’ll bring both. I’ve heard that they are really good,” he commented.

“Anything to sit back and curl up in your arms,” she replied, horrified of what she had to admit to him.

As she walked home, she rehearsed in her head the scene of her uttering the words “Alexander, I’m pregnant!” to him.

“Oh, that’s wonderful!” she pictured him saying as he lifted her and kissed her lovingly.

“You’re what? It sure is not mine — you little, filthy, cock-loving slut. Been sleeping around much, huh?” he would yell and slap her across the face. “Get out now!” he would then shout angrily.

Katie fought hard to hold back the many gathered tears, in her sad looking eyes, from falling. She could not know how he was going to react. She had to come up with a story. However, as many stories she came up with, the truth of what happened was always the most believable story and the only story that would gain her Alexandros sympathy.

Katie speedily tidied up her always chaotic apartment, relieved herself from her clothes and took a long, hot shower. She only wished the boiling running water could cleanse her soul as well as her body. She dried herself off and stood naked in front of her wooden wardrobe. Besides her work uniform and the crime against fashion as she called the dress she left Dayton in, she had only bought a few more items and only one was good enough for tonight's occasion. It was a fancy, red, tight dress she had found at the local thrift shop and even bargained successfully with the sales lady for a better price.

Putting on make-up had become a ritual with Katie. For too long had she been forbidden to wear any sign of it. Now, liberated from her biological father and her almighty heavenly father, she enjoyed every second she spent in front of the bathroom mirror applying her foundation, choosing from her many lip glosses and then applying her mascara before placing on fake eyelashes. She would sit there with a contented grin as she painted her nails and her toe nails in every color imaginable. Needless to say that more money was spent on beautifying herself than clothing and feeding herself. Her soul was more starved than her stomach. The result was stunning. Katie stood in front of her bedroom wall mirror, a fully grown woman, dressed in her best, ready for the ball.

She could not help but look down upon her tummy. Suddenly, the door bell shook her out of her daydreaming and pulled her back to earth. She walked into the living room slowly as Alexandros only rang the bell out of politeness. He had his own set of keys.

He walked in, carefree as always, pepperoni pizza in one hand and a small red nylon bag with two video cassettes sticking out from the other.

"Geia sou, mwro mou!" he winked at Katie and placed the steamy pizza and the movies on the brown coffee-table. She had gotten used to his greeting. It meant *hello my baby* in Greek. She ran into his arms and kissed him hard on his lips.

''Wow, somebody missed me,'' he laughed.

''We need to talk,'' Katie spilled out not being able to control her emotions and let him sit down and relax before ruining his night. Well, at least that was her plan up to the very minute she kissed him.

''What's up?'' he asked and did that thing he did with his eyes whenever he was thinking and feeling anxious.

''Sit down,'' she whispered as she lowered herself into the sofa trying to stop her knees from shaking.

''Come on, you're scaring me. Spit it out.''

''I'm pregnant!''

Silence filled the air and the few seconds between her short announcement and Alexandros' reply felt like millennia to Katie.

''You sure?''

''Yeah, peed on one of those sticks and they say they are 95% accurate,'' Katie answered with a flat tone, amazed by his coolness.

''Well, I know it's not mine... so I'm going to go out on a limb here, but I'm guessing this is why you ran away from home."

''No... Well... kind of... I did not know I was pregnant when I left... I only found out today... that is why I called you...''

''So you had a boyfriend? Where is he now?''

Katie took a deep breath and started performing just like she had rehearsed. She shook her head from side to side and started to cry.

''Alexander, I... I was raped! Gang-raped by four boys at my school.''

''What?'' he shouted out with pure fury in his voice. ''Why didn't you go to the police? Why did you run away? Katie this is serious...'' he continued yelling.

''Please, listen to me. It's ok. I wanted to leave my home town. My life was a living hell. My mother locked me in my room every night at nine and my father beat me for no good reason way too often. At school, I was mistreated daily, to put things lightly,'' she said and noticed the sympathetic look he was giving her. She was winning him over.

''As crazy as it sounds, that rape was the best thing that happened to me,'' she added and watched his jaw drop to the ground. ''It gave me the strength to get away. Here, I am living the life I have always dreamt of and it is all thanks to you."

''Katie, a child is a big responsibility and an expensive one too! I don't mean to sound like an ass, fuck the rent, but... how are you going to raise a child by yourself?''

''I have arranged through a relative to be sent a significant amount of money, out of which I will pay you rent and buy everything I need. As for work, I am sure I can sort something out with Mr. and Mrs. Reeve.''

He looked at her proudly; admiring her bravery. He leaned over and kissed her gently, right in the middle of her forehead and wrapped his arms around her.

''Katie, this is your house... and it will be your baby's home too! I can't say I'm the fathering type, but as much as I can help, I will.''

"Alexandre, I cannot believe you are so supportive. I am lost for words..." she managed to fight back tears and say with a brittle voice.

''After all, I am your boyfriend,'' he said with a tender smile that ran from ear to ear.

''Boyfriend!'' Katie cried out with joyful shock. She looked deeply into his eyes, whispered ''I love you,'' and fell upon his chest.

''Now that I have proven I am a good boy, can I eat some pizza? I'm starving!''

Katie started laughing and soon Alexandros joined her. As they dug into the delicious pizza and The Andromeda Strain started to play, Katie thought about how unbelievably lucky she was and wondered if in fact God truly does work in mysterious ways.

*****

Chapter 16

New York, 1984

Katie leaned on the newly installed, tinted glass counter and smiled as she watched the new girl take her first order. She remembered fondly how scared she was at just seventeen when she walked through the diner's doors. The new girl, also known to the rest of the world as Mary, was young too. Mary Williams was fresh at NYU, studying to be a primary teacher and spread knowledge and love to the children, as she stated. Katie, as a mother of an eleven year old boy, knew and valued good teachers. That was the main reason she had chosen Mary as the new girl and none of the other nine applicants for the vacancy. After ten years of working at Reeve's diner, Katie had developed an eye for good waitresses and had been promoted to manager. A position she held for the last two years. Since losing Mr. Reeve to a heart attack on Thanksgiving Day 1982, Mrs. Reeve decided to take it easy. Not that it stopped her from being at the shop every day, checking up on everyone and everything.

It was a slow evening and Katie stayed in the same position for quite a while; thinking of her life and how lucky she had been. Her son had turned eleven just last month and she was so proud of him — top of his class, tall, strong, handsome. Though her relationship with God never found its former glory, she still thanked the Lord everyday for her son and for Alexandros. Nothing would have been possible without Alexandros. He stood by her during her pregnancy and helped out with all the bills and newfound expenses. Shortly after she gave birth, he moved in with her and rented out his apartment down in Queens. Two years ago, he got an offer for the convenience store that he owned and ran for the last fifteen years and he decided to sell. He took great pride in the fact that he had retired before even turning fifty. He mostly spent his days between the Greek coffee shop in Astoria and home writing a book about an American who gets lost in time and travels back to ancient Greece where he meets heroes and Gods from Greek mythology. More importantly, especially to Katie, he spent time with her boy while she was at work doing long shifts. She wondered what the two were up to when Mrs. Reeve's voice was heard.

''Earth to Katie, Earth to Katie. Girl, where are you travelling?'' she asked and continued rambling like always without expecting an answer. ''Come see these books. The deliveries are all wrong. Told you Steward was not good for the job. Adrian, now there's a bookkeeper!''

''*Bet they are having more fun than me*,'' she thought, smiling as she followed Mrs. Reeve to the office in the back.

Alexandros had just finished writing how Hercules had helped his protagonist fight off Ares in a bloody and ferocious fight. He walked into the kitchen to grab an ice cold beer from the fridge.

''Hey Cricket! Finishing your homework?''

The young boy looked up from his math's book and replied "I have a name you know!"

"Yeah, I know. But I prefer Cricket. It suits you well."

"Whatever," the boy muttered as he looked back down into his school book.

"What was that?" Alexandros asked strictly, raising his voice.

"Nothing, sir," he managed to squeeze out from behind locked teeth. He didn't want another pointless confrontation. Alexandros was too generous with handing out discipline whenever his mother was away. He had grown used to being shouted at and even being smacked every now and then, but yesterday Alexandros' disciplinary ideas were taken to another level.

He had walked out into the living room from his room after a sweet midday nap to find Alexandros lying on the sofa, wearing only his boxers, drinking his third beer and watching some sports' results.

"I want to watch Sesame Street," he said sleepily and yawned.

"You are demanding to watch it?"

"Sorry, sir. *May I* watch Sesame Street, please?" he quickly rephrased his request.

"No. Now be a good boy and go make us a couple of ham and cheese sandwiches..."

“But I always watch Sesame Street at this time. Come on. You’re so unfair!” the youth retaliated.

He would have said more if he had not noticed the fury boiling in Alexandros’ eyes. He froze in shock as Alexandros got up and grabbed him by the collar of his pyjamas and forcefully dragged him towards the sofa. Alexandros sat down, furiously pulling him down too.

He found himself lying across Alexandros’s lap when he felt his pants being pulled down to his knees. He felt embarrassed, lying there naked and exposed. Alexandros started to smack him hard on his behind while yelling, “I’ll teach you to talk back, you little shit!”

The boy resisted crying out, not wanting to give Alexandros any sort of satisfaction from the sight of tears.

He must have smacked him a dozen times before releasing him and throwing him on the floor.

He quickly pulled up his underwear and pyjamas and ran into his room.

Alexandros sat there breathing heavily as he looked down on his hard on.

He stood up and looked towards the boy’s closed door. He took a hesitant small step towards it before stopping. He stood there for a moment, biting his lips before turning and walking into the bathroom, slamming the door behind him.

*****

Chapter 17

''Two weeks off work is paradise enough for me! I don't care where we go. I'm in!'' Amy had joked last month, back home in Dublin. Her brother, Conor, had sat her and their cousin –and best friend to them both- Patrick on his king size hazel sofa and stood opposite them presenting his *August-O'Brien-Holiday Plan* as he had titled his pitch.

''This island has it all! Look, clubs, bars,'' he said and started to show them pictures from a two-part brochure he had picked up at his local supermarket. ''Even the beach is called Paradise! Come on... yeah, it costs a lot, but we all work like dogs and even dogs deserve a break! What you say? Paradise is only 1862 miles away.''

''Cool your horses, Conchobar! Swallowed the encyclopedia of Mykonos have ya? This all sounds expensive. Two whole weeks?''

''Don't be a muppet, man. We'll stay at a decent two-star hotel and fly low cost. Trust me. This trip is one that you will never forget! And talking about forgetting, what better way to forget that Lucy bird for dumping your ass?''

Amy laughed out loud, only to receive a cold look from Patrick, to which she replied, ''What? She was such a gowl. I'm glad she's out of your life. Come on Patrick. It will be fun and I need some tanning. I'm probably the whitest girl in Dublin!''

The very next day, the three asked for time off work and in the evening, they all sat down with Amy's new Toshiba satellite laptop and booked their tickets.

Conor had even made up their daily program, which he photocopied for the two of them.

Wake up and eat breakfast.

Hit the beach.

Eat lunch.

Hit a different beach.

Eat dinner.

Shower.

Clubbing and drinking till falling asleep.

Repeat.

Both had laughed back then at his list, but besides a few hours of sightseeing and an evening of shopping during their first week, they had stuck to the schedule. Today, their 8th day on the alluring island was the day they would really break the rules of Conor's daily program. No clubbing today was decided unanimously. They had decided on a quiet night of drinking down at the peaceful away-from-it-all beach right in front of their hotel.

Conor, Patrick and Amy were returning from Mykono's town square just as the sun began to fade and soon the last sun rays were plummeting into the Aegean Sea. They were in high spirits having been on holiday for over a week now and they still had days to go. Amy, wearing pink sandals, a turquoise pareo tied round her thin waist and just her newly bought, ruby red bikini on top, walked in front of the boys swinging her hips side to side while singing out of tune that it was raining men. She had accomplished her mission on the island.

"Bronze tanning oil all day long equals a sexy Amy," she laughed at her brother's disapproving look whenever she was flirted and/or kissed by a guy in one of the many loud, crowded bars and clubs they visited. He knew he had no right to complain as the three made a deal before arriving on the island. No judging. All three were single twenty-five year olds and they were there to have fun.

Both guys wore their swimming trunks and brown beach sandals. Patrick was wearing a flowery red shirt opened up to reveal his hard earned six pack while Conor did not bother covering himself. Patrick was carrying in one hand the nylon bag with the snacks and in the other, a case with eight Corona beers while Conor was carrying the important bag as he claimed. Three extra large Guinness beers, a bottle of Jameson whiskey accompanied by a bottle of coke and a pack of plastic cups were the components of the *important* bag.

The three of them walked down the bricked path past their blue and white hotel and headed down to the beach. Besides an elderly couple that was packing up to leave, there was no one else on the beach. The three sat down in the sand at a spot that was provided with partial light by a nearby street lamp. Goods were placed between them and soon, alcohol was running through their veins. As the moon moved along the night sky, their singing got louder and their stories got funnier and more personal.

Up above behind them was their hotel, so they had no worries as to be in shape to walk back to their rooms. The Mykonos beach hotel was a two star, traditional Cycladic style bungalow complex. The many sky-blue and bright-white bungalows were spread out across the hillside overlooking the beach of Megali Ammos. Between the bungalows, wild flowers and bushes had grown and added to the hotel's charm. Little did Patrick, Amy and Conor know that during all their fun, two green eyes were lurking in the distance behind an overgrown bush. Two eyes that had been following them around for the last two days. A predator waiting for the right time to attack. An aggravated predator that had not fed in days.

''Alright, boys! That's enough for me,'' Amy said as she managed to stand up. ''I wanna get up early tomorrow and head over to Super Paradise in the morning. A girl's gotta work on her tan before heading back to cold, miserable Dublin!''

The boys both smiled, thinking that she was driving them mad with her tanning obsession and chuckled at her Dublin comment. If there was a committee for proud Dubliners, Amy would surely be president. They both watched her stumble her way up the path towards the hotel. As soon as she arrived at the first bungalow, she turned and waved, sure that her men would be keeping an eye out for her. Patrick and Conor waved her good night and continued drinking. Amy continued past the bottom line of bungalows, whose occupants were either asleep or out clubbing. Everything was dead quiet. She walked along the path towards her bungalow and that was when Amy noticed something laying in the center of the light circle formed by the hotel's overhanging path lights. She smiled as she got closer and suspiciously looked around her. She was alone. Alone with a fifty euro note. Right there on the path, just outside her bungalow. Sleepy and a step away from being totally drunk, she stopped and stood above it, rapidly closing and opening her eyes in an unsuccessful attempt to help her brain focus. With a naughty look across her face, she clumsily bent down and picked up the note.

Suddenly, the bush behind her shook and Amy felt something like a needle pushed hard against her neck and a hand covering her mouth and nose. Amy felt the will to stand up and resist as the needle penetrated her skin, but all the courage and all the reaction she thought she would have in such a situation went for naught. In a matter of seconds, Amy felt her whole body go numb and she fell to the ground. Fear instantaneously ran through her body and she screamed out loud or so she thought, as no sound broke the silence in the air. Her eyelids grew heavy and started to descend, covering her amber eyes. The last thing she saw was a shadowy figure towering over her. And then, total darkness.

He looked down at the motionless girl and sat on his knees beside her. He gently stroked her hair away from her face and faintly kissed her on the lips.

‘‘My Artemis! I have waited a long time for you. You and I are going to have so much fun together,’’ he whispered tenderly in her right ear before lifting her and throwing her across his shoulder. He walked through the darkness as fast as he could, yet being careful not to run. His excitement-caused sweat thinned out and was swept away by the calming Sirroco breeze. His boat was waiting for them, further down, in the next small bay. Luckily for him, no one was to be seen. No need for his fake smile and his rehearsed line of ‘‘that last shot of Tequila was too much for her.”

He walked into the water and struggled his way up to his boat. He threw the girl into the boat and climbed up himself. His blindfold and his rope were waiting for him. He tied up the girl’s arms and legs real tight with a double nautical knot, blindfolded her and stuck a curled-up sock in her mouth before passing a red cloth over her mouth and tying it hard behind her head. She probably wouldn’t wake up any time soon, but he was not the type to take chances. He had to leave her alone. He still had to catch Apollo. He frisked the girl and found her Blackberry fastened to her left thigh by her pareo. He looked through her contact list and was pleased to find only one listing of a Conor. That is what he overheard her call her twin brother.

He dashed back to his lookout and was glad everything was going as planned. Both boys had fallen asleep on the beach.

"Let's hope he hears it," he wished. He took out the girl's phone and grinned. He hated texting on Blackberries and their tiny keyboards.

Conor, hey...

Can you please come up to my room please... alone...

Don't wake Patrick up... it's important... we need to talk.

He pressed SEND and eagerly waited to see movement from the drunken youth. He had already placed the fifty euro note in the same spot with a portion of Blutack on its back.

"Come on, Apollo, come on," he whispered enraged by the idea of changing his plans. He knew he was choleric, yet he had to maintain his cool. This was not the time or place for mistakes. He decided to risk the boy's phone having an annoying and loud hip hop song as a ring tone and pressed CALL. Silence. And still no movement. The boys had passed out for good.

He stood up, looked around him and crept towards the blue railing of the path that led down to the beach. The moon had hidden behind a lonely, dark cloud providing him with shadows of darkness in which he could move unnoticed. Not that there was anyone around to notice him, but you could never know what eyes may be lurking behind curtains of closed windows. He ran back and picked up his note and went back to his bush. He attentively filled his trusted syringe with more of his horse sedative mix and hung his backpack on his right shoulder. He casually strolled down to the beach, with his eyes moving rapidly from side to side. He had to appear like just another tourist passing by as he headed through the open and down the well-lit path. He did not need any testimonials from witnesses that a strange man was loitering around the premises. As soon as the darkness of the beach consumed him, he swiftly sneaked over to the boys and sat down between them. He took in a deep breath and proceeded to give an 8ml shot into Patrick's right arm. Patrick grunted twice but remained motionless.

"What the..." Conor started to say and placed his hands in the sand, gathering the strength needed to get up. The thief, as he thought, rose quickly and jumped on his back, pushing him into the sand. He grabbed Conor violently by the hair and twisted his head to its side. In a matter of seconds, the same 8ml cocktail was flowing through his neck's carotid artery. Conor fought to get up, but soon felt drained of power. His eyelids fell and he closed his eyes, replacing his will to fight with a need to sleep.

Conor was carried along the same path in the same manner as his sister and tied up, right next to her. The boat engine roared as the Olympus Killer turned the key and with immense satisfaction written all over his face, he set off for the uninhabited island of Delos where no soul was allowed after dark. The 3.34 square kilometer island was home to a great number of archaeological sites and the Greek government decided not to allow any kind of tourist infrastructure on the island. At night, the island was closed to the general public. He smiled evilly at the thought of having all night with the twins.

He looked down at his vintage Rolex Air King –a present from his stepfather- and smiled at the perfect timing. The coast guard had just finished the late night round and the coast was literally clear. He followed the Delos-Mykonos sea road and soon his Enavigo 38 Racer was between Delos and the micro-island of Mikros Reumatiaris. The small docking bay was minutes near. He felt his blood moving around faster through his body as his heart raced at over one hundred beats per second. The adrenaline rush he felt each time he was about to kill had become his opium. He turned off the boat's engine and drifted towards the dock.

He had another three more hours of darkness before sunlight and the arrival of the island's museum guides, ready to welcome the morning's archaeological thrilled tourists. All guides agreed that the first on the island were always the ones most interested in the sites. Those who were amazed by the island's history and felt the vibe it sent out. Midday came the worst: the families and young couples. Parents that strolled through the ruins disciplining their offspring, interrupting the guide and bringing them just about to his or her breaking point and of course, complaining about the heat wave. Children that followed them with a PSP in hand, asking, "how long will this take?" and when were they getting back to Mykonos that waited for them with its sandy beaches, luxurious pools and Greek homemade, delicious, mouth watering ice-creams. Couples that pretended to listen to the guides and took photos for their profiles every now and then, but were mostly involved in lip locking and body grabbing. The day's work finished with the elderly, who as charming as they were, asked too many questions and complained about the lack of shade, the dusty air and the guide's fast-paced walking.

He unloaded the unconscious and now nude twins in the same manner he would have thrown any other cargo off the boat. A few bruises were nothing compared to the nightmare that awaited them. He dragged naked Amy by the feet all the way up the dirt track and leaned her, sitting down, against an ancient column of Doric order. He took out another piece of rope, passed it round her chest and behind the column. After tying her tightly to the column, he skipped back down to the dock to fetch Apollo. He whistled The Lazy Song by Bruno Mars as he followed the same procedure with Conor as he did with Amy. He had also removed all of the boy's clothing and stored them in the bottom draw of his tall, metal file cabinet that he kept on board, below deck. He squatted opposite the tied up twins and ate his fresh, green apple, eagerly waiting for the departure of his victims from dreamland.

Conor, though drugged second, awoke first. He felt dizzy and struggled to lift his head and slowly opened his eyes. The dark, shadowy figure sitting opposite him came forward, revealing himself under the moonlight.

''You! You're that guy from the club. What the fuck man? I said no and you fucking kidnap me?'' Conor started to shout at the man opposite him, who kept on eating his apple as if nothing was reaching his ears.

''Where the fuck are my clothes? Let me go!'' Conor yelled and wrestled with the ropes that were holding him prisoner.

''Conor?'' Amy's languid voice was heard. She felt drowsy and confused as to why Conor was shouting.

''Amy?'' he asked in shock and turned his head to face his sister. Panic kicked in for good. He thought his sister was in her room. Why was she here? And why was she naked too? Fears of his sister being raped ran free inside his head.

''Now, listen here, mister, you leave my sister out of this, this is between me and you...'' he firmly threatened the stranger.

''It was always about you both,'' the stranger hissed as he came forward on all fours and grabbed him by the neck, choking him.

''Help! Somebody help us!'' Amy screamed at the top of her lungs as she witnessed the life being squeezed out of her brother.

''Let him go. Please... We'll do anything you want. Please don't hurt him. Please,'' she begged.

Conor gasped for precious air when the stranger eventually released his throat. His evil laugh filled the cold air and his next words froze Amy's entire body.

“No one can hear you scream my goddess, but I do have a tendency of awful migraines. Scream again and I’ll kill you first,” he whispered calmly in her ear.

“Kill? First?” Her eyes opened wide and she began to breathe hectically, trying hard to fight back tears.

“Stay away from my sister, you freak!” Conor ordered with hate.

“Well, well, well.... Isn’t this lovely? You both want to protect the other. Touching. Now, whose fingers do you believe I will be cutting off?”

Amy shrieked repeatedly for help at the sight of the unknown man taking out of his backpack a pair of steel, diagonal pliers and grabbing Conor’s hand.

“Please sir, please... Don’t... Stop!” Conor shook his head side to side. He felt the cold blades of the pliers cuddle his thumb.

“Don’t stop, you say?” he laughed as he closed down the pliers and enjoyed their combined screams and frantic cursing.

“One down, nine to go,” he joyfully announced as Conor’s finger fell to the ground.

The next ten minutes were the longest of their lives. As he cut the last of his fingers, Conor lost all will to struggle. Blood dripped from his hands as he sobbed in sorrow over his lost fingers. He could not bear to look down at his mutilated hands.

“Next!” he shouted and ecstatically danced over to Amy.

“No... God... Please!” she wailed.

“God? God can’t save you now! I killed your father back in Crete days ago!” he laughed.

“My father’s in Ireland! What? How? Tell me what you have done with my father, you bastard! Answer me!”

He had no time to explain. He grabbed her by her hair and tilted her head to the side. He stared at her neck with its veins all tensed. He kissed the blade of his companion knife and stabbed her ferociously in the neck. Her whole body started to shake rapidly as the knife continued its journey of beheading.

“Amyyyy,” Conor cried out, not believing what he was witnessing. This nightmare could not be true. He longed to wake up back in his warm bed in Ireland and shake off this sick dream he was having.

But the nightmare continued. The stranger approached him, walking slowly, carrying Amy’s head in his left hand.

Conor closed his eyes and turned away in terror, in disgust, in grief. All will to live, had abandoned him.

“Kill me now... please.”

“Your wish is my command, Apollo,” he said and stabbed him in the neck. Blood sprang out high into the air. The feeling of blood on his face aroused him. He licked drops of blood from the corner of his mouth and howled in joy as he cut through the boy's neck.

He picked up Amy's head and a large rock and walked down the path towards the ruins of Artemis temple. There, in the middle of the temple, he placed the head and with all his strength, he started to beat it in with the solid rock. After a dozen or so manic hits, he stood up and looked down upon his creation. A crescent moon shaped head soon was laying in the dirt.

''One of a kind!'' he proudly said.

He danced back to Conor, singing to himself.

''I've got the moves like Jagger...'' he kept on singing as he collected all ten fingers into a small nylon bag and picked up Conor's head.

Apollo's temple was up ahead, a few minutes to his left. He glared at the temple's entrance –the only columns left by time to stand- and spat with no saliva on the ground. He walked through them slowly to the center of the temple. He carefully placed the *sun head* on the ground and one by one, he laid all ten fingers around it as sun rays.

''Perfecto!'' he whispered and loudly released a long breath. He had succeeded. The twins were dead. One by one, the Gods were dying. Soon he would be free.

*****

Chapter 18

There we were. Sitting up high on the Venetian rock walls –or what was left of them- enjoying our pita gyro. I had ordered a pork gyro with everything that should accompany the chopped up meat while Ioli ordered a chicken gyro with just tomatoes. I even ordered extra fries, which I had placed on the wall at my side. Ioli, proud of her home town and with good knowledge of its history, was informing me about the Venetian lighthouse that rose out of the untamed, deep blue, tumultuous waters right in front of us. Chania's port was a small graphic place with unique and colorful architecture. Yet, its beauty was not enough to calm us and fight off our disappointment and our irritation for failing to bring The Olympus Killer to justice. As I had predicted, the title was picked up by the Greek media and I had earned myself another twenty minute rant by the chief.

"... though heavily bombed during WWII, most buildings..." Ioli continued reciting her history lesson as she leaned over to grab a fry or two. I humorously slapped her on her wrist and warned her "You, my tomato-only friend are a fry-thief and these are mine!"

"Fries! Why don't you just call them chips like the rest of the world?" she joked as tzatziki dripped from my gyro down my shirt.

"Serves you right. Didn't they teach you in New York's kindergartens to share?''

"Shit... It was my last clean shirt," I admitted. I had not planned on staying more than four-five days. I had thought that I would pop down to Crete for a couple of days, check up on the case and be back in Athens giving my report to the chief as to where I believed the case was at and where it should focus on. Maybe even be as lucky to crack the case and bring justice to the loved ones of the victims.

"You change clothes?" Ioli asked sarcastically.

"Ha ha. What are you, ten?"

"Don't get me wrong; all your clothes look the same to me and they scream homicide detective from a mile. You are allowed colors, you know. Or maybe even live on the wild side and wear a pair of jeans!"

She was right. Shades of grey and brown pretty much formed my wardrobe. I looked at Ioli, with her faded blue jeans, her elegant pink shirt and her black short heeled shoes with the pink strass line on the side and I knew she was right.

"Down to Hallidon, it is with you!"

"I fear to ask, but I'll take a crazy guess and say is that a shopping street?"

"Bingo."

"Forget it!"

"Oh, come on. Take something from Chania with you. My treat. Well, the first item at least!" she laughed.

"Going away present?" the obvious sadness in my voice was heard.

She looked down and then gazed towards the sea for a moment before asking, "When did the Chief say you had to be back?"

"He didn't. But I can't stay down here forever working on a single case. My team needs me back home. This is your case, Cara. You'll be fine without me."

"I only wished you or I believed that was true."

"Ok, no more! The end! No more self pity! The case isn't dead yet. We are going to go shopping for an hour and then with two of the strongest coffees in hand, we are going to go over all the case from scratch. And I mean everything!"

"Really? We are going shopping?" she asked excitedly.

"An hour! That's it."

As we walked down Hallidon Street, I could not shake the feeling of living a normal life. I had not expected or even wanted to return to the real world. I had embraced my darkness which had entered my life and overshadowed all parts of it. I made a choice of dedicating myself to my work. A man with no fear of dying was a great asset to the police force. Some called them heroes, and some called them crazy.

I pushed the changing room's velvet curtain aside and walked in front of the sizeable oval mirror. Ioli sat on a yellow bean bag with a smile ranging from earlobe to earlobe as the sales lady, who remarkably perceived that everything in her store suited me announced, "Now this suits you well... Yes, yes... It's perfect on you... Don't you agree?" she asked Ioli, but did not wait for an answer before informing me that if my wife agrees, then I must buy it!

"Oh, we are not married, she's..." I began to explain.

"Oh, I know. Who gets married nowadays right? Though don't you leave a hot, pretty, young girl like this waiting too long mister or it won't matter how great your ass looks in these jeans!"

Ioli was still laughing as we exited the shop, having bought not one, not two, but three pairs of jeans and four shirts of different colors. She finally exhaled with a smile and wiped away her tears.

"That lady was crazy, but she sure did give us a good laugh."

"Glad you were amused. So, where to next?"

"Your hour is up, Captain. You promised me to go over the case and I realize how much you love shopping but a promise is a promise!"

"You're as mad as that sales lady if you believe I enjoy shopping!"

"Let's go shopping for clues then, Mr I'm-a-man-and-I-hate-shopping!"

*****

Chapter 19

There we were. Sitting side by side again. Whole different scenery though. We sat in the middle of the conference room in Chania's police station staring at the wooden notice boards that stood opposite us. The clock on the cheerful, cherry red wall had struck midnight an hour ago, and everyone but the overnight officer who was watching the late night news on rerun in the reception area, had gone home. It was six hours ago when, determined as ever, we flicked on the refulgent lights and spread out all the case files on the long, wooden table. Ioli had two officers roll in two notification boards and as they closed the aluminium and glass door behind them, she announced, "And let the games begin."

But before I could let the games begin, I did not resist remarking.

"Never saw a bright red wall in a police conference room before."

"My idea. Painted it myself. I went to a couple of lessons about colors and how they affect us and got inspired. This color increases your creativity and your memory."

"Ok, now that's out the way..." I said and walked over to the table.

I wrote 1ST VICTIM: ERIC BLAIR with my black marker on a white piece of paper and pinned it to the top of the first board. I pinned Eric's picture under it.

"Eric Blair. Age: 47. CEO of a major pharmaceutical company. Referred to as The God for his Midas touch in running his business. Cheated on his wife often. On holiday in Crete when drugged, tied to an oak tree and gutted. Killer tore open his head and lacerated his brains into half. According to the professor, the killer is re-enacting scenes from ancient mythology. Eric Blair was considered to be Zeus while his wife, victim number two, was considered to be Hera."

Ioli rose up from the blue office chair and pinned 2ND VICTIM: STACY ANDERSON-BLAIR under Eric's photograph and proceeded to pin Stacy's photograph under her title.

"Stacy Blair. Age: 33. Murdered in Samos. Several stabs to her heart. Pomegranate placed in her cut-open vagina. Not drugged. Believed to have been ambushed by the killer at the beach. None of her friends saw her with anyone and reported that she was going to take a walk down on the beach before returning to their hotel room."

"Alicia Robinson. Age:21. Stabbed in the back in Cyprus. Iron spike through her body along her spine. Arms cut off. Believed to have been positioned to resemble the famous statue, Aphrodite of Melos. Nothing in common with the previous two victims. She was British and much younger. Never been to the States and was in school last time the Blairs visited England. I highly doubt they ever met. We must assume that victims are chosen based on specific attributes. The god was Zeus. His cheated-on-wife was Hera. The model was Aphrodite..."

"And each *god* was murdered on an island which, according to myth, was their birthplace or at least their *special* island, as the professor said," Ioli added.

"Let's look through the list and make a possible next victim list," she continued.

"Good idea."

A few hours later we had covered the entire second board with our guesses.

The main problem was the vast scope both of area to cover and of possible victims.

We had the list of the Olympian Gods, but no pattern as to whom may be next.

"By the age of the Gods?" I suggested.

"Immortal Gods had an age?"

I cleared my throat and explained, "I mean, some pro-existed others. Aphrodite was the daughter of Uranus. Zeus and Hera were children of Cronos. Their kids followed after. Maybe he will kill the siblings of Zeus next and then his children."

"Could be. Maybe there's a pattern with the islands," Ioli said as she rolled open a well-preserved map of the islands.

"If there is one, I do not see it," I said after circling Crete, Cyprus and Samos with red and the rest from the professor's list in green.

"How did he find them, is my main question. I mean, he found a married couple who had traits of Zeus and Hera, a model for Aphrodite... these aren't random pickings."

"Social networks? Gossip sights? Quite a few mentioned the Blairs' divorce."

"1. Zeus... 2. Hera... 3. Poseidon," I murmured through the list.

"Poseidon doesn't have a specific island/city," I continued.

"He had the sea. Could be a fisherman or a marine biologist or whatever and killed anywhere in the Greek seas," Ioli complained.

"We could put out a warning to boat owners to be careful not to pick up strangers travelling by themselves or a general warning to not get on strangers' boats," I thought out loud.

"Yeah, and ruin the country's tourism. The chief would have us burned at the stake," Ioli said and took a much-needed sip of water.

"He's already pissed as hell with the media connecting the two murders between them and with the killing in Cyprus. He had not revealed that Stacy was Eric's ex-wife and that they were killed by the same man. Never mind mentioning Alicia in Cyprus. To be honest, I was hoping that with the pressure from the media, he would have assigned a bigger team to us. Maybe a permanent forensics officer or a profiler. I understand he is under pressure from the minister to keep things quiet as it is tourist season and all, but this is a serial killer!"

"We could write down a rough profile of the killer and fax it over to a professor I have in mind that taught us at the academy, to have a look at it. He was kind of an arrogant bastard, but as far as profilers go, he is considered one of the best."

"Ok, let's finish with the Olympian Gods' list and then work on a profile."

She nodded in agreement as I read the fourth god from the list.

"Demetra. Could be a farmer or a farmer's wife. Again, too vast. 5. Athena. Anyone he would consider intelligent. Holy city: Athens. With a metropolitan area of over 3 million!"

"Could you imagine putting out a warning, *all clever women please stay at home*?" Ioli said smiling.

"That's one way of dealing with the traffic," I said, recalling the endless hours of waiting in my car on my way to work.

"He has only killed foreigners so far. Do you think that is part of his MO?"

"Good observation, Cara. I think tourists are easier targets for him. Maybe if our killer is as I believed a foreigner with knowledge of the sea and the islands, he doesn't speak Greek and approaches tourists speaking English..."

"Believed?"

"Well, yeah. I thought the killer was an American based on thinking that he knew the Blairs. Now, he could be Greek."

"But definitely still a boat owner?"

"For sure. Though he did travel to Cyprus by plane."

"6. Hestia," Ioli read.

"Also Crete. Known for giving health and protecting doctors. He could target anyone working in healthcare," she added.

"We have to be honest with ourselves. We don't have anything to continue on. If he is going to kill again, there is no stopping him. Look at the next ones. Apollo and Artemis. Born in Delos! An uninhabited island. Will it be a double murder?" she continued in despair.

"Most likely. Doubt he would kill one and then the other. He is too clever for that. He knows we would protect the other twin and have men guard Delos day and night. God damned papers. Running the Olympus Killer story. Now, he knows we have connected the murders and the whole mythology idea behind his killings. Now, he will be even more careful."

After she exhaled, she said, "out of the rest on the list only Hephaestus has an island, Lemnos. Aphrodite was killed. Ares, towns of Sparta and Mani and Hermes, no island or town."

I took a minute before saying, "Ok, we will alert Delos' coastguards to be extra careful and check all boats passing near the island. Maybe even put extra routes... and... What would you say about a change in headquarters?"

"Lemnos?"

"Yep. I have a hunch he will murder again on an island. And even if I am wrong, he will eventually and we will be there when he does. He is fast. Fastest serial killer I have ever faced. Just days between kills."

"I'll call Lemnos' police too. Warn them to double check all new boats in their harbours. We could get lucky."

I nodded back at her as she flipped open her laptop to start typing up a profile of the killer based on our assumptions and fax it over to the expert.

After discussing the profile, the rest of the hours passed by in silence as we both sat reading through police reports, testimonials, autopsy reports, crime scene photographs and drinking strong Greek coffees. Not strong enough, I thought as I was awoken by the voices of the morning officers passing outside the door. The precise clock's hands fixed at seven and twelve.

"Cara. It's seven in the morning," I called over to Ioli, fast asleep and leaning on the table.

She slowly lifted up her head and mechanically stretched out her hands.

“Fuck,” she said as she rubbed her eyes.

“Well, good morning to you too, sunshine!”

*****

Chapter 20

I froze, for a quick second, at the sight of the white and blue Reims Cessna F-406 aircraft of the Hellenic Coast Guard.

"Could it be any smaller?" I shouted across to Ioli as we fast paced across the runway towards the plane following a speedy junior grade Lieutenant.

As we got closer, the aircraft's engine came to life. The thin, young lieutenant stopped before two metal steps that were hanging from the plane's narrow entrance. He helped Ioli up and smiled as I waved that I was fine to step on board by myself. He hopped on after me and secured the door behind him.

I fell in one of the grey leather chairs, strapped myself in tightly and closed my eyes. The twelve meter, twelve passenger seat plane was a claustrophobic nightmare to me.

"You ok?" Ioli asked and sat beside me.

"Yeah, fine," I lied.

The lieutenant signalled a *thumbs-up* as he sat down beside the dark platinum-haired pilot with the black shades on. Soon, the plane was sprinting down the short runway. My heart beat was racing too. I felt the kick of the escape from the ground's gravity and once again, during a flight, I exhaled deeply.

"We could have flown commercial if you couldn't handle this," Ioli said politely.

"Yeah, wait hours to catch a flight to Athens to wait more hours to catch a flight to Myconos. And have the chief show up to bark for a few hours at the airport till the next flight. No, thank you," I answered irritated.

"Just saying."

"This is pissing me off big time!"

"The plane?"

"The whole body here-body there situation! It seems like all we are doing is hopping on planes and going island to island to see this guy's mess."

"At least the flight lasts only an hour," Ioli tried to cheer me up.

"Good night," I replied, closed my eyes and travelled to my happy place.

Thankfully, the smooth flight came to end within fifty minutes. I was awoken when the plane's wheel met with the ground in Mykonos.

It was eleven o'clock in the morning and the colossal Mediterranean August sun was sizzling. The local police lieutenant stood in the shade by the small, dilapidated, bricked building that was used only for emergencies. He walked forward to greet us and take us to his car. It was only a few minutes drive to the port where the coast guard's speed boat was waiting to take us across to Delos.

"Lieutenant Douka, when was the killing reported?" Ioli asked as he turned the key of the vehicle. All we had received was a call from Mykonos requesting whoever was in charge of the Olympus killer case to come to Delos; the killer had struck again.

"Killings," he corrected her. "There are two bodies."

"Of course!" I said. "Apollo and Artemis! Have you identified the victims yet? Were the victims twins?"

"No. Not yet..."

"Do they look alike?"

"Erm... Ok... You haven't been told any details, I presume. The two bodies were decapitated. One head was found in the temple of Delians and the other, which was beaten to an unrecognisable state, was found in an area further down where a temple dedicated to Artemis used to stand. From their bodies, I would say they were young, could be the same age, but as to whether they were twins or not, I cannot say. I believe they were tourists. The boy does not look Greek at all and the girl has an Irish flag tattoo on her right thigh."

"Is the coroner here yet?"

"Nope. I think that they are going to fly someone over from Athens."

"Great!" I rolled my eyes.

Only after he parked and we exited the patrol car did I look around. The white and blue houses, the sea of people strolling up and down and the road filled with motorcycles carrying beach clothes wearing teens. The outside atmosphere was in total contrast with the car's atmosphere. A group of loud, teenage girls passed beside us wearing the shortest skirts imaginable. Hell, I'm pretty sure I have belts longer than those checked minis.

As we walked down the cement paved road towards the coast guard's speed boat, two voices were heard.

"Captain Papacosta?" the smartly dressed woman called over as she approached me.

"Ioli?" the familiar male voice came from the opposite direction.

"Yes?" I replied, stopping to face the busty, intelligent-looking redhead.

"Katerina Galani, I am with the local press. If you could have the courtesy of answering a few questions for me before the major outlets arrive?"

"No comment," I replied and turned to leave.

"Do you realize how many tourists are going to cancel their trip to the islands due to your failure to catch this killer?" the assertive journalist snapped, disappointed by my dismissal.

"What people don't know can't hurt them. It's people like you, who love publishing all the gory details to sell more prints that are damaging tourism," I answered quite proud of myself for remaining relatively calm.

"Are the tourists safe, Captain?"

"They could be if you would let me do my job."

"May the Gods be with you," she shouted, watching me walk away. Ioli had her back turned towards me and was engaged in conversation with a man. I could not see his face, yet he gave me a *familiar* feeling.

"Giorgo?" I asked, surprised to see the young Cypriot officer standing there in shorts and a *no fear* T-Shirt.

"Captain," he replied with excitement and extended his hand towards my direction.

"What are you doing here?"

"On holiday with friends. Saw all the commotion and came down to see if I could be of any assistance. I told the local authorities that I worked on the case in Cyprus but they wouldn't let me help out until your arrival."

"I was just explaining to Giorgo that we cannot allow him to help out as anything he would find or touch would be considered contaminated evidence by the court," Ioli said as she gave me a look as to say *back me up here*. She disliked beggars. I felt for the kid, though. This could offer more experience than years of police academy training.

The eager cadet was waiting for my reply.

"You know she is right... you are not even..."

"I promise I will just stand aside, no talking, no touching..."

"No talking, no touching?"

"Cross my heart and hope to die."

"Interfere in any way and you just might get your wish," Ioli whispered from behind closed teeth and tramped off towards the police boat.

"Stay close to me and be careful. Anything you have to say tell me when we return, got it?"

"She doesn't like me, does she?" he fired the question of disappointment at me.

"Focus, Georgiou!" I said, and we both boarded the boat saying no more about the matter.

The speed boat fought against the fierce waves and the wind howled in our ears. The vivid sun rays danced upon the wild waves of the vast open sea. I was having problems of my own trying to avoid Ioli's long, black hair that kept on striking me across my face.

"Medusa, move up."

"No joke is saving you for bringing that kid along after I had already said no," she retorted and I let her be. Her hair kept on whipping me until suddenly the wind stopped and the boat relaxed in the calmer waters provided by Delos Island. The dried up rock with the paramount temples was facing us. I could only distinguish two police officers on the island. As we approached the wooden dock, I saw another officer standing above two seated uniformed women.

"Must be the tour guides that were first to the island at seven in the morning," Ioli said and started to brush her tangled hair back with her hands.

Lieutenant Douka leaped off the boat first and waved for us to follow him.

"Everything is as we found it. I personally photographed the crime scenes and put two men out to search the rest of the island."

We stepped off the wooden dock onto the sandy beach and headed uphill.

All four of us instinctively stopped at the sight of the two tied up, decapitated bodies. Douka stepped aside while Ioli and I carefully moved forward.

"Mary, holy mother of..." Ioli said as she raised her D800 Nikon DSLR camera and began taking photographs of the boy's headless body. She zoomed in on the complicated knots of the rope.

"Check out the knots," she called over as I leaned beside the girl's body. The knots were similar to Eric Blair's.

"I want an expert on this or Google it if you can. I want to know what kind of knots these are."

"They are called double sheet bend knots," Douka called over. "Grandfather was a fisherman," he explained as I looked over.

"No tape?" Giorgo, who stayed a step behind Douka, asked.

"The whole island is our scene," Douka replied without his eyes leaving the bodies.

That's when I realized how calm Giorgo was at the sight of the decapitated bodies. I remembered my first murder case. An old prostitute, who was violently gang-raped and beaten to death, was dumped in an abandoned car yard. I stood there trembling, trying to keep my chicken sandwich in. It was probably the only time I regretted adding mayonnaise. No training prepares you for the sight of real life, in-your-face, dead bodies.

"Breathe through the mouth; it helps. Here, have some cherry flavoured chewing gum," the detective whose name eluded me advised.

A crazy thought spawned in my head. Giorgo. Strong, black hair, green eyes, American roots.

"Costa, have you noticed this?" Ioli asked, pointing at the boy's missing fingers.

"They are with the head," Douka said, sickly.

"I'm no forensics, but these cuttings on the neck appear to have been made by our imperial knife," she continued.

I stood up and walked towards her.

"Doubt he would have persuaded them to follow him here. We have to wait for the autopsy reports but I'll bet my wage that they were drugged. He tied them up and waited for them to wake up. Or did he kill them in their sleep?" I thought out loud.

"I wish they had such luck," my kind-hearted partner answered my thinking. "If they are twins, he must have been in Mykonos searching. You don't just bump into twins every day. Lieutenant Douka, we need to start interviewing everyone on the island. Hotels, bars, clubs. Focus on men visiting the island on their own. Get your men to make a list of men staying alone that checked out yesterday or today. Have them ask about suspicious boats. He must have docked somewhere. I doubt in any popular bay. No flight or ferry leaves without checking all single travelling men. Emphasis on black hair, green eyes, masculine build. Oh, and don't forget to alert the coast guard to stop every one-crew boat."

She looked up and smiled gently as she saw Douka taking notes in his brown diary. She knew she talked fast, but there was no time to waste.

"On it," he replied, took out his cell and wandered off to give orders to his men.

"Find out when the forensics team gets here too if you can," the tasks kept on coming. Douka gave her a thumbs up to which she shouted, "Thank you, by the way."

My own phone came alive at that moment and I answered, knowing who it was without looking.

"Good morning, Chief."

"What the heck do you find good about it? Damn it, Costa. I got the Prime Minister's office down my throat. Can you imagine what's going to happen when this gets out to Euronews and the BBC? Welcome to Greece, enjoy your stay, and don't forget your head! Fucking hell! Where you at? What have you got so far?" he bawled without a single pause for breath.

"I'm here, Chief, at the scene with the bodies. We are collaborating with the local department. We are getting the whole island of Mykonos on lockdown, the forensic team and the coroner are on the way and Ioli and I are examining the bodies. Going to go to their heads as soon..."

"Where the fuck are the heads?" he snapped.

"Heads were found in temples further down. We believe the boy was killed as Apollo and the girl as Artemis. Looks like the same knife and the knots in the rope are identical to the ones from Eric Blair's scene. The bodies haven't been identified yet, though I am positive that they will be twins..."

"Get this bastard, Papacosta and get him quick! And keep me..."

"Informed. Yes, sir. Of course, I will be..." I managed to say before the call got disconnected.

"Bet he was a bundle of joy," Ioli patted me on my right shoulder.

“If we don’t catch this killer before he kills again, the chief is either going to have a heart attack or burn down all the news outlets.”

“Do you think he removes their clothes so as to not leave DNA evidence behind, to not leave personal items to identify them by or is it a way to disgrace his victims?” Ioli asked.

“Could be all three. Might even be because it is the way he pictures the gods to be. Most sculptures and paintings do depict them in the nude or with few clothes on.”

When the scorching midday sun came right above us, I spotted a shimmering light playing around in the dry leaves of a burned to death bush. I walked over, put on my white, latex gloves and bend down.

“Oh my!” I said and cautiously lifted up the heavy, hidden object.

Ioli looked over.

“Is that real gold?”

“Looks like it,” I replied and held up the solid, gold mask with the inscription ΑΛΕΞΑΝΔΡΟΣ ΒΑΣΙΛΕΥΣ ΜΑΚΕΔΟΝΩΝ.

“Alexandros, king of the Macedonians,” I read.

“Guess we are adding rich to our profile,” Ioli said as she took the ancient artefact into her glove covered hands.

"Or smuggler," I added.

"You think he wore the mask while he went all sleepy hollow on them?" Giorgo said as he stood between us.

We both turned and gave him cold looks.

"Yes, he held a five kilogram mask to his face with one hand and decapitated them with the other!" Ioli could not resist showing her irritation.

"Douka," I called as I saw the lieutenant approaching.

"I found this mask, hidden in a bush over there. Get one of your men to ask the tour ladies for any info. Without touching it, obviously. Then run it for fingerprints."

"I'll handle it."

"No, you are now taking us to the heads. Let your men handle it."

"Gianni!" he called over the rather short and corpulent office that was at the beach down below.

"Yes, sir?" he asked as he ran up with great effort towards Douka, who began instructing him on how to proceed with the mask.

As the flushed face, heavy breathing officer zigzagged back down the path to the dock, mask in hands and mission in mind, we turned to follow Douka upwards to the first head.

"Now there's a sight you don't see every day," Ioli said, stopping at the entrance of the ruined temple.

On the ground in front of us laid the male victim's head. Around the bodiless head, forming a depiction of the sun, ten fingers were placed.

"Apollo. God of the Sun," I said and took my first steps ahead. Ioli took her time before closing her eyes, exhaling deeply and steadily walking towards me. Douka remained still while Giorgo sat down on a nearby rock and ducked his head between his legs. He swallowed loudly, obviously trying to keep his breakfast in.

"Check out the neck," Ioli said as she pointed and focused her camera.

"Needle entry most likely. He was drugged," I replied.

"Sadistic bastard," Ioli mumbled to herself. More curses followed as she photographed all angles of the scene.

"So much hate towards people he never met. Such violence is normally seen in revenge cases. The murders must mean something to him in relation to his past. Something must have happened to him. This is not your average psycho killings. The mythology connection is of great importance to him," I once again thought out loud.

"Douka?" I interrupted myself.

"Yes, Captain?"

"I know we have been driving you mad with orders, but can you please find out when the coroner and the special forensic team are going to get here? It's a shame to leave the head lying here."

Flies had already gathered and were wandering upon his face, up his nostrils and into his opened mouth.

"They haven't notified me yet," he replied as he looked down to his phone.

"Let me take you to the girl's head and I'll call them to see where the team is at."

We speedily followed him up the dirt track, paying no attention to the ancient ruins that thousands pay hard earned money to travel around the globe and see.

"Jesus Christ! Just when you thought things couldn't get uglier!" an opened mouth, dropped jaw Giorgo declared as we approached the next victim.

The head had been beaten to an unrecognisable state.

"Must have taken considerable force to break the bones like that," I commented.

"We found the bloody rock used for the... erm... beating. I've bagged it and have it down at the dock. It has blood all over it so I thought I leave it to the forensic team to see if any fingerprints can be lifted off it."

"Let's hope they can. Though I believe our killer is too careful to slip up like that. I bet he wore gloves," Ioli replied and continued taking photographs.

"It's a crescent moon, right? Artemis was the goddess of the moon," Giorgo stated the obvious.

"Yeah. He managed to complete a double killing and got away again..." I said and I leaned down close to the bodiless head.

"I can't make out a needle entry mark, but logic would have us believe she was drugged too. He brought them here by boat, most likely from Mykonos. And we fucking told the coastguard to be more alert!" Ioli complained.

"Douka, didn't the coastguard get..." she continued, but the lucky lieutenant avoided her rage as he had already wandered off on the phone to the coroner.

"I'm going to go and pick them up from Mykonos," he shouted and ran down to the dock.

"I'll come with you," Giorgo shouted and ran to catch up.

"So much for the help!" Ioli murmured.

"Well, you did tell the boy that he was not allowed to move, touch or breathe! Anyway, I guess he wants to follow the forensic team around. He wants to get involved in Criminalistics."

"Really?"

"Yeah, he mentioned it as we walked here. He said it twice as you did not hear him the first time. Guess you did not hear him the second time either."

"Shall we go to the witnesses before the team arrives?" she asked, ignoring my remark.

"He just wants a bit of your attention."

"Well the case takes up 99% of my attention, thank you very much."

"Who gets the 1%?"

She smiled as we walked down to the dock and said, "I'm going to regret telling you this, but after dinner, in Cyprus, the professor promised to try and come to Crete. He wants me to take him sightseeing to Knossos and such places."

"Interesting. Sightseeing ancient ruins. Sounds like your kind of date."

"I did say I would regret telling you," she said and opened the aluminium door into the guide's office.

Mrs. Nikolaou and Mrs. Beaumont were sitting down nervously on the old, worn-in green sofa that took up a large amount of the little space in their container turned office. The two of them looked stunningly alike and if I did not know that one was Greek and the other French, I would have sworn that these two forty-something, blonde, medium height, attractive ladies were related. Maybe it was their unofficial uniform that confused the mind. Both wore a white sleeveless shirt, black skirts that fell knee high and black sandals. Around their necks hung their work's laminated identity card.

We introduced ourselves and asked the ladies to relax. Mrs. Nikolaou looked like she was ready to throw up while Mrs. Beaumont was ashen. I would say like she had seen a ghost, but I would think that between two decapitated bodies and a ghost, these ladies would have chosen the latter.

"Would you like some water or anything else?" Ioli asked politely.

"That's kind of you sweetie, but by all means can we just get this over and done with? I can't wait to get home and do my best to erase this morning's image out of my head," said Mrs. Beaumont.

"As if such a possibility exists! Those poor children... what kind of monster does such a thing?" Mrs. Nikolaou said in disgust as she raised her head and looked straight at me.

"The kind of monster that we are trained to catch and bring to justice, Mrs. Nikolaou."

"Call me Anna. Mrs. Nikolaou is my mother."

"Juliette," Mrs. Beaumont added with an attempt of a smile.

"What time did you arrive this morning?" Ioli asked.

"Seven o'clock give or take."

"How do you get here every day?"

"We have a deal with Mr. Gianni. He runs a service of sea taxis. He picks us up from the port at quarter to seven, Monday to Saturday," Anna replied.

"That was the worst!" Juliette said. "We got off the boat, careless as the wind, waved him goodbye and found ourselves stranded here with two dead, beheaded bodies!"

"Did you touch or move anything?" I asked.

"No! As soon as we saw the bodies, we started screaming and ran back down to the port shouting for Gianni to come back, but he was too far out by then."

"We were so scared that the killer could still be here, so we locked ourselves in here and called the police. We did not open the door until the police's arrival."

"Did you see anything suspicious? Anyone leaving the island? Any boats as you were on your way here?" Ioli inquired.

"No, no boats."

"Did not see anyone either. Sorry we cannot help more."

I smiled slightly and asked about the mask.

"Ah, the golden mask of Alexander the Great," Anna said in admiration. "If it is not an imitation, which I doubt, the bodies aren't the only reason we are going to make the news."

"You never heard of it?" Juliette asked as both of us did not make any sort of remark upon hearing Anna's statement.

"No, can't say I have," I answered in all honesty.

"It made the headlines a few years back... Well, at least amongst our circles it did. The mask is considered to be well over two thousand years old and probably even forged during Alexander's lifetime. The mask disappeared during Ottoman times and only reappeared in 2007 when Christie's included it in one of its auction lists. Greece demanded that it was returned to its rightful owners, the Greek people. Christie's denied claims of looting and despite strong evidence provided by the Greek authorities and a lawsuit through European courts, the auction house went ahead with the sale. What was even more remarkable was that it was purchased by a Greek!"

"For four million English pounds!" Juliette added.

"Of course, the Greek government thought that a wealthy Greek man bought it to return it to his homeland and generously donate it to an archaeological museum. However,no such move was ever made and Christie's never revealed the identity of the buyer despite pressure by the Greek government," Anna continued saying.

"This time I must call Jimmy," I said to Ioli as I remembered that I was supposed to call him about Eric's sister's list. Not that I had any hopes that path would lead anywhere. The identity of the buyer now is a whole different story. Could this wealthy man be our killer and why would he leave the precious mask here?

"Thank you, ladies. If we need you for anything further or if you remember anything, anything at all..."

"We will call you at once!" Juliette announced rather happily. Probably happy to be leaving the island. Doubt either of them would continue working here.

"You can return with the police boat. It is on its way with the forensic team."

"Thank you, sweetie."

They got up simultaneously, smiled a goodbye and walked down to the dock, eagerly watching the speed boat approaching.

"Do I look like a *sweetie*?" Ioli asked me, imitating the French woman's voice.

"I'm sure you could be if you tried."

We stood there watching as Doukas, the Athenian coroner, an excited Giorgo and the four member team of specialists got off the boat. Introductions were made swiftly and casually as I knew most of them from old cases of mine. The coroner, Dr. Jacob Petsa, was one fine fellow. Large in appearance and in character. He was a few inches taller than me with broad shoulders, an enormous, round Santa Claus type belly and a pair of tree trunks for legs. His hair was whiter than I could remember him by and he had changed his glasses. A thin silvery skeleton glasses with thin lens now decorated his honey brown eyes. He had studied and taught in the States during the nineties and loved the fact that he could talk to me about places and events that he went to during his time there. As a matter of fact the doctor enjoyed talking just for the sake of talking. He must have punched in enough words for a thesis last time we were together during an autopsy of a murder victim. The four member team included two men known to me and a man and a woman who I had not met before. Captain Phillip Dionysiou, Athens's best crime scene manager, greeted me with a smile and asked how I was doing.

''Murder,'' I replied to the rather short, chiselled faced, dark haired man with the stocky build.

Next in line was the always joyful DNA specialist Matthew Cosma. He had not changed a bit in the two years since our last common case. Chubby, baby faced and chattier than most Greeks, he took the liberty to introduce the other two officers that followed.

"This is Dr. Helena Argyriou, our department's new forensic biologist. She specialises in blood pattern analysis."

"How do you do?" I said and extended my hand for a shake. She answered with a slight nod and a flat smile and acted as if she did not see me extend my hand.

"And this is Alexis Andreadi. *The* Alexis Andreadi."

"Ah, the fingerprint specialist. Rumours say you're the best. We are going to need your skills with a bloody rock," I said and shook hands with him.

"I hope I can be of assistance," the shy, modest, muscular young man replied.

“This is my partner, Ioli Cara,” I said and it was then that I noticed that another man was standing down at the dock.

Captain Phillip caught my eye and said “That’s the profiler. Chief chose him himself. Highly recommended. Why don’t you go talk to him while your lieutenant and Douka bring us up to date with the case and the scene?”

“Yes, let’s get going,” Dr. Helena snapped as she walked over to the bodies, looking left and right. She had stunning green eyes, but she was not particularly beautiful. However, she was what I liked to call presentable. A self-assured woman who knew how to carry herself. She had that confident aura that most women in the force learned to have as they deal with their male counterparts who still lived in a man’s world fantasy or more appropriate, in a man’s police department.

The group moved onwards and I briskly walked down to the beach to meet the profiler.

“Chief finally decided to put his hand deep in his pocket,” I thought as I studied the well-dressed, tall, middle age man who stood still on the pier, gazing the horizon. He turned around upon hearing my footsteps on the rattling wood.

“You must be Captain Papacosta,” he said as he reached out. He had a firm grip.

“Yes. And you are...”

"Doctor Simon Romas. You can call me Doctor or Roma if you must." He paused for dramatic effect.

"I teach psychology at the University of Athens and applied criminology at the police academy," he added, looking straight at me. I noticed his furrowed face. Though I doubt these were lines of age. Lines of over thinking I would classify them.

"Are you familiar with our case?"

"Oh yes. Followed it through the media and last night the Chief had the case files and your notes sent to me. I have come to many conclusions. However, if you don't mind, I'd rather walk around the scene, see the bodies and then inform the team of my profile."

"Yes... sure..." I said and watched the pompous ass and his air of superiority wander off. I never cared much about the characters of the people I worked with. My only demand was that they were good at their job. I just hoped that one of these specialists would help crack the case.

*****

Chapter 21

New York, 1984

"Bye, boys," Katie cheerily shouted as she ran out of the bedroom door, dressed for work.

"God, I'm late," she said as she saw the burgundy clock strike two.

"Relax babe, it's just down the road," Alexandros calmed her from the sofa where he was sitting with Cricket watching the midday programs on the box. Katie kissed him on the lips in a hurry, then Cricket on the forehead. He did not even bother to turn and look at her, not that Katie paid much attention to him when Alexandros was around. She loved her boy, but she loved her man more. He always felt a distant second in the race for her affection and he knew that telling her about Alexandros' abusive behavior would bear no fruit.

"See you tonight!" she said and with a thud, she closed the door behind her.

Alexandros got up, walked over to the TV and started to flick through the channels without asking Cricket if he wanted to see something in particular.

"Only shit on again," he complained and switched off the television.

"Want to play a game?" he asked the boy.

"What?"

"You deaf or what? A game. You know, play, have fun."

"I meant *what* do you want to play?"

"We could Greek wrestle."

"Greek wrestle?"

"Yeah, let me show you. It's an Olympic sport, you know. Only the bravest Greeks and Romans wrestled. Come on, get up. Stand here. Bend your knees like mine and open your arms like this. Good... Bravo... You're a fast learner."

The boy smiled and felt good that Alexandros was being nice to him for a change.

"Now, move in closer to me like this... great... and I'll try to tackle you," he said and pulled the boy close and twisted his arm, throwing him to the floor. He held the boy's arm behind his back as he fell on him.

"Ah, that hurts... get off!" the boy begged.

"Come on you pussy, I said only the bravest... be a man," he said as he gradually got up and commanded "Again!"

"I don't wanna play this anymore, it's stupid!" the boy retaliated.

Alexandros slapped him hard across his face. The force of the hit threw Cricket to the cold floor. Alexandros kneeled beside him and frantically started to remove the boy's clothes.

"What are you doing? Let me go!" the boy started to shout.

Alexandros grabbed him by the throat, choking him just enough to make him stop shouting.

"Now, listen here, you little shit. I'm trying to teach you Greco-Roman wrestling here. The ancient Greeks fought naked. Humble beneath Zeus. If you shout one more time or disobey me again, I'll give you the beating of your life. Understood?"

"Yes, sir," he replied, accepting the fact that he was powerless against Alexandros' rage. He stood up in the nude and took the wrestling position Alexandros had just taught him. He remained in the same position as Alexandros took off his blue shirt and pulled down his ripped jeans. He was not wearing any underwear.

"Now, attack me again like before," he commanded.

As the boy approached, Alexandros picked him up off the ground and slammed him to the floor, falling next to him. The boy tried hard to absorb the excruciating pain in complete silence.

"That is called a suplex! And this is a headlock!" Alexandros joyfully explained, then laid on top of the boy and wrapped his arm around the youth's neck.

Silent tears fell from his face. He felt ashamed to feel Alexandros' naked body rubbing against his. As Alexandros released him, he sprang up and ran to his room. This time, Alexandros followed him.

"Please, leave me alone," he implored.

Alexandros acted sympathetically and sat down beside the frightened boy. He hugged him around the shoulders with his left hand, while his right journeyed down the boy's chest to his genitals. The boy shivered and tried to jump off the bed, but was held down tightly by the grown man's arm.

"Lay back and be quiet. You think I don't know you jerk off all the time, you filthy little shithead? Don't go acting like you don't like it," he said as he masturbated the petrified boy.

"You know, in the ancient temples of Greece, it was considered an honour for young boys like you to serve the priests who were representatives on earth, of the gods themselves. Let's play another game since you didn't like wrestling. I will be Zeus and you will be a temple boy. Now *you* will serve *me*."

*****

Chapter 22

The team had split up.

After an hour on the tree-less island, we all returned to Mykonos and went our separate ways.

Ioli and Captain Phillip were heading to Mykonos Beach Hotel where a young man from Ireland had reported to the receptionist that his cousins were missing and that their cell phones were switched off. If the two missing youths were our decapitated Apollo and Artemis, Captain Phillip wanted to process the hotel scene and anywhere the killer could have attacked them.

The coroner and I were on our way to the hospital for the requisite autopsies.

Doukas and his two men were out investigating and interviewing the public while the three specialists had been set up, with their gadgets and findings from Delos, in separate rooms at the local police station.

As soon as Captain Phillip parked outside the hotel, an old, dyed-blond man dressed in a shiny grey suit with a pink bowtie, jumped out of the hotel's door, rushed over to the patrol car and discreetly tapped it on the window.

"Yes?" Captain Phillip asked, having lowered his window.

"Good day officers," he smiled anxiously. "I am the hotel's owner. If I may kindly request, can you please park your vehicle over there behind the palm trees. You see, we get a lot of young ones passing by on their motorcycles looking for a room and a police car is not that... encouraging, let's say."

The owner stood there pleased as the Captain parked where he was instructed to. They both exited the car and walked over to the owner waiting by the glass door entrance.

"I am Andreas Makropoulos. Anything you need, just ask," he said as he shook their hands with both of his.

"Oh, the poor young boy. Dreadful state he is in. Woke up and missing his cousins. I told him they are probably... *sleeping* elsewhere... it is Mykonos you know! But alas, he is sure some wrongdoing has been done. Oh, but let's not have you two standing out here listening to this old fool. Come in... come in, my darlings."

They followed the bubbly senior who never stopped nervously talking through the hotel's door and into the main reception area.

"Took him to my office and gave him a good, strong Greek coffee to calm him down. He said he would only calm down if I called the police... and here you are. This is my partner Thomas," he introduced the muscular, elderly man behind the reception desk.

"How do you do?" Ioli politely asked as she walked past Mr. Andreas. "We will take it from here, thank you. I'm guessing this is your office," she said, pointing with her glare at the glass door with the golden *OFFICE* sign.

"Coffee, water... vodka?" Mr. Thomas asked.

“No, thank you,” the Captain replied and followed Ioli into the office.

Patrick O’Brien sat curled up in one of the office’s plastic, see-through chairs, rocking his body back and forth with his hands placed between his legs. He stopped at the sound of the door opening and with teary, red hungover eyes, he looked up to watch the two strangers walk in.

“Patrick O’Brien?”

“Yes?”

“I am Lieutenant Ioli Cara and this is Captain Phillip Dionysiou,” she introduced them, but doubted the frustrated man cared much for their strange, foreign names.

“We are with the Greek police. I have been told you have reported your cousins missing?” she continued saying as they sat opposite him on the soft, sea-foam, lemon yellow sofa.

“Yes. We were all down at the beach, just here in front of the hotel, drinking last night. Amy left and went to her room and Conor and I slept down at the beach. I woke up and I was alone... neither of them was in their room and their mobile phones are turned off...”

“Couldn’t they just have woken up before you and decided to hit the beach? Probably somewhere soaking up the sun and...” Captain Phillip started to say.

Patrick shook his head rapidly from side to side.

"No, no... they would have woken me up. And besides, we always have breakfast together, Conor loves hotel breakfasts. He even sets his alarm clock so he doesn't miss it! Something's wrong, I'm telling you..."

"I believe you," Ioli firmly said. She had noticed something during his shaking of the head. She could not keep her eyes away from the small, pale purple and slightly swollen bruise on his neck.

"Amy and Conor were twins right?"

"Yes, how did you know? I'm right ain't I? What's up? Where are they?" he anxiously demanded to know. He was just a step away from screaming out the string of questions at them.

"Do you have a photo of Conor on your phone?" Ioli asked, noticing his Samsung Galaxy in his right hand.

"Oh God, he's... he's..." Patrick started to breathe in and out in a panic.

"The photo... please," Ioli smiled in an attempt to calm the boy down.

"Here," he said after flicking through his phone's images.

"Is it him? Is it him? Tell me!" he raised his voice as the two officers stared at his phone in silence.

Captain Phillip raised his finger in front of Patrick, silently asking for a minute. He leaned towards Ioli and whispered, "don't tell him yet. I need him to show me the exact spot they were down at the beach. And you need him to remember everywhere they had been, everyone they have talked to... he is already in a mess... you tell him and we lose him."

"I can't... he deserves to know."

"Well, let him show me and then do what you like!"

"Patrick, can you please show the Captain where you were last night and the route to your rooms? And then come back here. I'll answer all your questions," she honestly said.

The two men exited the room; she stood up and walked over to the window. It surely was a fine, hot day. When she started out in homicides, everyone she knew asked the same first question.

"Are you ok with being around dead bodies?"

For Ioli, that was the easy part. The dead were dead, and her dead bodies were murdered; it was her job to bring justice to them and their loved ones. The hard part was the living: the ones left behind to deal with the pain of loss. She hated uttering the words "He's dead" and watching the glow diminish in their eyes. The sincere "I'm sorry for your loss" that never sounded sincere, but came off as a lousy movie cliché or a mother crying over her dead son, a man losing his wife... and now a boy on holiday about to learn his friends' tragic end.

A tingling feeling on the back of her neck informed her that she was not alone.

She turned round quickly and found Patrick standing at the door.

"Searching for the right words?" he asked with a toneless, dry throat voice.

"Excuse me?"

He sat down and looked up at her.

"You promised me answers."

She pulled one of the see-through chairs and sat opposite him.

"The boy in the photo you showed me was murdered last night..."

The words hit Patrick hard. The worst case scenario came alive. He struggled to speak, but emotions overwhelmed him and he choked as he tried to say a simple "No, God, no!"

Ioli watched his face shrivel up. Soon, uncontrollable tears were running down his cheeks.

"Who would do such a thing?" he finally managed to say in a broken voice.

"We believe it was a serial killer which we are currently pursuing. I promise you we are doing our best to bring this bastard to justice and..."

"Amy! Where is Amy?" the thought abruptly kicked in.

"Let me show you a photo of her," he said and frantically picked up his phone.

Ioli took in a much-needed deep breath. She had promised him answers.

"Patrick, a second body was found. A young girl, but the body was in an... unrecognisable state. Did she have a tattoo of the Irish flag on her thigh?"

He nodded yes and fell back into the chair. He turned his hollow eyes towards a map of Mykonos that was hanging on the white office wall.

"Conor promised us paradise... and that's what he got."

Ioli let him be for a few minutes before interrupting his thoughts, whatever they could be at such a time.

"I know this is a hard time for you; it's just that the first memories and thoughts are important and I know you want to help catch their killer... So I must ask, what do you remember from last night?"

"Nothing! That is what pisses me off the most! Amy left around one o'clock, I think, to go to her room and we stayed down at the beach and continued drinking. Conor fell asleep, so I thought OK, a night at the beach it is and fell asleep too. I woke up and he was gone. How is it possible someone took him without me noticing? I am quite a light sleeper and I wasn't *that* drunk!"

"Don't be too hard on yourself. Did you notice that mark on your arm?"

"Yeah, I guess I must have hit it somewhere..." he answered puzzled.

"I believe you were drugged. Just like your cousins. That is why you did not wake."

Her answer gave minimal satisfaction to Patrick, who could not stop blaming himself.

"Why him and not me?" the most common question of the living was asked.

Ioli took a second and replied, "He wanted twins. It's a part of his evil, twisted plan. This is why I believe he stalked you. He must have bumped into you somewhere. At a bar, at a club, maybe the beach. Did any strangers approach you? A man on his own?"

"They died because they were twins? Well, as funny as it sounds. I'm glad they went together... neither would have coped with the other's loss."

"I know what you mean," Ioli replied, thinking she had no idea of the pain the boy must have been feeling.

"As for strangers... it's Mykonos. We met dozens of people. Most were here with their friends," he answered disappointingly before shouting out "wait! At that club, the biggest one on the island, can't remember its name. Amy met a local boy, erm Costa, yeah, he was called Costa... he flirted with Amy and they ended up kissing and they met the next day at the beach too. I remember Amy saying his uncle was the bouncer."

“Ok, we will look into it,” she answered as she wrote down everything he had said.

“Anything else?”

He shook his head. Ioli took out a folded piece of paper and opened it up.

“Have you seen this man before?” she asked, holding up the sketch from Pissouri.

“Is that him?”

“Maybe. This is based on an eye witness.”

“Never seen him before,” Patrick managed to say before starting to weep.

“Patrick, I think you should call home. Don’t go through this alone. Here is my card. Call me, anything you need, anything you remember. I’ll help with all the paperwork needed to take your cousins home.”

“Thanks.”

She smiled at him, stroked his shoulder and walked out of the room.

Mr. Andreas was pacing nervously up and down the reception area.

“Ah, my good girl, how is he?”

“Devastated. His cousins are dead.”

"Dead? My God, he was right to worry... The poor thing."

"Yes, and until his family arrives, you have to be with him. Help him with anything he wants. He is only a boy and is all alone, in a foreign country and his cousins have just been murdered. His family should be needing a couple of rooms, too..."

"Yes, yes... sure. Anything they need."

"You're a good man, Mr. Andrea."

She looked around.

"My partner?"

"Down at the beach he went. Come, let me show you."

She followed him through the wide balcony doors and out to the spacious dining terrace. She looked down towards where Mr. Andreas was pointing and saw Captain Phillip on all fours digging in the sand.

"Thank you," she said and marched down to Captain Hound.

She smiled as she realized she missed Costa. He would have enjoyed the joke. Captain Hound.

"Captain Phillip?"

He raised his head to face her, stood up, shook off the sand and pointed to the ground.

"This was where they lay. See the prints of the towels in the sand? I've picked up all their trash, mostly alcohol bottles. We'll have them fingerprinted, though I doubt he would have touched anything. No hair, no blood or any signs of a struggle. The sand looks calm. Too many footprints around the area, but look here. See, this set of footprints leading up to the path?"

"Deeper," Ioli commented.

"Right! They are deeper. Like someone overweight or someone carrying something heavy."

"Size?"

"Forty-four. Ten and a half, if the American asks."

"I'll call Douka to send you some silicone rubber to make a mold of the print."

"Good. Call him while you follow me. There is only one route the girl could have taken to her room. I've got something interesting to show you."

As per the Captain's wish, she walked behind him while talking to Douka over the phone. She requested the silicone rubber and informed him on Patrick's account of the young man named Costa. When she hung up, Captain Phillip announced proudly, "here!"

"Here, what?" Ioli asked.

"This is where he took the girl. Which means he stalked them. He knew her room. He knew she would pass from here. Look at this," he said and fell to all fours again.

She kneeled down beside him and stared at the faint, watery mark on the rock pathway.

"Blutack," he said and sneezed out loud. Louder than anyone Ioli had ever heard before. She opened her mouth to wish him a simple bless you, however, the Captain paid no attention to the sneeze and continued with his theory.

"Killer must have pinned something to the ground. Maybe money as to make the victim stop. As drunk as she was, I doubt she gave much of a fight. He hid here, in this bush. Look for yourself. I found many broken twigs. Unfortunately, nothing else."

"Our killer makes no such mistakes," Ioli said once again. "Bless you by the way," she added.

"It's all this sand. I feel like there is a sandstorm swirling around my nostrils!"

Douka had just got off the phone with Ioli. His men had gathered around him. So far, nothing suspicious had been revealed with their search of nearby hotels. He gave them instructions on how to proceed and watched them walk off to their respective missions.

"Biggest club, town center? Space club, here I come," he said to himself and headed upwards through the crowds that were busy window shopping and choosing the *right* souvenir.

"Good day," he said to catch the attention of the petite elderly lady that was busy sweeping outside the closed club. Leaves and leaflets decorated the grounds of the club's grand entrance.

"Eh?"

"Good day, I said."

"What do you want?" she snapped.

"Anyone else here?"

"No. Why? Ain't I good enough to talk to? Think that this old lady is stupid or can't remember things eh?"

"No, madam. I would never think that..."

"You officers, always coming round about fights and drugs... as if anything will ever change. And tell me this, boy... if you closed the bars and got rid of the drugs, who will continue coming to Mykonos? We live from the tourism you know!" the callous woman said.

He was in no mood to get into a heated conversation with the cranky old lady and her twisted logic.

"Not here about fights or drugs. I'm here to see the bouncer."

"Which one?"

"These old ladies know everyone," he thought and replied, "the one whose nephew is Costa."

Only then did she stop sweeping and looked at him.

"You want the bouncer or Costa, Mr. Officer?"

"By the way, how do you know I am with the police?" Douka asked not being able to shake the thought.

"A cop's face is a cop's face. Talk! I asked you something, boy."

"Costa."

"What for?"

"About a young girl he met."

"Ah. These young sluts they come here dressed with nothing on, flirting with our men and when they get what's coming, they remember their forgotten morals and cry rape. My Costa raped no one. My boy can have whoever he wishes, girls with open legs in the club every night..."

"Twisted logic you have there, grandma. *Your* Costa huh?"

"My one and only grandchild!" she declared proudly.

"I'm sure he is a good boy. No, the girl was not raped. I just want to ask him a few questions about her."

She read him for a moment before shouting out loud.

"Costaaaaaa!!!"

A head popped out the window from the floor above.

"Yes?"

"Get your ass down here boy. Now!"

Soon a young, skinny, fresh looking twenty year old was standing opposite him.

“Yes?” he asked with anxiety colored all over his voice.

“Costa, I need to have a word with you about an Irish girl I believe you met a few nights ago, here at this club.”

“Amy?”

“Yes, Amy. So you did meet her?”

“Of course!” he answered, smiling as he thought of her. “What’s wrong? Is she ok?”

“How many times did you meet her?”

“Well, we met at the club, then the next day at the beach and grabbed a bite at a kebab shop later that day. I wanted to see her last night, but she said she had something planned with her brother and cousin.”

He stared at Doukas with vast curiosity. Thoughts of what could be wrong ran freely through his mind, but none of the illegal and immoral scenarios he thought of came anywhere close to the grave, ghastly truth.

“She was murdered last night. Her brother too...”

“Costa was here all night. We had him fill in for a useless waiter who did not show up again. Ask anyone...” his grandma rushed to say in his defence.

"I am not here to accuse your boy. I'm here to see if he can help us in any way."

"Help?" Costa asked, and he quickly wiped away a lonely tear that had formed in the corner of his eye. *Men don't cry* was grandma's opinion, and he did not wish her to see him cry over a girl he had just met.

"We believe someone might have been following her. Did you notice anyone let's say peculiar looking at you, someone who came up to talk to her? A man on his own..."

"No, can't say that... wait..." he closed his eyes reconstructing the moment in his head.

"The night we met, we sat down on the VIP couches. I wanted to impress her, you know. Anyway, there was this guy sitting just below us, just sitting there and not moving. He did not seem to be enjoying himself much. Well, I had this feeling that he was listening in on us. At that moment, I did not think much about it as..." he rolled his eyes and looked towards his grandma before continuing saying that "we started kissing and fooling around as my grandma calls it."

"What did this guy look like?" Douka asked.

"Wait, that's not all. This man, he finally got up and the next time I looked around, he was at the bar talking to Amy's brother."

"Was her brother alone with this man? The two were there with their cousin, right?" Douka asked, hoping Patrick was there.

"Yes, Patrick. No, he was not with Conor at that moment."

"Tell me all about this man. Everything you can remember. Face, build, clothes, age."

As Douka listened to him describe a tall, fit forty year old with black hair, miles away the coroner turned on his tape recorder and wore his gloves.

"Nice and cold in here... lovely."

I smiled and agreed with him, "Yes, the heat is unbearable during the summer."

"Though I would prefer to be somewhere air-conditioned with an ice, cold beer than in here with you and a couple of bodies!" I added.

"Medical examiners can have a beer too, you know," he said as he lifted the cheap, white, hospital sheet to reveal Conor's headless body. His head rested on a silver side table next to the large metal table.

"Autopsy number one. Conor O'Brien. Age 25" he started to speak to his recorder. Ioli had texted the victim's age and names.

"Beheaded. Time of death around twelve hours ago. The wounds to the neck indicated that the victim was still alive when stabbed, thus it is pretty safe to say that cause of death was bleeding out from the decapitation. The small bruising on the neck indicates a violent, forced needle entry. Blood from the victim is being processed to determine the drug used."

He called me over and pointed to slight markings on the belly.

"Slight bruising underneath the thorax. The victim was carried by the murderer over his shoulder," he said and lifted his finger from the recorder.

Jacob Petsa picked up his favorite little chisel from his instrument case and cleaned out the nails from what seemed like sand. He placed the sand in a sealed test tube and said "sand, but I'll have it tested anyway. No defensive wounds, Costa. Your theory of them being drugged seems about right. Here, help me lift him," he asked as he placed a rubber brick called a body block upon the cold table. The two men placed it under the body and Costa knew it was time for the deep Y incision to be made.

"No visible tattoos or birthmarks..." he continued into his voice recorder as he picked up his autopsy blade and wore his goggles.

I cringed as Jacob began the incision.

"At least the body is fresh and doesn't smell. Remember that one, a few years back. The homeless guy or at least that was what the police thought at the time... must had been in that tunnel for a good couple of months before being discovered. Oh, that smell as we cut him open, appalling stench it was... and the worms... and the rat bites..."

"Anything new? How is the family?" I asked, in an effort to prevent the talkative fellow from continuing down memory terror lane.

“All the same, all the same, just getting older. Daughter is in Uni you know, thinks she is all grown up now and doesn’t need to listen to an old fart like me, sleep all day she would. She goes to parties that outlive the night, but her grades are great, so what can I say? Pediatrician, she dreams of. Wants to help people, she said, not like me... my patients are already dead!” he laughed out loud and I joined in.

He continued cutting away and now and then he reported to his recorder, yet he mostly talked about the motorcycle riding, tattoo filled, long hair chimpanzee his daughter was currently dating.

“And get this; she took him round my mother’s house last week! The poor old woman thought he was an ugly girlfriend of hers with all that hair!”

After the second wave of laughter died down, he asked, “You know why there is so little blood during autopsies, Costa?”

“Ah, you *are* getting old! You asked me this during our first date with a body. With no cardiac function, gravity is the only blood pressure!”

“Smart ass... yes, yes... you always had a good memory. Now you say, talking about memory, I was trying to recall a place during a dinner party last Saturday. What is that place with the amazing steaks down on 46th street, the one with the bull on the sign?”

“Sparks Steak House?”

"That's the one! Bravo to your memory. Now, that is a place I've missed. Don't you miss..." he began to form the question but regretted attempting on asking and swiftly switched the conversation to memories of beer, wine and of course steak.

I endured another hour of mindless but humorous chatter and watched as shears cut through the chest cavity, organs were exposed, the heart was removed and the stomach and intestinal contents were examined and weighed. To top all this off, the head was neatly cut open, and the brain was examined, accompanied by a joke about a blind guy in an all women's bar.

"Nothing extraordinary then?" I asked as the coroner took off his bloody gloves and threw them in the metallic, black lid bin.

"Besides the gap between the head and body?"

"You know what I mean."

"Nope, nothing extraordinary. Stabbed and beheaded."

As I exited the room, eager to get down to the twins' hotel, I heard the good doctor say "Victim number two. Amy O'Brien..."

*****

Chapter 23

Douka had set up the team at his grandmother's little, but sufficient and of course blue and white painted inn that was situated on the outskirts of town.

"Everywhere in town is fully booked," he apologised out of fear of being accused of using tax payers' money to his grandmother's gain.

"No need to apologise," Ioli said. "We perfectly understand that it's August. Besides, I personally love these old-fashioned inns that are family run. Good food for sure," she said as she looked at the rest of the team.

"Okay, so let's head to the inn for a good night's sleep and we will recoup in the morning. We will begin presentations at nine o'clock sharp," I said.

"I have made my own arrangements thank you. My taxi is waiting," Dr. Roma dryly said and with a dull, sleepy ''good night'', he left us.

"Guess five star hotels aren't fully booked," Matthew, the DNA specialist, joked and gained our laughter and smiles. Besides Dr. Helena's, who proved incapable of showing any sort of human emotion.

At the inn, the nerds –as Ioli fondly called them- scattered to their rooms, and I wished Ioli a good night.

“Screw sleep, I’ve got Mrs. Douka to cook up a real Greek island meal!” she announced, thrilled by the opportunity of a toothsome feast.

“You do have an appetite!”

“You think I can run on junk food take-away eaten at the station? I’m a home-cooked kind of girl. Anyway, want to join me?”

“You dare risk me eating your food?”

“Come on, big guy.”

She hit me on the shoulder and led me to the warm and cozy traditional kitchen of Mrs. Douka.

“It gives you a very homey feeling, right?”

“I love it!” she said exhilarated as we sat down on the wooden and straw chairs that were so familiar in coffee shops around the Aegean islands. I do believe *food* would easily top any ‘Ioli list’ of the top things that provided pleasure.

Mrs. Douka walked in, Greek village salad decorated with feta cheese, oregano and olive oil in one hand and tirokafteri, a dip made of feta, red peppers and garlic in the other. Bread was already sitting on the table, placed neatly in a hand-made straw basket.

“I made the bread this morning,” she said.

I looked up at the elderly woman and admired the force in her emerald eyes. Her face was etched with deep wrinkles and despite a cloud of worry that graced her face, you could sense that she was a proud lady.

She hobbled quickly out of the room and reminded me of my own grandmother. Dressed in black, limping about tirelessly. I guess a lifetime of work did that to you.

"Just like my grandmother," Ioli commented as if once again, she was wandering inside my mind. "Never could sit still, though towards the end, her back kept her resting most of the time."

"My back has been killing me the last few days. Makes me feel old."

"Eat better and work out and you will be fine. You're not old; you're a couch potato!"

"A getting-old-fast couch potato," I complained.

A rich, deep, aromatic, peppery smell reached us and evoked our senses, watering our mouths.

"Here you go my young ones," Mrs. Douka said as she left the perfectly grilled lamb chops in front of us. "Bougatsa for desert, is that ok with you?"

"Bravo! Perfect choice!" Ioli replied with colors of happiness sprinkled over her words.

"Thank you so very much, Mrs Douka. You are too kind at such an hour."

"My boy, besides my guests, I have seven children and God has blessed me with sixteen grandchildren," she announced with a wide smile and continued, "out of which twelve are boys. You think I am not used to cooking at all hours of the day?"

"Pretty sure you are," I laughed picturing herds of hungry teenage boys returning from clubs at dawn and playing the sympathy card to receive grandma's exquisite meals.

"I am glad to meet a man who can still throw back his head and laugh. Too many worried faces nowadays and especially in your line of work. A beautiful girl like you should not have sad eyes!" she waved her hand at Ioli and exited the kitchen.

I looked at Ioli and thought myself a fool. She was truly troubled.

"What's wrong?"

"Nothing," she said and just as I opened my mouth, she humorously snapped, "and it is not one of *those* women's *nothing* that means everything! I had to tell the remaining cousin of the deaths. He was just a kid. End of story. No point in discussing anything to do with the case as we are only going to repeat it all in the morning. Let's enjoy our meal like two normal people."

"Fine, don't bite my head off! So what do *normal* people do over dinner?" I asked.

"I have no idea whatsoever!" she laughed and her warm laughter filled up the room.

The next day was such a Greek day. The golden sun rose from the ocean at twenty past six and started its fourteen hour journey above the islands. The sky was clear; the air was pure and even the birds sounded happier than usual.

"The less night time, the less sins," Mrs. Douka, with her long, silver hair tied up in a bun, joked as she served us our delicious and much healthier breakfast and asked how we took our coffee.

"Greek coffees, you order from me. Fancy cappuccinos and modern frappes you order from my grandchild Peter, who will be with you in a moment after finishing with the Germans."

Various breads, butter, honey, apricot and cherry jam, warm milk, yogurt, turkey ham, freshly cut tomatoes and cucumbers, olives, orange juice, cooked pita bread with olive oil, feta cheese, tyropita, spanakopita and last night's sweet and creamy bougatsa were laid out across the long wooden table.

"I remembered reading an article, in the New York Times I believe, about how people in Greece lived longer due to our breakfast and generally our diet. I think it was called something along the lines *islanders that refuse or will not die,*" Dr. Jacob mumbled away as we dug into our plates.

"Greek breakfast in my town, Parga, is a strong coffee and a cigarette!" Dr. Helena said and we all laughed, though somehow, I sensed she did not mean it as a joke.

Ten minutes later, Douka was standing above us declaring that he had came in a mini bus to pick us all up. We all stood up to leave before sitting immediately back down as Mrs. Douka ordered: "sit!"

She kissed him loudly on the cheek and asked, "had breakfast?"

"Yes, grandma."

"Coffee and a donut?"

His guilty look gave him away.

"That is no breakfast! Sit! Eat!" she ordered him and of course he complied. No point, in Greece, discussing whether families were patriarchal or matriarchal. They were, without a doubt, granniarchal!

Another ten minutes later and we were all thanking her for her hospitality and her well-prepared food.

"Good luck on your murder hunt. Hope you hang the bastard!"

"Grandma!"

"What?"

"No one hangs people anymore."

"Well, they should!" she said as she kissed him again and told him off for not visiting more often.

"And bring that nice little lady you're dating... it's about time I met her!"

"How do you..."

"I know everything boy. Thursday at eight. Dinner just the three of us. Now stop standing there, the people are waiting on the bus. Get going!"

We parked outside the police station and one by one, stepped off the beige, ten seater mini bus and walked into the newly renovated building.

After a few minutes of organizing papers and slides, we were all ready to get the show started.

A speaker's stand was placed center and front of the narrow room and twelve chairs formed rows of fours in front of it. All sat down as I presented the case. The Blairs, the model and now the twins all passed by, slide by deadly slide. All details, all info collected and everything was mentioned.

"So who wants to go first?" I asked, feeling like a school teacher.

"Don't know about first, but I will be speaking last," Dr. Roma said as he entered the room and sat down in the back row with no apology for being late or no good morning for that matter.

"Let's go by age," the coroner joked as he got up and gave us all the gory details of the decapitation and the brutal smashing in of the head.

Next up was Captain Phillip Dionysiou. He got up, fixed his navy blue shirt's collar and coughed to clear his throat. In contrast to the talkative coroner who joked and changed tone now and then, the captain spoke calmly, maintaining the same rhythm and same tone throughout his presentation on how the killer had ambushed Amy by tricking her into kneeling to the ground and how he drugged the two boys down at the beach.

"It is in my belief," he continued, "that the murderer carried the two victims to his boat that was waiting for him just around the corner, in the next bay."

"The only piece of significant physical evidence is the killer's foot size. Size 44."

"Ten and a half," Ioli leaned over and whispered to me as the DNA specialist Matthew Cosma succeeded Captain Phillip to the stand.

"Well, erm..." he started to say as he scratched the back of his neck awkwardly.

"I don't really have much to say. This is one careful killer. No foreign DNA was found on the bodies or the mask. You realize as the island of Delos is a tourist attraction that any DNA collected from the beach or the ruins could belong to anyone and it would not stand in court."

Alexis Andreadi was more enlightening.

"I lifted two sets of fingerprints from the mask," he said and suddenly everyone went quiet. I leaned forward in my chair, eagerly waiting for good news.

"One set is very clear and due to the density of the ridges, I would say they belong to a woman. The other was not so clear, but I... well, I won't bore you with the process... I managed to overlap some partials and create a whole. This set is larger and again due to the density, I would say that they probably belong to a large man but not an overweight one. Both sets have been sent to Athens and are being run through the system; however, no hits have yet to come up. I will be checking through police and state records as soon as we are over here. Hopefully, I will have better luck."

Dr. Helena Argyriou placed her hands firmly on the wooden stand. She was the first to bend the switched off microphone out the way. She looked down at her notes for a few seconds before placing her USB on the laptop that was connected to the projector. Images of blood spatter in the sand from various angles flashed before us accompanied by the dry narration of Dr. Helena's.

"... and as you can clearly see here, the common carotid artery was cut and blood squirted upwards. From the gap between the blood, here and here, we see that the killer was on his knees right in front of the victims. This is pretty uncommon in cases of decapitation, as normally, if there is anything normal about a beheading, the executioner would stand behind the victim avoiding the blood. I guess the blood might give our killer a thrill, but such psychological explanations are not my field of expertise," she said as she nodded to the profiler.

Dr. Simon Roma strolled pass us and as always, he was looking straight ahead. He held notes and did not seem interested at all in the projector.

"I realize by everyone's rather short presentations that most of you are eager to get back in the game, the *field* as you say. This is a murder hunt and you have a job to do. However, may I have your full attention for the next few minutes as I describe your murderer to you. My previous work speaks for me and I have never been wrong. I say this not to show off, but to stress the importance you take into full account the details I am going to share with you. As for outer appearance, I am in full agreement with Captain Papacosta. The killer is a man, he is tall, and he is what most would agree upon as being handsome. He lured the model down to the beach. He probably opened a conversation with Mrs. Blair so as to get closer to her. He knows how to have a conversation without showing an apparent psychological or psychiatric disturbance. This is a result of his higher education. You should look for someone with a master's degree or a PHD. Most likely a degree in the arts. He did not need to study. He wanted to. He is a wealthy man and only studied to better himself and for a further knowledge in an area that sparked his interest. I place him anywhere over thirty five and surely under fifty. He is someone that people would describe as confident. I believe he is Greek or of Greek origin in some way yet fluent in the English language. He feeds his high intelligence with all the little clues he has left behind for the police to reach the conclusion of the mythological connection of his murders. He wants the reason of his murders to be known. I would say the title *The Olympus Killer* would find him in agreement. All clues left behind were for this reason. He was careful as to leave no incriminating evidence. Though, the signature characteristic of each murder, the naked body, is a part of the whole mythological angle and not part of hiding evidence. He leaves them naked just like the Gods are depicted through art. The naked body arouses him, yet, he has not had intercourse with any of his victims. I find this rather strange and would expect that in the next murder or an unknown previous crime, some sort of intercourse would have taken place."

"Let's hope there isn't another murder," Dr. Helena commented to the obvious disapproval look of Dr. Romas.

"I'm sure we will get this bastard by then," the good hearted Matthew added.

"I would not expect the intercourse to be anything but normal as this individual is a very disturbed one when it comes to sex. Abused and neglected as a child, he has had trouble connecting with people his whole life. Maybe an orphan, a foster home kid or someone who ran away from home at a young age and had to make ends meet on his own. Our serial killer is motivated by revenge. Fame, money and curiosity mean nothing to him. He has an inner desire to accomplish his goal, which is to kill the ancient Greek Gods. He has a great deal of rage in him, most likely caused by traumatising events at a young age. For some reason, he has connected these traumatising experiences with the Gods of Olympus. Closing, I would like to say that I am positive that he will kill again and that he will not stop killing until he has exacted all his revenge. Thank you."

The professor stayed behind the stand –he was used to accepting questions at the end of his speeches. As the team, myself included, asked for various clarifications about his conclusions, I noticed that Ioli had exited the room and was pacing up and down the corridor, phone at her ear. Satisfied by the profiler and the whole team's work, I opened the door to find Ioli sitting on the floor with her head against the wall looking rather gloomy.

"It's my grandma. She had a stroke this morning. My mama called from the hospital. Things are not looking good."

I sat down beside her, placing my hand around her shoulders.

"Go. I'll be fine."

"I can't leave. Not without..."

"You are leaving. Today. Go catch the next flight. I will keep you in touch. Get back as soon as possible. Anyway, judging by the DNA that grandma passed down, I am sure she is one tough cookie and will be out of the hospital in no time."

She hugged me and placed a gentle kiss on my cheek before standing up and walking off without saying another word. Soon, she was back in the air on her way to Crete.

*****

Chapter 24

In the wealthy and prestigious area of Colonaki, Bill Aggelopoulos or Mr. Rich as the Greek media referred to him, woke up after only two hours of restless slumber. Today was going to be the big day. As his custom-made, dream machine alarm clock went off, he immediately rose to his feet. He picked up his wooden cigar box from his bedside table and slowly and steadily walked towards the caramel and latte damask curtains. He blandly pulled them aside, turned the golden knob and walked out, barefooted, onto the balcony. He leaned against the Syrian stone balustrades and looked down upon the vast city of Athens. A few groups of clouds lingered in the sky; an unusual sighting for the beginning of August in Athens, but then again, this was not going to be an ordinary day.

He smiled as he remembered standing in the same spot, eight years ago, with his wife in his arms and a lively, chatty real estate agent who couldn't stop talking about the exquisite fireplace of the master bedroom and let them enjoy the city skyline and the vast ocean on the horizon.

He took in a deep breath, offering his nose –probably for the last time- the remarkable and overwhelming sense of pine from Lycabettus Hill which bordered his estate. The seven bedroom mansion truly had a magnificent view. Not that he cared anymore. Ever since his wife, Christina, put a gun in her mouth last December, the whole place was just a colossal mausoleum. The mansion's spacious rooms, once decorated and furnished with much joy and love, felt cold and alien. Silence filled the air between the walls as the maids, the cook and even the live-to-sing gardener moved around like ghosts through the corpse of a house. Christina was the heart and soul of the place and one bullet changed all that.

He placed his 13-top cigar box on the balustrade, opened the hinged box and took out one of his Cohiba Esplendido cigars. They surely were splendid. Mr. Money –an alternate name used not to bore the public with Mr. Rich- was a firm believer that Cuban cigars were and would always be the best in the cigar market. He never used lighters. Old-fashioned soul as he was, he always used matches. He never smoked regular cigarettes for that matter. He sniffed in the rich aroma as he passed the cigar under his nose. He lit his Cohiba and inhaled deeply, filling his lungs with smoke. He exhaled and thought that if he cried, this would most likely be the time he would shed tears. But he was tough. He had no time for tears. Having left New York at the tender age of only seventeen, he came to Athens, where he got involved in shipping. Soon, he was one of the market's top players. He was definitely the youngest. Now at forty-two, he was the top.

He flicked his cigar away and watched it as it journeyed down to the interior court yard's swimming pool and landed in the still tranquil waters.

"Won't be using the pool again, I guess," he smiled with sadness. He walked back into the master bedroom to get ready, as ready as he could ever be. Normally, he would follow his morning ritual with devout punctuality. Now, he didn't even bother to shave or brush his teeth. He stood and stared at himself for a second in the bathroom mirror wall before splashing some cold water upon his face and through his black hair. A rich and powerful forty year old that was once the envy of the city's so-called good society. Now, too many worry lines graced his forehead and the area around his once vibrant green eyes.

He wore one of his many black suits, a plain, but as expected expensive white shirt and he skipped the tie.

"Not a formal occasion."

He took the house's glass elevator down to the basement, beeped open his black Bugatti Veyron and then the garage door. As the garage door reached its destination, the car roared into the street.

The First Cemetery of Athens was only ten minutes away, but traffic always made that fifteen. He parked opposite the main entrance where the two archangels majestically looked down on the human race. He bought a dozen purple carnations off a polite senior lady selling flowers outside the cemetery for a living. She had helped him choose which flowers to buy as she explained carnations symbolised pride and beauty. His Christina was a grounded, proud person and beauty was an understatement to say the least.

He always laughed at the idea that the First Cemetery was the cemetery for the rich and famous. A luxurious resting place for the well off. He also thought the name of the street was humorous too.

He looked up at the street sign. Οδός Αναπαύσεως - Eternal Rest Street! Now, the whole idea did not seem so funny anymore. He walked past the cemetery's notable interments, politicians, singers and actors, heading towards Christina's grave. He took comfort in the fact that she was buried near her all time favorite actress, Melina Mercouri. He sat down beside her and placed the flowers under her angel sculpture. The cypresses offered much welcomed shade as he looked at Christina's sun faded photograph. Bleached blonde with dynamic blue eyes and French facial characteristics; she had been the love of his life. They met at high school and as soon as they graduated, they ran away together from New York to Athens.

"Wish you were here to guide me, baby. I've done so many wrongs... I hope my next move is a right," he whispered, kissed his fingers and placed them on her photograph.

"A prayer for the wild at heart kept in cages," he poetically read her tomb's engravement. Christina's favorite quote by Tennessee Williams.

Before leaving, he entered the cemetery's church, not the main one of Saint Theodore but the smaller one of Saint Lazarus. He had no faith but Christina did, and that was good enough for him. He lit a single candle, and whispered, "for Christina" as he placed it amongst the others in the sand filled round, golden container.

He placed his black shades back on and walked back to his car. He drove around for a while in silence before heading down

Vasileos Conctantinou Avenue towards the Syntagmatos Police station.

"Great. No parking," he said as he searched for where to abandon his car.

His eye finally caught a spot on his left and he quickly maneuvered and parked as many were in the same situation as him.

As casual as he could be, he strolled into the crowded police station and stood in line behind an obese ginger lady shouting rudely about her neighbour's dogs that were driving her mad. He waited patiently and without realizing, he started whistling as the kind, young police officer behind the reception explained to the lady how to fill in a complaint form.

"Yes, sir?"

"Good morning," he smiled to her. No response.

"I'm here to turn myself in," he continued.

She looked up into his eyes.

"For what, sir?" she asked, not expecting his next words.

"I am the Olympus Killer," he said firmly and continued on smiling.

*****

Chapter 25

New York, 1986

"Nooooo," Cricket screamed as he woke up once again in a cold sweat.

He sat up in his bed, kicked the blue sheets away from his body and wiped the sweat from his forehead. His hands were still shaking as he tried to pull his mind away from the dream. It was not something unusual to him. He dreamt almost every night of the horrors he lived with Alexandros during the last two years.

Tonight he dreamt once again about the first time Alexandros raped him.

He was only eleven at the time. As always, Katie was at work. Night shift until two after midnight. *Katie*. That's what he called her. He hadn't called her mum in over a year. She thought it was a teenage outburst, but the truth was that the thought of calling her mum turned his stomach inside out.

Alexandros was busy writing his never-ending book in his bedroom.

"A good chance to shower and go to sleep without seeing him," young Cricket had thought. It had become unbearable to undress and head for a shower as Alexandros would always have him *perform* in the nude.

One time he had to be the god Hermes and run around, the other he had to be Hephaestus and limp around. On one occasion, he forced him to drink a whole bottle of red wine and danced naked shouting "I am Dionysus!" while masturbating. The worst was when he had to be Aphrodite. Alexandros always demanded fellatio when he was Aphrodite.

He hopped in the shower and started to wash speedily. Unfortunately, the door had no key. As he heard the door open, he closed his eyes in sadness. He had given up on fighting and yelling.

"Yes, Father Zeus?"

"My sweet Poseidon!" a naked Alexandros replied.

"*Makes sense, I am in water*," the boy thought with slight relief he was not Aphrodite.

"Let me help you," Zeus said as he stepped into the white bathtub and stood behind him.

He picked up the bar of soap and slowly started to wash the boy's body. He then picked up the shampoo, shook out a blob on his hand and caressed Poseidon's hair. Suddenly, he grabbed the boy violently by the hair and forced him to bend over, hands placed on the tiled wall. Poseidon felt Zeus' hands washing him between his buttocks. Zeus stood right behind him and said in his almighty Zeus-voice, "and now you will accept your father god in you!"

He struggled to get away, but he was no match to Zeus. The more he struggled to free himself, the more it hurt. The more he hurt, the more Zeus seemed to be enjoying himself.

"Thank you, Poseidon," he said minutes later and casually walked out the bathroom, leaving him curled up in the tub as blood from his insides became one with the running hot water. He did not move for what seemed to be a century before managing to lift himself up, dried his aching body and slowly and painfully carried himself to bed.

He never showered again without Katie being home. Not that that saved him from being raped every other fortnight either in his room or on the living room sofa.

Two years of pure hell. Cricket knew well that this could not go on any longer. He had begged Alexandros to leave him alone, yet to no avail. All he received was a punch in the face and a kick in the stomach for even asking. A week later, he tried tactfully to speak to Katie.

"Can I come with you to work?"

"Baby, you got homework to do. Besides, at work... I work! I can't keep an eye on you for eight hours!"

"I don't want to stay home with him. He is mean to me."

"Baby, he loves you. Have you any idea how much he has done for us?"

"He has done enough alright!"

"What's wrong, baby?"

"He... he..."

"Well, spit it out."

"He hits me. And he shouts and curses me. Yesterday, he slapped me hard for listening to music too loud and he... he..."

"Baby, he is just stressed bout his book. I am sure if you are quiet and well-behaved, like I know my good boy is..."

"You don't understand! He hurts me! He's a mean bastard and you're a whore for abandoning me day and night with him!"

Katie slapped him hard across the face.

"Now, you watch your language young man! No wonder he hit you! I am so ashamed of you right now! Such language! If I ever hear you speak like this again..."

"What? Gonna get your boyfriend to beat me?"

"Go to your room!" she screamed.

"Gladly!" he said calmly and walked off.

At school, he hoped for a kind teacher to notice his bruises and scars, but as he was always getting into fights with his classmates and older boys of the school, nobody gave his marks a second thought.

He was alone.

He was the one that had to fight back.

He quietly got out of bed, opened his door and tiptoed through the living room to their bedroom's door. He could hear them laughing away. He kneeled down and peeked through the void of the keyhole. They were both naked and rolling around tickling each other.

"Make love to me," Katie whispered, and he felt nausea at the thought that she wanted him inside her. He was shocked to see how much pleasure he gave her. He stood up. He knew he could not get rid of him as long as she was around. They both had to go.

He was always good at planning.

''Straight A student like me should have no difficulty giving birth to a bulletproof plan."

"*Bullet*proof," he repeated and his wild thoughts excited him.

He tiptoed through the kitchen door and stared at the small window that lead to the outside stairway. He then walked back into the living room, over to the locked wooden buffet meuble and lifted up the purple glass vase to reveal a little shiny key. With the key, he unlocked the top drawer. He pulled it open as slowly and more importantly, as quietly as he could. He looked down at Alexandros' Smith & Wesson Model 19-3 357 Magnum revolver and smiled evilly. He took the loaded gun in his hands and sat outside their door, waiting for them to quiet down. Half an hour later, he was still sitting there; alert and with a guilty grin.

Alexandros' snoring signalled the beginning of the end.

He got up, walked into the kitchen, closing the door behind him. He opened the window, looked around to make sure no one could see him and stepped out onto the fire exit stairs. He pulled down the glass window and tapped it with the gun. A faint crack appeared. He tapped again putting a little more strength this time. He did not want to risk waking them up. Lightning lines appeared across the glass.

"Third time lucky, as Katie always said," he thought as he hit the window again and smashed the glass just enough to be able to put his hand through and unlock the window from its hook. He lifted up the glass window and hopped back into the kitchen. He took a deep breath, opened the kitchen door and stood outside their bedroom. The sound of snoring filled the air.

"*No more!*" he screamed inside his head and entered the room gun in hand.

He stood at the end of their king size, oak-wood bed and looked at them for a while.

"Alexander the Great Greek General shall die tonight! And you will have no salvation! I will kill all your Gods too, you sick motherfucker!" he said as he lifted the gun and aimed at Alexandros.

"What the..." Alexandros said sleepily as he was woken up by Cricket's words.

"Goodbye," he said and pulled the trigger, shooting Alexandros just below the left eye and blowing off part of his face.

Katie jumped up terrified by the loud bang and started to scream at the sight of her dead lover. She froze as she turned and saw the shooter.

"He raped me, you dumb bitch," he said calmly and pulled the trigger again. The bullet flew through the room and hit Katie's chest.

Cricket then quickly opened all the drawers of the bedroom dresser and the wardrobe doors, pushed things around and quickly ran to the bathroom where he carefully washed his hands. He then dashed back to his room and hid under his bed.

His heart was pounding away with excitement.

Fifteen minutes later, he heard the door being kicked in by the police force.

"*I knew I could count on Mrs. Horowitz to call the cops*," he thought as he saw black boots moving around the apartment.

"Police! New York Police Department! Come out with your hands in the air!"

"Help! Help me!" he began shouting and watched as the boots filled his room. The lights were flicked on and that was his cue. He slid out from under the bed and stood there in front of the armed policemen, gun in hand. The officers raised the guns and ordered him to drop his weapon. He obeyed and then fainted right in front of them.

Half an hour later as the paramedics lowered him gently down on the hospital bed, he felt truly happy, probably for the first time in his life.

He drank, ate his hospital meal and informed the nurse that he was ready to see the detectives now. She smiled at the brave little boy and used her pager to call the attending doctor.

He listened in as the doctor advised the detectives to take it easy.

The curtains were pulled aside by the curvy nurse with the crooked nose and the tall doctor calmly introduced the two similarly dressed detectives.

"Is mummy and daddy ok?" he asked stressfully.

The two detectives looked at each other.

"He shot them! Are they OK?" he cried and interrupted their awkward moment.

"Who shot them?"

"The man in black. I saw him in our living room."

"Where were you?"

"I was sleeping when I heard something like a glass break. I got up and as I slowly opened my bedroom door, I saw a tall man dressed in black opening the drawers in the living room. He then walked into my parents' bedroom and that's when I heard Dad shout and then I heard the *gunshots*" he said as tears fell down his cheeks. He closed his eyes and started to sob.

"I know this is hard for you, but what happened next?" the detective on the right asked.

"I hid in my wardrobe, praying he would not come into my room. That's when I heard him jump out the fire staircase. I ran into my parents' room and saw all that blood... I picked up Dad's gun from the floor and ran back to my room. I stayed under the bed just in case he came back. That's when the police came."

"My dear boy, I am sorry to have to tell you this, but your parents did not make it," the detective on the left said sympathetically, admiring the plucky -as he thought- teen.

"Mummy's dead?" he said in a broken voice and started to weep.

The nurse hugged him and wiped the flow of tears falling from his eyes. They all looked at him with sadness and sorrow written across their faces. If they only knew that the tears were ones of joy!

*****

Chapter 26

Ioli watched as the flickering bright light ran up the numbers before settling on six. She was finally home. The elevator doors opened slowly. She felt exhausted as she dragged her aching body along the narrow corridor and searched for the keys to her apartment. She had gone straight from the airport to the hospital. Her parents were not answering their phones and her mind thought of the worst. She had been close to her grandma at a younger age, during a time when her parents worked, what seemed to her child's eyes as all day and all night. Grandma picked her up from school, grandma cooked for her and later on, during her adolescence years, grandma listened patiently to all the whining about silly boys. She gave good advice too. Ioli wondered if she would hear such advice again and felt guilty for having neglected her grandmother due to her career. Thankfully, her grandmother was alive and kicking when she arrived at the hospital. She just had to "take it easy from now on" as the doctor put it.

Old age scared Ioli. The feeling of being inadequate. Of having to be cared for like a baby and slowly losing your body, your mind, the essence of being you.

"And the downhill begins... poor grandma," she whispered tiredly and closed the aged door behind her. She had missed her apartment -her 49 square meter home. She did not have many things or much of an art sense. No paintings or ornaments of any sorts, yet the place had a certain sense of warmth about it and had everything

Ioli needed, besides food that is. She always forgot to shop, forcing her to give in to late night take away meals. Though, when she did cook, everyone complimented her cooking. Generations of Cara secrets had been handed down to her and there was not a Greek dish she could not handle.

She sat down on her single bed, took off her black heels and rubbed her feet gently. She resisted an inner feeling of lying down to sleep and gradually stood up and undressed. A hot shower always helped her enjoy a better sleep.

As she closed her eyes, twenty minutes later, she thought of Costa and picked up her phone. No news from Costa. Only four missed calls, all from her best friend Polina. She would call her in the morning. Now, she was in the company of Morpheus.

She needed no alarm clock to raise her from her eight hour sleep. The banging on the door brought her back into the world of the living. Polina was outside the door at nine o'clock sharp.

"I know you're home. Your mother told me. Get up sleepy!" her voice journeyed through the thin walls and entered Ioli's ears.

Ioli smiled as she sat up. She had missed Polina and missed living normal for a while. The last couple of years, she had gone from one case to another and what she feared had happened. She lived for her job and her job only.

"Breakfast?" Polina asked as she waved two cereal bars in Ioli's face. The two girls hugged and sat down on the living room sofa.

"Girlfriend, where have you been the last couple of weeks? Every time I called, you didn't pick up or the stupid phone redirected me to voice mail. Your mum said you were in Cyprus and then Mykonos..." Polina complained.

"It is a murder case. And no, I can't talk about it. I'll be leaving tomorrow again, so let's talk about your favorite subject, you!"

"Bitch!" Polina laughed out loud.

"Well, I have been busy too. Between the shop and Vasili, I don't have much free time."

"Oh, the joys of marriage."

"Shut up. I love my time with him. You know he is talking kids already?"

"Really?"

"Yeah, but don't worry. I told him that I would chop it off if he dared. The cupcake shop is really taking off now and I can't afford to be away. By the way, Petro came round the shop asking about you."

"Hmm."

"Come on, don't be like that. He really fell for you."

"That's *his* problem. And yours for setting me up with Vasili's friend."

"Come on; you really want to grow old and fat and live with ten cats?"

Ioli did not answer, but Polina could read her like an open book. It was a talent of hers since nursery.

"Why are you looking down?" she asked and then suddenly opened her eyes wide.

"You met someone!"

"Well, not exactly. He was a witness at the scene in Cyprus. An American professor..."

Polina frowned and snapped, "Cyprus! American! Girl, find yourself a local, please. Stop setting yourself up for un-attachment. Anyway, go on, was he cute?"

Ioli laughed and as she started to describe Michael, her phone rang.

"It's him!" she said in disbelief.

"Hello?"

"Ioli? Good morning!" his joyful voice echoed through the phone.

"Good morning, Michael! So funny, I was just talking about you!"

"Really? Hope only about the good things."

"I haven't seen the bad yet."

"Well, you might just have a chance to see my naughty side tomorrow!"

"Tomorrow?" she asked in a panic and pushed Polina's face away from the phone.

"You forgot our date? You promised to take me to Knossos. If you're busy, it really is fine, I understand. I just called you out of the blue and expected you to be available and..."

"Calm down," she laughed. She never would have thought of blowing off work for a man and her next words surprised her. "I can arrange to be free tomorrow. When are you flying in?"

"Tonight. Basically, early morning round three. I have booked at the Cretan Dream for two nights. I will call you in the morning then, to arrange to come to pick you up."

"No need to rent a car. I'll pick you up."

He hesitated for a minute before reluctantly agreeing, "Ok, I can't wait. See you tomorrow."

"Tomorrow it is! Bye Michael."

She checked that the line had gone dead before speaking.

"Shit, what have I done? I'm on a case and I..."

"You took time off for your grandmother! No one will judge you! And besides, the bodies will still be there in two days, dream boy won't!"

"I feel guilty..."

"Well, don't. Now, get dressed! Let's get you ready for tomorrow!"

The following morning as she parked outside the five star hotel, she laughed at her racing heartbeat. Strong, free-willed Ioli was acting like a school girl.

She stood by her car and watched a smiling Michael walk all confidently towards her. She smiled back and took a step forward to kiss him on the cheek as all Greeks do. A very American Michael interpreted this otherwise and soon she was placing a soft kiss on his lips.

"Good morning," he said and his wide smile never left his face. "You sure you don't want me to drive? It is a two hour drive to Knossos and I feel bad forcing you..."

"Forcing me?" she laughed as she sat in the car. No one had ever forced her to do anything in her life. All successes and all failures were all due to her own doing.

Knossos was a majestic city that was once one of the greatest of the known world. The palace of mighty king Minoas was envied throughout ancient Greece. It was king Minoas, who ordered Daedalus to build him a vast labyrinth in which he placed his enemies' greatest terror, the Minotaur. However, as all great empires, it was doomed to be defeated by time. Decades turned into centuries and the city lingered into dismay and soon the ruins of the once great city were covered by dust, only to see the light of sun in 1878. Today, the whole city is Crete's most visited tourist site. Flocks of tourists defied the heat and walked through the city's gates and head on up to visit the palace and its exquisite throne room.

Ioli had visited the site many times in the past. First with her parents, then with school, the third time with family visiting from the mainland and then again with her high school. She did not expect to learn something new but then again, she was in the company of a history professor. She enjoyed the way he held her hand and guided her through the city with his map in hand as he recollected all his knowledge from his studies. His excitement was obvious and Ioli admired people who loved and were passionate about their job. If only her mind would let her relax. Costa popped in her head now and then as guilt kicked in for leaving him alone. More guilt built up as she thought of her grandmother. She tried to distract her thoughts by focusing on the sun rays caressing Michael's golden blond hair.

"Am I boring you with too much history?" he asked, smiling.

"No, of course not."

"You seem a bit distracted..."

"Oh, it's nothing. My lieutenant's mind has trouble switching off."

"I hope it switches off later on. I am taking you out to dinner tonight, Miss Cara!"

"Are you now?"

"Yes. I have already booked!"

"Where are you taking me, Mr. Johnson?"

"It's a surprise!"

"I hate surprises," she admitted. She truly did. Her mother always retold the story of how she planned a surprise party for Ioli's 8th birthday and how Ioli walked through the door, froze in shock as all her friends jumped out, shouted *surprise* and how Ioli ran into her room, crying from the rush of the excitement. She finally came out and enjoyed her party, though she did make her parents promise her *no more surprises*.

Michael just flashed his white teeth at her and walked on with a smile, ranging from ear to ear. He had planned a magical night for her, but one phone call changed all that. On their way back to Chania, Ioli's phone rang.

"Hello?"

"Ioli? It's Costa. How's your grandmother?"

"Thank God, she's fine. Just has to take it easy from now on, you know."

"That's good to hear. I had a debate with myself and concluded that if your grandma was not well, I would not tell you the latest."

"We've had a breakthrough?"

"More like a quantum leap... the killer turned himself in half an hour ago at a police station in Athens..."

"You're fucking kidding me, right?"

"I'm taking the next boat out; can you make it by tomorrow morning? The chief wants us to be the first to interrogate him."

"I'll look for flights as soon as I get home," she replied and rain started to fall hard on Michael's parade.

*****

Chapter 27

Minutes before my call to Ioli

I sat alone in the cubicle of an office that Douka hardly used. The walls begged for a touch of fresh paint and the furniture cried for retirement. Little did I care as I went over the case files and the findings of the team while filling up my lungs with my good old poison, Marlboro Lights. Ioli had just left, on her way to Chania's district hospital and I could smoke without her judgmental look. Four cigarette buds occupied the round, greenish glass ashtray and soon a fifth came down to join them.

I looked up at the wall clock that hung tilted to the left, calculated the time difference and picked up my cell phone to call Jimmy.

"FBI, how may I help you?" the female voice said in an upper Midwest accent.

"Erm..." she had caught me by surprise.

"Sir?"

"I was calling on agent Jimmy Miler's cell?"

"Agents that are unavailable tend to switch their cells to the main operator. Who may I say is calling?"

"Costa Papacosta."

"Concerning which matter?"

"Err, just tell him my name."

"Please, hold."

A horrific modernized version of a Bach -or was it a Mozart- symphony started to play as I was forced to hold.

"Costa, my malaka, long time no hear," Jimmy's familiar voice brought a smile to my face.

"How you doing, bro?" he continued with obvious excitement coloring his fruity voice. Jimmy never accepted the fact that I did not plan on returning to New York. He blamed himself for not really being there for me after Gaby's death as he was busy with a shit-load of cases as he had put it. There was nothing he could have done to make me stay and I wish he would realize this in time.

"I'm fine, Jimmy. How are Cecilia and the boys?" I replied, feeling good to hear him again.

"Fine, fine. All is how you left it. So how's your holiday in Greece going? Keeping busy?"

"I actually may be up against my most difficult case yet," I said and gave him a synopsis of the case and explained how I needed his help to find out who had purchased the golden mask and to check if anyone from Mrs. Blair's list had left the States in the last month.

"So is this Ioli single?" he asked after I had finished with all the details of the Olympus Killer's case.

"Jesus, man. Out of everything I said that is what you focused on?"

"What do you want me to say? The things you asked for are easy and of course, I'll help. Now I am more interested in you. This is the first person in Greece you sound like you are fond of..."

"I am. Not in that way though. That would be the last thing on my mind."

"You are too young to retire from women," he argued back.

"She has a boyfriend," I replied to get him off my back.

"Really?" he said in disbelief. "You don't sound sure."

"She met him on the case. An American professor on holiday named Michael Johnson. She said they would be meeting up again."

"Do you hear how *not* serious this all sounds?" Jimmy continued, sure I was interested. Maybe I should have gone light on the praise for her during my case description.

"What's that noise?"

"Listen, I gotta go. Chief's calling me on the second line. Call me if you find anything out."

"Will do bro, take care."

I pressed the 'switch call' button on my cell and raised it back to my ear.

"Papacosta?"

"Yes, chief?"

"Bill Aggelopoulos just walked into a police station and gave himself up."

"Mr. Rich? For what?"

"He claims to be the Olympus Killer. Now pick up your jaw up from the ground, get that young lieutenant of yours and get your asses in Athens. You will be interrogating the suspect first thing tomorrow morning."

*****

Chapter 28

Hundreds of reporters, local and international, had already gathered outside of police headquarters in Athens. Tens of minivans with all sorts of antennas and dishes on top, illegally parked, formed a line all the way down to the hectic traffic lights. A significant number of the police force's members stood on the steps leading up to the building's main entrance as a warning to whoever may try to breach the building. The news of Mr. Rich turning himself in had spread like wild fire in a hay field and had caused a media frenzy like no other in Greece.

"Bill Aggelopoulos, the richest man in Greece, turned himself in today at Syntagma Police Station. We are here live outside police headquarters..." a brown eyed, petite reporter was saying.

"...no official statement has been released and rumors are running wild..." another continued.

Further down, a boisterous, beautiful brunette was finishing off her report with "Could Mr. Rich be the Olympus Killer? The public would be in disbelief if the news came just a year ago. However, after his wife's unexplained suicide and his withdrawal from public life, Bill Aggelopoulos has not been the same. Stay tuned for the latest."

A lifetime channel next to her was listening in and soon went live with a report how Bill Aggelopoulos went crazy with grief over the loss of his gorgeous wife and was being interrogated for the crimes of the Olympus Killer.

We stood opposite, watching as the hyenas quarrelled between them for a better spot.

"Ever been here before?" I asked Ioli.

"Once. They brought us on a day trip back in my academy days."

We crossed the busy road as all cars slowed down to see what all the commotion was about. Buses were making strenuous efforts to reach their destinations in time as reporters had even parked in the bus lanes. Not so easy was the passing through the technicians and their black wires and it took us a few minutes and a few dirty looks before we managed to head towards the entrance. The security guards prepared to intercept us and I even saw some fingers head for their triggers as I put my hand in my pocket to pull out my identity card.

"Captain Papacosta and Lieutenant Ioli Cara," I declared and smiled a good morning as we passed through the opening provided by two officers who stepped aside.

We placed our guns in the small, white plastic basket and stepped through the metal detector. There, the chief's charming secretary greeted us and informed us that *they* were waiting for us on the second floor in conference room one.

I knocked on the heavy wooden door and before receiving a reply, I opened.

"Ah, here they are," the Chief said, standing up.

“These are the officers in charge of the case,” he continued and introduced us as he brought us to the center of the room in front of the long table.

“Full house,” I thought, looking across at our audience. The Minister of Public Order, the Minister of Justice and the spokesman from the Prime Minister’s office stood out amongst other important public figures and police majors.

We were then bombarded by questions from the get-go. None of my sentences managed to reach their end as I was constantly interrupted for clarifications, judgmental suggestions and questions on how we planned to proceed.

“Do you believe he did it?” the domineering minister of Public Order asked first.

“It is not a matter of what I believe; it is a matter of finding the evidence to support...”

“Of course he did. He admitted it, didn’t he?” the serious-looking spokesman of the Prime Minister asked.

“People say many things. For a case to stand up in court, we will need to...”

“The Captain is right. We cannot risk any chance of this getting thrown out of court. Do you understand what this is doing to our already fragile economy? He owns some of the biggest companies in the stock market. Since yesterday they all took a dive and soon they will be swimming at the bottom of the ocean,” the extroverted, sensible Minister of Justice told them with a worried cloud darkening her eyes.

"Maybe I am a bit ignorant about the whole process, but he is not a suspect, he is not being blamed by someone else, he said he did it. He has admitted being the Olympus Killer. Chief, this needs to be wrapped up as soon as possible," the bald, stocky Minister of Public Order said raising his voice.

"We will know more about what we are dealing with after interrogating the suspect..."

Once again, I was interrupted. I gave up on the idea of finishing verbally any of my thoughts and stood still watching them discuss the matter between them.

"Is it true he has given up his right to be represented?"

"Really? I thought we would be up against an army of top notch solicitors!"

"Doesn't that shout guilty?"

"Well, he had the means to do the crimes. He owns God knows how many yachts and boats."

"And it is not like he has an everyday '9 to 5' job and he was missed at the office."

"What do his house employees say about his whereabouts?"

"Doesn't he have a son somewhere?"

"GossipTV should know everything by now."

After forty long minutes, the Chief finally spoke.

"Gentlemen and lady," he smiled at the Minister of Justice "we appreciate your time and fully understand your concerns, but the officers must be on their way now. I am sure we will have more to tell you after the interrogation. Trust me; you will be kept in the picture all the way."

As the three of us stepped out of the room, the chief exhaled deeply.

"Quick, follow me before the sharks get hungry again. They have been driving me mad since yesterday. You think the media outside is bad? You should see what is going on at Syntagma police station."

He talked as he trudged towards the elevator's door. I glanced at his right leg that seemed to be holding him back.

"Stop staring, Costa! My hip had been working double shifts, that's all!" he growled. "Now you've gone and interrupted my thinking. What was I saying? Oh, yes. Thank God, we had him transferred from there before the reporters' arrival," he added. The crisp sound of a bell signalled the opening of the elevator doors.

"Transferred?"

"Yes, to another police station. No one knows," he lowered his voice and pressed the button to the basement.

A black minivan with tinted windows and opened doors was parked down below. The driver did not move a muscle as we climbed in and as soon as the doors closed, we were on our way.

"Agios Dimitrios police station. Take the back roads and park behind the station," the chief ordered the driver.

"So you're the bright young star I've been hearing about?" he threw the question at Ioli.

"Just doing my job, sir."

"Hmm, modest too," he commented and picked up the phone to order the suspect to be taken to the interrogation room.

"I'll speak to him first. Five minutes. Then he is all yours. I want all loose ends tied up. This is a case that can make or break careers. Get everything from him on tape. Confessions to every murder, to every move, to every word."

"We also need the murder weapon. I want proof, not just words."

"You don't believe it's him?" he asked with his small eyes rapidly moving side to side, reading my every expression.

"He could be and he could not be. Everything is possible. You taught me that. For this case to close, I need him to provide hard, cold, undisputed evidence."

In his holding room, Bill Aggelopoulos sat alone with his thoughts, counting the cracks in the pale wall. He was not used to staying still. He never sat in the same spot for more than an hour, which made business meetings odd or interesting, depending on how his counterparts took it. Most attributed it to *billionaire's bizarreness,* but truth be told, he could never sit still. He worked long, endless hours, both day and night to succeed. Every time he accomplished one goal, another was already set. He could hear Christina's voice joking that he was a shark and would die if he ever stopped swimming. Now, he wondered what it all was for. He looked up on the sound of the thick metal door being pushed open.

"Stand up and turn and face the wall," the towering officer commanded.

He obeyed and stood there as a second officer entered the room and handcuffed his hands tightly.

"Is this really necessary, officers? I have shown no signs of..."

"Be quiet! Save your talking for your interrogation."

"Interrogation? I have already given myself up and pleaded guilty."

"Silence. Walk."

"*Great. More sitting!*" he thought as they ordered him to sit and used a second pair of handcuffs to cuff his right leg to the chair. Both exited the room without saying a word and he was alone again. He looked around at the lack of color: freshly painted white walls, white chairs, white table. In contrast, the video camera and its tripod in the right hand corner were black. The intense fluorescentt light was tiring to his eyes. He closed his eyes and held them closed until hearing the door open. He rubbed his eyes as the chief entered the room. He stood opposite Bill and placed his hands on the table.

"Mr. Aggelopoulos, I am Giannis Iordanou, Chief of the Hellenic Police. The two investigators in charge of the case will be with you shortly. I consider you a clever man and I know you realize the damage that will be caused if for whatever reason you are lying. The damage to the economy, to the victims' families, to our chances of catching the man responsible for these vicious crimes. So I have one question and one question only; are you *the* Olympus Killer?"

Bill looked at the chief straight in the eyes and answered a simple "Yes".

The chief exited the room, saying no other word. Through the left opened door, Ioli and I walked into the interrogation room and sat opposite him.

"My name is Costa Papacosta. I am a Captain with the Hellenic Police. This is Lieutenant Ioli Cara. I am going to be interviewing you today, Monday the 12th of August, 2013, in relation to the murders of Eric Blair, Stacy Anderson Blair, Alicia Robinson, Conor O'Brien and Amy O' Brien. The entire interview will be video-recorded and both officers present will be taking notes purely for our own references. Is this all clear to you, Mr. Aggelopoulpos?"

"Yes, very clear. Please, call me Bill."

"Please state your full name and your date of birth for the camera."

“I am Vasilis –Bill- Aggelopoulos, born in New York in 1973.”

“Can you please confirm that you understand that anything you say here may harm your defence and may be used against you later on in court? Anything you say can be given in as evidence. Do you understand?”

“Yes, of course,” he smiled slightly.

“You have the right to be legally represented Mr Aggelopoulos”

“Oh, yes. I have been told so, but I don’t need a lawyer. I admit to all murders. I killed all of them. Every single person you mentioned, I slaughtered them. And please, call me Bill. I will not be answering any other questions, asked to Mr. Aggelopoulos.”

I stared deep into his chartreuse green eyes and his soul did not move an inch as he pleaded guilty to all five murders. He remained tranquil as a windless sea. Ioli broke the moments of silence that followed.

“Tea? Coffee? Before we get started and you explain to us exactly how you killed five innocent people.”

“Coffee would be fine.”

“Two coffees for us, too,” Ioli spoke to the tinted glass window.

“We have an audience,” Bill said.

“Before Captain Papacosta discusses with you the how and the when, I have one very simple question for you. Why?”

"Why not?" he replied coldly.

The door opened and coffees were served in silence. I picked up mine and took a long, slow sip.

"Eric Blair," I said and placed a photo of Eric's body tied to the oak tree in front of him. He did not bother to look down.

"Wanna share your story, Bill? This is truly a work of art." I played to the tune of his sadistic mind.

"Art? Yes, you could call it that. No story really. Saw him, drugged him, threw him in my rental car and drove up to the hills. The result you can see."

"What day was this?"

"Wednesday, the 24th of July."

"How did you get to Crete?" Ioli asked. "We found no records of you travelling."

"I have my own, one crew boat. I am quite the sailor if I may say so myself."

"Where is the murder weapon?"

"My Bowie knife? I threw it overboard in the open just a few miles out from Delos."

"Why?" I asked.

"Did not feel like killing anyone anymore."

His calmness was annoying me. Arrogant answers and a confession to all those hideous crimes and not a single sign of remorse.

"Thought you were going to kill all the gods," I commented.

"Ah, the Olympus Killer. Yes, I am a huge mythology fan, but I am sorry to disappoint you. There was no specific meaning to the way I killed them. I just felt like killing and thought to be creative. You see, I have not been myself since my Christina passed away."

"Going to go for an insanity plea?"

"Excuse me? No, no. I am fully sane, I can assure you."

"Your wife did not pass away. She put a gun in her mouth. Found out about your sick side, did she?" Ioli snapped and at last, he moved slightly forward and raised his voice.

"My wife had troubles dealing with reality. Her mental state was not the best. She committed suicide in a moment of weakness. She has nothing to do with this and I forbid you to talk harshly about her. I killed and killed for the fun of it!"

I laid all the case photographs in front of him.

"Look at them! Is this your idea of fun?"

"Suum cuique pulchrum est."

"To each his own is beautiful," Ioli recited after him.

"An educated woman! I love a woman who knows her Latin."

"So this is your preference for a good time huh? You admit to all these hideous, inhuman crimes?"

"I do!" he replied to her.

"For the tape. You admit that on the night of Wednesday, July the 24th you murdered Eric Blair?" I asked.

"Yes."

"And you cut open his stomach and head?"

"Yes."

"And on the night of Friday, July the $26^{th,}$ you murdered Stacy Anderson on the island of Samos?"

He placed his hands on his legs and wiped his sweaty palms.

"Yes."

"You stabbed her in her heart and tore her vagina?"

"Yes," he said, lowering his voice.

"Cyprus, late Tuesday night, early Wednesday morning of July the 31st. You lured young, beautiful, innocent Alicia and you stabbed her and chopped off her arms like a butcher with a swine." My nerves were getting the best of me.

"Why are you telling me all this? I know what I did. I planned it for crying out loud."

"Delos, 8th of August..."

"Yes, yes, yes! The twins. Heads cut off. Yes, yes, freaking yes! Are we done now?"

"I will tell you when we are done. Where is your boat Bill?"

"I set it on fire and put it in drive, just off the coast of Mykonos."

"How convenient. No murder weapon, no boat."

"I was covering my tracks."

"Why? You were planning on giving yourself up."

"Maybe I wasn't at the time!"

"What do you think your wife would have said? Proud of her murdering bastard of a husband. I would have killed myself too if I was dumb enough to have married you," Ioli provoked him.

He smacked his hands hard on the table's surface, knocking over his untouched coffee.

"Now listen here. You have no right..."

"What about those people's right to live?" she threw the photographs at him. "Their mothers' right to not have their kids slaughtered by a sick fuck like you."

"Leave me alone! I enjoyed killing them and I have admitted to all murders. Stop with the questions! I have no reason for what I have done. I'm crazy!"

He let out a high pitched scream which ended in a howl and started to drub himself on the head with both his hands. The door was pushed open and two men restrained his hands.

"The time is 1500 hours and the interview is concluded."

I stood up and walked to the video recorder. I ejected the tape and took it over to the table.

"This is the tape of your interview. I am sealing it in your presence."

"Take him away," Ioli said, in disgust.

As I sat back down and closed my eyes, the chief came flying in.

"Well done to you both. We've got him on tape for all murders."

I turned around and gave it my best effort to smile.

"Cheer up, Papacosta! The case is closed!"

*****

Chapter 29

Ioli pushed open the rusty old door and walked out onto the roof. The sizzling sun blinding her as she looked to find me. I did not even bother to stop smoking. I leaned on the safety bar and gazed down, replaying the *breaking news* inside my head. The chief gave the performance of his career. With overwhelming enthusiasm, he announced that the Olympus Killer was in custody and that the islands were safe once again. He assured them that Bill Aggelopoulos was the killer and he provided the fingerprints found on the golden mask as evidence of this.

The cameras and the endless flashes suited the old man who was always better at politics and running things at headquarters rather than being out in the field. Playing golf with the mayor every other Sunday did not hurt his career either. I took out another cigarette, placed it between my lips and lit it with my first cigarette before it burned out.

"Annoyed are we?"

It was a difficult question to answer. I was annoyed, but I just could not pinpoint why exactly. Was I annoyed for not catching the killer myself? Was I annoyed at the chief's impatience to shout from the rooftops that the case was closed, even when all we had was a testimony? Or maybe I was angry at my mind that was incapable of comprehending that Bill Aggelopoulos was the killer.

"Are you thinking of an answer or are you just blanking me?"

“Did he do it, Cara?”

“He says he did. He certainly knows every detail about the murders and his fingerprints were on the mask. *His* mask, according to your FBI friend.”

“I know what he says. I want to know what you say. Your mind, your heart, your gut.”

“I’m guessing yours are telling you that it’s not him.”

“I cannot shake the feeling that this is not over.”

“Ok. Let’s, for the matter of argument, say you’re right. He is not our killer. Then that means he knows the killer right? He knows things about the victims that were not in the news. Maybe he is an accomplice. We never ran the thought that there could be two murderers,” she said.

“How about we pass by his cell on our way out and ask him a few off-the-record questions?” she then asked.

Luck was in our corner as the cell block guard happened to be an acquaintance of mine. Bumping into people you knew was something not so unusual in Greece. You could easily get talking with someone and find out you have the same roots and end up being third cousins from your mother’s side.

He opened the door for us and whispered in a guilty voice. “Five minutes... tops.”

"You two again? Missed me already?" Bill asked, looking up at us.

"You're so charming; we couldn't resist. So charming that we have difficulty believing that someone so charming is the Olympus Killer. What is it Mr. Aggelopoulos? Need for attention?" Ioli answered him.

Clouds formed across his face. He squinted his eyes and looked right at us.

"No wonder crime is so high. People give themselves up and you don't believe them and send them on their way. I did all the murders. What you believe or don't believe is your problem. I don't know what else to say to get it into your thick police heads that I am the Olympus Killer."

"If you are our killer why did you stop? You want to prove you're guilty? Tell us why? Give us a good story, Bill," I said.

"Who said I stopped?" he replied enigmatically. "You like stories, Captain? Well, here is a nice, short one for you. I am not a Christian. As a genuine Greek, I still believe in the Twelve Gods of Olympus. But what did they do for my Christina? They let her go mad and take her own life. That was when I decided to kill the gods. Revenge them in a twisted way. Now get the fuck out of my cell. I know my rights; you cannot interrogate me here. Leave now or I will scream. Mad people do crazy things you know."

As we walked to the car, Bill's words were playing like a broken record.

"Who said I stopped?" I whispered.

"You got the feeling that was a hint?"

"It was something in those green eyes of his. I felt like he was saying that the murders will continue."

"He sure has the means to make things happen."

"Did I tell you that the Chief has given both of us two weeks paid complementary leave?"

"You don't say!"

"I can't tell you how to pass your vacation time, but I have heard that Lemnos is lovely this time of year."

"Only island left on the list. Hephaestus."

"Right! And this time we are going as the killer and not as police officers. We will look through the media, local registration offices, Facebook, Twitter and I don't know what else and find possible targets. It will be a man that has a limp and has something to do with metals and/or fire. How many will fit that description?"

"Only one way to find out," she smiled at me and I felt glad that she was coming along with me on something that would most likely end up a wild goose chase.

*****

Chapter 30

I had spent the last two days reading through the local registration office's documents and all tourist bookings for arrivals during the last week and the week to follow. I had two criteria to highlight a name. Either medical problem noted or professions like blacksmiths, craftsmen, sculptors or a profession that dealt with metals, fire or volcanoes. These were all believed to be under the protective wing of Hephaestus, the god who according to myth, was thrown by his mother Hera from the heights of Olympus down to Lemnos. Only an infant at the time, the fall caused him severe damage to his legs and he was often depicted in art as having a limp or carrying a walking stick.

Lemnos had a population just shy of seventeen thousand and welcomed roughly twenty thousand tourists during the month of August. So far, I had managed to slim down the numbers to a pool of one hundred and sixty two.

"Call off the search party," Ioli called over from my sofa where she had slept the last two nights. I offered to take the couch and give up my bed, but she would have no word for it. She had been playing around with her tablet, looking through newspaper clips and social media.

"This is our target," she said and placed the fragile gadget in my clumsy, technological non-friendly hands. I held on to it tightly and tried to make out the tiny writing.

"Zoom in," she advised me.

"Does it have voice command?"

"Give it here."

"It is from a local newspaper; the Voice of Lemnos. *Fire-fighter* Jason Vlahos, aged 29 was released from the hospital today after three weeks of fighting extensive burns to his legs. A huge crowd waited for him outside and as he *limped* out, they all cheered and gave him a hero's welcome. The young fire fighter risked his life last month when he ran into a burning building to save two children aged three and five. Unfortunately, Jason Vlaho will no longer be able to work for the fire station as doctors ruled out any chance of his legs regaining their formal strength. An upbeat Jason told reporters that even though he loved his work, 'saving those kids was more important. Besides that, thank God, I will be making my father happy as I now plan to take over the family business, Vlahos *Blacksmiths*.' The mayor of Myrina, the capital of Lemnos, has officially invited the youth to the town hall where he will be receiving a medal of bravery in a ceremony dedicated to all local heroes."

"A crippled fireman who is a blacksmith! Well, I will be damned if he's not our target."

"Check this out too. Cheap morning flights and I found a good three star hotel near the harbour where all the fish taverns are."

"You and your love for food!" I joked.

"I have already searched and found out that Lemnos is famous for its unique Kalathaki cheese and its natural creamy yogurt."

*****

Chapter 31

The plane landed on the flat plains that made up the outskirts of Myrina. We were surrounded by Athenians looking to get away from the suffocating heat waves that made Athens so unbearable during August. The exodus of millions of Athenians took place during the days before the holy day of August the 15th, the day of the assumption of the Virgin Mary, a holiday most Greeks spent in their grandparents' villages or on an island.

Once again, I exhaled heavily and closed my eyes, finding religion as I thanked God for another airplane journey that came swiftly to an end.

"Still not used to planes by now?" Ioli complained.

"Nope! And never want to get used to them. I had enough planes, the last month, to last me a lifetime."

The wind was menacing outside, helping the island live up to its name -Lemnos, the wind-ridden island. The wind also helped to keep the temperature down. The 6 degrees Celsius -or 42 Fahrenheit if you prefer- difference with Athens in combination with the island's thirty sandy beaches made it a desirable getaway destination amongst mainland Greeks.

For a woman, Ioli travelled light and just like me, she carried her luggage on board. This gave us an advantage against our co-travellers who soon would exit in the hundreds and fight for one of the only twenty available taxis. We exited the building first and took the first taxi in front of us to our hotel. Ioli had booked two adjacent rooms and as soon as she unpacked, she came banging on my door.

"Come on; we haven't got all day."

Myrina was more fascinating than I expected. The quiet harbour, the stone-paved alleys, the stone-built houses of neoclassical design, the shops and the restaurants that maintained their traditional look and the friendly people all added to its magic.

"Do you feel the town's magnetism?" Ioli asked and sustained my belief that she could read my mind.

I did not manage to reply as she had already stopped a teenager that was showing off with his skateboard to a group of female peers.

"Excuse me, can you show me where Vlahos Blacksmiths is?"

"Sure. Down that alley there. All the way down and turn left. It will be on your right. Can't miss it really."

"Thank you," she said and winked at the boy as she shook his hand, leaving money scrabbled up in his palm.

"Here's five Euro for your help. Now, go buy that pretty girl in the blue dress an ice-cream."

His whole face brightened and his eyes opened wide.

"Thanks lady!" he said in excitement and in a great hurry, he rolled through the square towards the ice-cream parlour.

“Why didn’t you Google it?” I sarcastically asked what she always asked me.

“I did. It wasn’t listed,” she replied to my disappointment on having no revenge.

We walked through town and through time, looking like another couple of tourists enjoying the sights. Everything was well preserved and if it wasn’t for all the electricity wires, you could swear you were back in the fifties.

I was happy just to be able to wear shorts and a T-shirt. Ioli looked casually wonderful with her pink flowery sun dress.

We stood outside the blacksmith’s shop, window shopping. We entered through the green wooden door and were greeted with a vast smile and a warm welcome.

Jason Vlahos was a tall, built up, young man with handsome facial features and thick, rich black hair. A *manly man* as my mother would say. He put down his tools and asked if he could assist us.

“Just looking around for souvenirs,” Ioli said smiling.

“You have to see our metal olive tree set,” he said and limped with difficulty across the shop.

“Nice shop you have here. Yours or do you just work here?”

“Family business. I took over so my poor father could retire in peace.”

"What time do you close?" Ioli asked.

"Around seven."

"And what time do you open in the morning if you don't mind me asking," she continued.

"Eight, well, eight-ish," he admitted with a grin.

"I really like these, but I can't make up my mind. I'm thinking of coming round in the morning and shopping without my brother. Will you be open tomorrow or do you close for the holiday?"

"No, I will be open. Can't afford to be closed with all these tourists around. I will open right after church."

"See you in the morning, then."

"Brother, huh?" I said as the door closed behind us and we were back on the street.

"Preferred husband?"

"Bravo on getting his schedule. Now we need a place to spy on the place."

We were in luck as diagonally to the left was a colorful little cafe with a large front window.

Now all we had to do and all we could do was wait.

*****

Chapter 32

The 14th and the 15th passed rather uneventfully and it was my belief that Ioli started to have doubts that the killer would strike again. The news and the talk in town presented the case of Bill Aggelopoulos with every gory detail. Public opinion had already convicted him and his enemies enjoyed the steep fall of his stocks. Was I the only one who suspected otherwise? Too many *ifs* occupied my stream of thought.

"Good morning!" the gregarious owner of the cafe greeted us. He must have thought that we really liked his cafe as this was the third day in a row that we had chosen his establishment — something rare amongst holiday makers.

We sat in silence, enjoying our Greek coffees and staring at the blacksmith's place opposite. Jason Vlahos was not the most punctual guy, but at least he made stalking him easy. Home-shop-home was his daily routine with a small stop yesterday at the Cathedral of the Holy Trinity.

Ioli's phone started to vibrate, and she smiled as she looked down to see the caller.

"It's Michael," she said, got up and walked outside.

I watched her as she walked up and down the street, smiling and laughing and remembered my own youthful days with Tracy.

She fixed her hair as she walked into the cafe and caught her breath as she sat back down.

"Well, you won't believe this," she said.

"What won't I believe?"

"He's here."

"The professor? He is here in Lemnos?"

"Yes. He called me to see how things were going with our case in Athens. I said fine, you? Still in Crete? And he replied no, took the boat to Tinos for the assumption of Mary's celebration and then the ferry to Myrina. He is somewhere called the Hill of Poliochne. He sounded excited. A site from the early bronze age. His kind of party, I guess."

"That is convenient."

"What do you mean?"

"Sure he is not following you? I mean, you don't really know the guy..."

"Excuse me, *dad*. How long do I have to know a guy to know he is not a stalker? Besides, how can he be following me? He thinks I am in Athens!"

"Don't get upset. I was just trying to..."

"Never mind. Anyway, enjoy your coffee. I'll call you later. I am going up to surprise him on those Poliochne hills."

"You did not tell him you are here?"

"No," she said and rushed off to find a taxi.

The route to the ancient site was not the most scenic - dried-up valleys on both sides for the entire twenty minute drive, with the only interruption being the small village of St Dimitrios.

Ioli stepped out of the taxi and wondered what madness had come over her. She pulled out her phone and texted, "Costa, sorry I left like that. I still believe the killer will strike. Let's hope not today. See you tomorrow."

She felt better after pressing *send* and scanned the horizon. A group of Japanese tourists was living up to the cliché and were taking countless pictures of every rock and column. A few elderly European couples were strolling casually amongst the ruins and in the distance, one tall, handsome, blond, blue-eyed forty-year old was standing still with his back to her.

She crept up behind him and wondered what was so fascinating in the inscription he was preoccupied with reading.

"Excuse me, sir, but I seem to be lost."

"Ioli? Ioli!" he screamed and swooped her off her feet. "How the hell? You own the police helicopter or what? How? I can't believe you are here."

"Me neither," she laughed and kissed him gently on his soft, warm lips.

"Seriously, how?"

"I was already here, silly. My partner, Costa, has family here and he invited me to visit the island before heading to Crete. The chief gave us a two week holiday for closing the Olympus Killer case."

"No more nasty business and beheadings? Perfect! And I have you all to myself?"

"It seems so, Mr. Johnson."

"Fancy going swimming and then to an idyllic fish restaurant that I found just outside of Myrina?"

"Sounds perfect to me!"

As Ioli enjoyed her day, I wandered up and down the street, always keeping an eye on the blacksmith's shop. He was having a slow day with few customers, mostly couples and old ladies, looking for souvenirs.

I counted the benches, the street lights, the shops and the people passing by — anything to keep my mind from going over the case for the millionth time.

Jason Vlaho's closing time found me with a pita gyro with extra pink onions and tzatziki in my hand, sitting on a bench just a few meters away from his shop. I followed him to his building and watched him enter. Soon, the shutters of his second floor apartment were rolling up and lights were flicked on — lonely life for such a young man.

"The soul needs more time to heal than the body," my grandmother always said and she was -on most occasions- right.

I felt lonely too. And exhausted. My back and my knees were begging for rest and I was angry at the fact that my Athenian couch potato life had taken its toll.

Ioli, on the other hand, had company and she was terrified of what her next move would be. Michael had invited her up to his hotel room. Ioli had few rules in her life, yet important ones. One was that she was not what you would call an *easy girl*. Out of her friends, she lost her virginity last at the age of twenty two after dating Panayioti for over a year. Two yearly relationships followed, with a year in between, and now she was in an elevator going up to Michael's room after only a few dates.

"Rules were meant to be broken," she thought and felt guilty for trying to reason with her moral self. She was an adult who felt that what she had with the professor could progress into love and she needed an escape from the murders.

Half an hour later, naked between the white hotel sheets, she started to regret sleeping with him. Not for moral reasons though but for the lack of imagination on the professor's part. And to top that off, he fell asleep minutes if not seconds afterwards. The room was suffocating her and she did not feel like spending the night there. She slipped out of bed, quietly collected her clothes off the threadbare red carpet, got dressed and exited the room. She walked down the dark stairs and began to text Costa.

"*Where are you?*"

Seconds later, the answer came.

"*Sunset Club. Vlaho's cousin came round and forced him out of the house.*"

"*See you in five.*"

I beamed as I read her text and ordered her a strawberry margarita and my second whiskey and coke. I was not on duty and thought "*to hell with the no drinking on the job*". I sat there with one eye always on Jason and with the other enjoying the view from the beach bar. The palm tree lined road that ran parallel to the dark ocean, the clear sky with the bright moon journeying across it and of course the energetic, upbeat, well dressed, and young at heart locals and tourists that made up the crowd of the smoky club with the bright neon lights. Everyone seemed to be enjoying themselves. Vacations can always be relied upon to have that effect on your mentality. Even the couple on a blind date next to me, engaged in drone-like first date chatter, seemed comfortable. Everyone but Jason. Jason Vlaho sat awkwardly in the corner of the bright green couch. His friends all spoke loud, sang and poured drinks in a futile attempt to liven him up.

"Oh, margarita! Perfect! Strawberry or cherry?" Ioli asked and brought her glass to her lips without waiting for my answer. "Strawberry," she said quite tonelessly.

"Prefer cherry?"

"Most times, yes. But strawberry is fine. Nice club."

"I was thinking that too."

"So what have I missed?"

"Not much. His friends are really doing their best to cheer him up. My money is on the waitress though," I said and smiled as we watched her approach the five man group.

The waitress, wearing a short black skirt and a deeply displayed cleavage, flirted with him every time she brought over more alcoholic beverages to the glass table. A few straight whiskeys later, she even managed to earn herself a smile from the low spirited, crestfallen Vlaho.

"It's not every day you get a hero smiling at you," she whispered in his ear, bit his earlobe and passed him her number.

"I'm no hero. I was just doing my job."

"There are quite a few *jobs* that I would love to do with you," she said in her intriguing, luring, husky voice. She then took him by the hand, winked to his cousin and dragged him round to the shadowy back of the bar.

His friends all raised their glasses to each other and wished that their friend would be returned to them just as he was before the *incident* as they referred to the fire that burnt up their friend's life loving spirit.

Jason was pushed against the wall and he let the passionate redhead kiss him with force as her hands travelled down to his zipper. He closed his eyes and tried hard to act normal. His leg was killing him and he stood with difficulty as she knelt down. Her full, hot lips touched the head of his erect penis and sent shivers down his spine. His instincts took over and he placed his hands in her hair and guided her back and forth until he ejaculated deep down her throat.

He zipped himself up and searched for the right words. Thankfully, words were not needed. The unknown girl blew him a kiss and walked off to the ladies room.

I discreetly watched the skilful young lady please the troubled man from a distance and ran inside to inform Ioli that we were leaving. Jason had wandered off down the dark, rough beach.

We followed his limping shadow up the narrow stone steps and onto the busy street, realizing that he was heading home.

We shadowed him down dark, dim, little stone, brick alleys and watched him startle scruffy stray cats that were feasting on overflowing, smelling trash cans. Suddenly, he stopped and turned to see who was following him. Without a second's pause, Ioli pushed me up against the dirty wall and acted kissing me on my unshaved neck. With one eye on each other and one eye on Jason, we waited as he disappeared down the next alley. We held hands, maintaining the fable of being a couple returning from the bar and turned left behind him.

A loud, penetrating sound made us jump as a trash can was knocked over and cats ran in every direction, hissing as they disappeared into the darkness of the surrounding brick walls.

"Bloody cats, nearly gave me a heart attack," I said to no response.

Ioli had momentarily frozen.

"Stop! Police!" she shouted and ran down the narrow alley.

Jason was on the ground and above him stood a towering shadow. The starlight was shining on his menacing hypodermic needle that crowned the blue liquid filled syringe.

I took out my gun and ran beside Ioli.

"Stay with Jason. You have no weapon," I ordered her and sprinted after the fleeing murderer. I was right. "Who said that I have stopped?" Bill had said.

"Stay where you are!" I yelled and fired a warning shot into the night sky.

The Olympus Killer raced into the busy street and crashed into a red Fiat. I waved to the people inside of the car to remain still and walked slowly round the car, gun in hand.

"Freeze, you piece of..." I began to yell, but he was gone.

I looked hectically around and saw his figure running down a side street. I continued chasing him, ordering him to stop. He was quick and I was panicking at the thought of losing him. I heard him jump over a tall, wire fence and ran to follow him. As I approached the fence, a black Doberman was barking at me from behind it, saliva running down his sharp, white, dog teeth. For a moment, I was tempted to shoot the poor animal, but my sense quickly took over and I ran around the fenced property. Breathless, I reached the other side and to my dismay, realized that I had lost him.

I ran up and down the street with my eyes travelling 360 degrees. I was alone.

This was not the time to feel sorry for myself. I picked up my phone and dialled all the numbers I had prepared for such an occasion. I called the coastguard, I informed the local police, I called Athens and then Ioli who informed me that Jason was out cold and she had alerted the paramedics. I made it clear to everyone that I wanted the 477 square kilometer island on lock down. The coast guard was commanded to stop and search every ship. No flights were to leave the next day and no speed boats, jet skis or any other means of transportation by air or water would be up for hire.

I was not going to lose him again.

All hell broke loose. I never understood that phrase until this night. The chief called yelling down the phone, cursing me for leaving him in the cold. He did not sleep well that night if he slept at all. The sleepless night provided him with enough time to prepare his press release explaining that the police was looking into the possibility of a copycat or maybe even a second killer. In no way did he want a theory of Bill Aggelopoulos' innocence going viral.

Two Hellenic police helicopters circled the island while seven coast guard speed boats patrolled the winding coastline. On land, police officers were awoken and called to duty. Hotels and rooms for rents were searched and documents were checked.

Ioli accompanied Jason to the local hospital and when he recovered, she explained to him what had happened. He had no recollection of the events leading up to his awakening in a hospital bed. I was working side by side with the local authorities, co-ordinating the mission. Minutes turned into hours and my anxiety grew, turning me into a smoking, swearing, and unkind, rude monster. My *M.r Hyde* had been awoken.

With the break of dawn, the first positive news came in. The coast guard had found an abandoned ship in a small, isolated rocky bay; anchored behind steep rocks.

The *Christina*. Bill Aggelopoulos' Enavigo 38 racer yacht.

An hour earlier, I was joined by Ioli, who also stayed up searching hotel receptions and guest lists. As the news of the boat came in, we both ran to the first police car and shouted at the driver to step on it. The first sun rays hit us in our eyes as we stood at the edge of the cliff, looking down at the yacht. No one had responded to the coastguard's calls of "come out with your hands above your head".

Specialist marines swam with caution in the deep waters and reached the silent boat. Soon all three of them were on the boat, ordering the killer to come out and surrender peacefully — still, no response. The white, wooden door was kicked in and the marines went below to the yacht's cabin. Minutes later, all three re-appeared in obvious disarray. One managed to give a thumbs up and signalled that all important *all clear.* The yacht was hooked up to the coastguard's main ship and towed into Myrina's serene graphic harbour.

I stepped onto the boat first, followed by Ioli. The smell was near unbearable: a cloying and pungent stench like no other. We both placed on medical masks to cover our air portals and walked through the kicked-in door. Our eyes first fell onto the naked male body lying face down in the bath tub. A plastic trident, similar to the ones used during the carnival, was placed beside the decomposing body. The skin had taken an ill green color and was blistered all over. Most parts of the hair had fallen off alongside a dozen teeth and a few nails. The intestines were pushing to come out and maggots had made their appearance on the outside after their feast on the inside.

"Poseidon," Ioli managed to say as she lifted her photo camera and began flicking away.

"Based on its overall appearance, I would say the body has to be at least three weeks old. Probably longer."

"It out dates Eric's death," she commented and swallowed deeply.

"This kind of decomposition is over a month old," I said changing my estimate as I leaned in closer to the body, searching the white porcelain bathtub for clues.

"No stab wounds or any wounds of any sorts. Maybe drugged and drowned?"

"He looks young," she said.

Ioli stood up and looked around the small room. No luxuries for such a rich man on his yacht. One room below with a small, wooden closet that housed the toilet, a bathtub, a worn in, ripped around the sides armchair, a microwave, a fridge, a 24inch TV and a large chest freezer that would otherwise have smelled of fish. This was his alone-boat. He had his 377 foot super yacht with twelve rooms, two swimming pools and thirty member staff for his luxurious travels. This was his fishing boat.

Ioli walked over to the refrigerator and yanked open the lid. She gasped for air and took a step back. She turned away for a second in disgust before forcing her eyes to look back into the freezer.

"This one is even younger!"

I walked over to see another naked male body. His penis had been cut off and had been placed in the victim's mouth. A broken wine bottle was beside the victim. He seemed to have been stabbed repeatedly with the glass bottle. The freezer was still running. Due to the low temperature, the body was in a far better condition than the bathtub's body.

"Read the name of the wine," Ioli said.

"Dionysus. The god of wine. We will need the coroner to establish exact times of death."

"Holy fuck!" she said as she leaned into the freezer and stared at the young man's face. "I don't believe it!"

"What?" I asked.

"You don't read many gossip magazines do you? This was Greece's soon to be most eligible bachelor. Turned eighteen a few months ago. Most magazines featured the party and were judgmental at the extravagant party that took place so soon after his mother's death."

"Don't tell me this is..."

"Alexander Aggelopoulos. Bill's one and only child and heir to the Aggelopoulos fortune."

*****

Chapter 33

By midday, every muscle in my body cried for sleep. Ioli's red-shot eyes begged for the same. We were at the local police station having a much-needed fifth, Greek, rich-aroma coffee and being informed that they had come up with nothing. The majority of holiday makers were families and groups of friends. Most tourists had flown in from Athens and had not visited any other island. All tourists were not even in the country during the past murders. No local or tourist man fitted the description given and if not out at a bar, were fast asleep at the time of the attack on Jason Vlahos.

The search would have to continue without us. We were waiting to be taken to the airport where we would escort the bodies to Athens. I was eager to interview Bill Aggelopoulos again and get answers from the coroner.

"Your car is ready," the husky local lieutenant with the wiry hair informed me.

"The search is still on, Andrea. Don't disappoint me. Check everyone. No one leaves without being questioned, papers checked and items searched. The killer is still on the island."

"Yes, sir."

We walked outside and approached the parked vehicle. The young officer rushed to carry our bags for us.

"Ioli?" Michael's voice came from a distance. "You're leaving?" he asked out of breath as he ran over.

"I have to. We had..."

"I know! I heard. The police came by the hotel asking all these questions about where we were, whowere we with, how long have we been here..."

"When did you leave the states, professor?" I asked.

"Flew into Athens on the 27th and the next day, I flew to Cyprus. What terrible business. Two more bodies? Baby, are you ok?" he stroked her arm.

"I'm fine. It's my job..."

"So you are going to Athens *now*?" he interrupted her again.

"Yes, I will call you when I can."

"I am leaving in a few days. I have to get back to work," he said, lowering his voice and looking to the ground.

That was when it hit her. It was not going to work out. She had fallen for the most unavailable guy. They both loved their jobs and she could not imagine either of them quitting.

She smiled, slightly lost for words.

"Give me a reason to stay. I'm flying to Athens late tonight. I understand you are busy, but I would love to see you before flying back."

"And then?"

"And then, we will see. I could better my Greek and..."

"Michael, this is not the time or the place. I really have to go. I'll call you in the morning," she said and turned away without a goodbye kiss.

The professor stood there on the sidewalk and watched the car being driven away. For a man whose mind was always travelling in the past, he now found himself preoccupied with thinking of the future.

*****

Chapter 34

The nightmare kept on playing over and over. A single bullet would flying through the air and across the road from the black Lincoln and I, like a second superman, stood in front of a frightened, crying Gaby.

"Save me, daddy. Don't let me die again!" she would beg, but the bullet would just travel through me every time and end up hitting her. The first bullet hit her hard in her chest.

Then, like an old tape, the whole scene would rewind to five minutes previously and I would live the torment once again. This time the bullet hit her in the face and I watched motionless as half of her head broke off. Rewind. Again. Rewind, again. A modern day Sisyphus.

The ringing of the phone saved me from my own personal hell.

"Hello?" I grunted.

"Costa? You did say to call you as soon as I woke up," Jacob Petsa started to excuse himself. I looked over at my cheap living room clock. 06:25. The sun was just waking up as well.

"Morning, Jacob. Meet you at the morgue in twenty? You finished examining the bodies last night?"

"Yes, didn't get home till one o'clock last night. Still waiting on most lab results, but I can tell you everything you want to know before interviewing Bill."

"Thanks a lot mate. I owe you one."

"Didn't you hear me right? One o'clock I got home and I was up at six. You owe me two. Pork chops and a beer would be nice."

"For sure," I said and closed the phone. Footsteps behind me made me jump up from the couch.

"Nice boxers," Ioli joked as she walked out of my bedroom, fully dressed, black shiny hair brushed, high heels and make-up on, and wandered into the kitchen.

"Get dressed and come to breakfast," she ordered.

"In twenty at the morgue," my words followed her into my -on the verge of derelict- kitchen.

"I heard. I was awake. Been up since five, thinking."

"This case owes us sleep," I said and walked into my bedroom to get ready.

By the time I walked into the kitchen, ready to go, Ioli had not only brewed coffee, but she had also boiled a couple of eggs and prepared toast. She had even taken the liberty of cleaning the kitchen counter and wooden table while she was at it.

"You're one hell of a Greek woman, Cara," I laughed to cover my embarrassment of having her stay in a dirty man's den.

"So what was on your mind and you've been up since five?"

"Coroner said anything specific?"

"Only that lab results aren't in but he could tell us everything that we need for the interrogation."

We bit into our honey-laden toast and sipped our coffees. A few eggs and another round of toast and we were ready to go.

I loved Athens before eight o'clock in the morning. It was calmer, it felt normal, and it felt liveable. Soon, the storm would hit and millions of ants would run around, creating traffic jams and Greek-swearing conflicts around each set of traffic lights. Some loved the chaos and fell in love with the big city. Others accepted it as a necessary evil and reminisced living in the pacific periphery or even better careless on an island where they hoped to relive the halcyon days of their parents.

We arrived at the morgue before Dr. Petsa, who showed up ten minutes later. He had trudged down the stairs to find us outside his door.

"Morning," he exhaled.

"There is an elevator, you know," I said.

"I steal moments of exercise. I haven't got time for a gym or the will to stop eating. I was reading this article in this men's magazine how to keep fit with a few changes in your life and using the stairs was in the top three," he said and unlocked the door. "Come in, make yourselves at home," he joked.

"No, thank you!" Ioli said, looking at all the little silver lockers, each with its own unfortunate individual. An old lady who died quietly in her sleep. A twelve-year-old boy who was hit by a drunken driver as he rode his bike home. A middle-aged man who did not cope with a third heart-attack. And of course, our two murdered bodies. Dr. Petsa rolled them both out and stood between them, facing us. The scars from the doctor's incisions were pink in contrast to the pale bodies. All the blood inside had travelled south and the skin was rotting away.

"Body number one. Identified as Alexander Aggelopoulos, aged 19. Stabbed to death with a broken wine bottle. It's hard to determine how many times he was stabbed exactly as the stabbing was erratic and in multiple areas. He was stabbed in both his legs, the lower and upper abdomen, his back and in his right arm. Unfortunately, the cutting of his erect penis happened while he was still alive."

"Erect?" Ioli asked.

"Yes. He was raped, too."

"Raped?" we both said.

"Now this is something new for our killer," I said.

"Dionysus was the god of orgies, to put it bluntly. And the phallus was a symbol used during his worshiping," Ioli said.

"That would explain the cutting of the penis which was stuffed down his throat. There are no marks of being tied up and as I don't believe it was consensual intercourse and having in mind our killer's

M.O., I would say he was raped while drugged," the doctor said and his voice gave away his lack of sleep.

"DNA?" I eagerly asked.

"Again, nothing. Gloves, condoms and wiped clean are how I imagine the killer's way. Nothing to go on."

"Date of death?" Ioli asked.

"Seven to eight weeks ago. Both the bodies."

"So they were killed together and from the bodies, we know of, they were killed first. A few weeks before Eric Blair," I thought out loud.

"The second body?" Ioli asked, looking down at her watch. At nine we were interrogating Bill.

"Body number two," he said and pulled back further the white thin sheet. The sight of the rotting body was appalling. While the first body was placed in the freezer, the second was left in the water-filled bath tub.

"The body has yet to be identified. I would place his age around twenty-five. Thirty tops. Caucasian. Maybe Greek, could be Latino or anything Mediterranean I would say. Cause of death? He was drowned. Also, no defensive wounds or marks to imply force. As before, given our case, he was most likely drugged and placed in the tub. Slowly his lungs filled with water and he died of suffocation. We will know more when the labs come in."

"No water was found in the tub, but I guess this is a Greek summer right?" I asked.

"Yes, the water would easily have evaporated during the last two months."

We thanked the doctor and we swiftly left the premises. We were up for the next round with Bill Aggelopoulos.

"What kind of monster carries two bodies around with him for months? I mean, just the stench..."

"Exactly, Cara. A monster. Seven bodies. Seven!" I said and started my car.

"Do you think Bill killed his own son?" Ioli said and strapped down her seat belt.

"As I see it, we have two scenarios. Either Bill is lying and has not killed anybody, thus the killer in Lemnos is our real Olympus Killer and he is the one who killed all seven victims or there are two killers, Bill and the killer in Lemnos, and we have to determine who killed who."

"Let's hope we get the truth out of Bill."

"Whether he wants to or not, today he is spilling the beans. No more monkey business. We have seven dead bodies on our hands, maybe more and we still have a killer on the loose."

Bill was moved again. This time he was taken to Korydallos prison where he was isolated in a cell away from the prison's main population. Bill was not informed about our visit. For him, it was just another day in detention awaiting trial.

I drove up to the main prison gates and stopped in front of the armed guard.

"Captain Papacosta and Lieutenant Cara," I said and passed him our papers.

"Good morning, sir. The warden is expecting you. Drive on up and turn left. Park in the visitor's parking. Someone is there ready to escort you," he commanded peremptorily in military fashion.

I nodded a *good day to you, too* and drove as commanded. I parked next to a black-suited man with a short neck. He was leaning up against a Mercedes with government plates. The man with the dark shades on was smoking a cigar while listening to Beethoven playing from the car's stereo. He dropped the cigar to the cement ground and did not bother stepping on it. He walked over as we stepped out of my car.

"Captain Papacosta?" he asked in that manner you ask anything that you already know the answer to.

"Yes?" I answered his question and added tones of *who are you.*

"I am the warden. Spyros Costopoulos," he extended his right hand. He smiled at my face that revealed so clearly that I was surprised by the welcoming committee.

"Did not expect the warden to be out here?" he said and shook Ioli's hand. "You're more beautiful than your file photos, Miss Cara."

"Been reading up on us?" she replied to his somewhat inappropriate statement.

"I always know who comes and goes in my prison."

"I must say, no, I was not expecting you," I said.

"I like the parking lot. It is probably the only area on the premises with fresh air. Well, before my cigar that is. Good place to think, too. Prisons are always so dank and depressing. But that is enough rambling on my behalf. Now, you talk. Follow me and tell me all about Bill Aggelopoulos. And not gossip that I already know from the media; what I need to know. I like to know my *guests*."

"To be honest sir, I'd rather not discuss the case. It is still open and Bill has not been sentenced yet..."

"You believe him innocent?" he asked and stopped walking for a split second before continuing on a slightly faster pace.

"I said no such thing. Maybe we should discuss things after the interrogation."

"Hmm..." he grunted, not satisfied with my answer. Surely a man used to getting his own way. In one perspective, prison wardens were truly kings of their castles. Especially ones with political ties, which was the rule and not the exception here in Greece.

“How is the old chief?” he changed the subject.

“Fine. As fierce as ever.”

“Give him my regards and remind him that the mayor and I will be expecting him for golf on Sunday.”

“I will remind him,” I answered, thinking what boring sport golf was. In my youthful days, basketball was all I played.

“Do you play golf, Captain?” he then asked.

“Oh, no. I horse ride on Sundays at the country club,” I replied to earn Ioli’s trademark smile of satisfaction.

“Second door on your left. Order coffee to the guard. Aggelopoulos will be with you shortly,” he said annoyed, and wandered off, barking orders down the cold, unfriendly corridors.

“Horse riding?” Ioli laughed as we sat down while I ordered coffees.

The coffees came before Bill and that was the only positive thing about the day. Well, that and the revelation of the truth. The door opened and Aggelopoulos was led into the small room.

“Not you two again!”

“Sit down, Bill. This time I’ll be doing all the talking.”

“Yes, sir,” he sarcastically remarked and sat down, looking bored.

"The camera is rolling, you know your rights, now listen carefully. I know you are *not* the Olympus Killer," I said with certainty.

"Oh, not all this again. I have admitted..."

"And I know this because yesterday we caught the Olympus Killer in Lemnos."

Now I had his full attention. He sat up straight and placed his palms on the cool table surface.

"Who did you catch exactly?"

"The Olympus Killer. He attacked a local blacksmith. Hephaestus, I would presume. We haven't identified him yet. He is not talking, *yet*."

He lifted his palms from the table, leaving sweaty imprints behind and looked me straight in the eye, trying to figure out if I was lying or not. I gave him no such time.

"Found your boat, too. You know the one you said exists no more?"

"My boat? Really? You found my boat?" he said, his voice a mixture of joy and sadness. He was trying to keep his cool and failing. As I remained motionless, he turned to Ioli and begged.

"Please, please tell me the truth. Did you find my boat? Tell me!"

"Yes," she replied. "We found your boat. We found your son, too."

He closed his eyes and tears fell down his cheeks.

"Alexander. My boy. Thank God. Is he ok?"

Now, we were taken aback.

"Excuse me?" I replied baffled.

"Alexander, where is he?"

"Mr. Aggelopoulos, your son has been *dead* for over two months now. *Butchered* and *raped* by the *Olympus Killer* who *you* claim to be!" Ioli said with subtle rage underlying every other word.

Shock hit him hard and he let out a high pitched cry.

"Nooo! I don't believe you. How many lies? I demand to see my son," he shouted and waved his arms in the air. He was only chained at the ankles.

"We can arrange a visit to the morgue even though your house maid, Miss Maria Evripidou, has already identified the body. It is your son. However, you might help identify the other body found on your boat. A tall, dark haired, handsome man under thirty?"

"This can't be happening. I did everything right," he sobbed and lowered his arms upon the table. We left him in peace to cry. It was obvious he had no idea his son was dead. All we could do was wait for him to find the strength to tell us his story. Moments later, he punched the table with his right fist and lifted himself up slowly.

"Is the tape still rolling?"

"Yes" Ioli answered.

"Please do not interrupt me with questions. I have no will to answer them. I want to tell my story to help bring justice to the victims and their families. Then, I wish to return to my cell and mourn my son."

"Agreed," I said.

He raised his voice and started to unravel the true events surrounding him, his son and the Olympus Killer.

"My name is Bill Aggelopoulos. I am not the Olympus Killer. I have never killed anyone in my life. Two months ago, my son, Alexander Aggelopoulos and his lover, Giuseppe Acqua asked for my boat. They planned to spend the summer together, sailing around the Greek islands. Alexander wanted to show his boyfriend the beauties of Greece before moving to Italy to study philosophy. Four days after they had set sail, I received a DVD in the post. FOR BILL-SEE IT ALONE it had written on it with capital letters. I could not believe my eyes when I pressed play. It was videotaped on my boat. Alexander and Giuseppe were both tied up naked on the floor while above them stood a tall man, dressed in black and wearing a rubber carnival mask over his head. He took out a knife and held it to Alexander's neck. He told me that if I did everything he asked for, he would not hurt them and that by the end of August, I would have my boy back safe and sound. Since then, I received e-mails instructing me what to do. The last e-mail instructed me to give myself up as The Olympus Killer and not to tell the truth untill Alexander was released. And the whole time my boy was dead!"

"I am sorry for your loss..." I started to say. "It is never easy. It is only painful when you lose your child, your only child."

He wiped his watery eyes with his shaking hands. "Maybe it's better this way. He belongs with his mother," he said, strikingly calm. He took a moment and asked maintaining his new-found calm tone of voice, "so you arrested the American then?"

"American?" Ioli asked.

He gave her an angry look and snapped at her.

"Yes, American. You haven't heard him speak? Pretty damn obvious if you ask me."

"He is refusing to talk to us," I lied again, feeling immoral.

"Does he look like me?" he asked.

"Why do you ask such a thing?" Ioli answered back with a question.

"When I wrote back to him, offering him millions for my boy, I asked *why me*? He replied that it was because I was so handsome and in parenthesis, he added *we look so much alike!*"

"I wouldn't say you resemble much," I kept on feeding the lie.

"I want to go back to my cell now."

"Of course," I said and called in the guards.

Bill walked off a broken man with touches of sorrow, grief, regret and hopelessness painted in his eyes.

*****

Chapter 35

The next morning came with news for Ioli. Some surprising, some not so surprising. I stood before her and announced what I had learned and what I planned on doing next.

“Bill hung himself last night in his cell with his bed sheet.”

“Money truly can’t buy you happiness. He lost his wife, then his son,” she said with hints of the pessimism of the world’s state in her voice.

“Lemnos called. No success at all at apprehending Jason’s attacker.”

“No surprises there,” she said and fell further back into the sofa.

“And... no questions allowed, I am going to New York for a few days.”

“What?” she said and her face lost all its sweetness. “Why?” she raised her voice as I did not respond.

“I did say no questions.”

“Family?”

“You can stay here if you like. You could go back to Crete. Officially, we are still on vacation. The chief is keeping everything hush-hush on the new developments and Bill’s death will suit him fine. It closes the Olympus case in the media’s eyes till we catch our killer.”

“I’m lost for words.”

"Well, that will be a first."

"Please, don't joke," she said quietly.

"I'm sorry," I said and sat beside her.

She hugged me with both arms and laid her head on my chest.

"I trust you. Do what you have to do."

*****

Chapter 36

Ioli was torn. She had never felt so lost of clear choices. Not that she was a fan or even a believer of astrological signs, but one thing she did agree upon was that as a Virgo, she wanted everything to be in order. She loved having a schedule and she kept to it. This was her first case that required leaving home; leaving Crete. She was now faced with the dilemma of staying in Athens or returning to her island. The thought of going back to Lemnos or maybe even traveling to find the next murder location and victim spawned in her mind.

The midday gossip shows playing on the TV were not helping with her state of mind either. She sat in the middle of my black leather sofa feeling lonely and without a purpose. She turned and glared at her made-up suitcase next to the bedroom's door. She did not wear self-pity well. Suddenly, vibration sounds echoed through the room, interrupting her thoughts. Her phone was moving across the old, wooden coffee table. It was Michael. The call fed her pity and anger. She had promised to call him and she had not been in touch with him since she left Lemnos so abruptly.

"Hey, sorry I did not call. I was..."

"No need to apologise. I miss you," his gentle voice came through the receiver.

"Miss you, too."

"Where are you?"

"Athens. You're still in Lemnos?"

"Yes, still here. I am flying out in the evening to Athens. My flight home is in four days. I hope no murders happen and I will get to see you more than a day at a time."

"I'm free for all four days!" she answered, having decided to let him fix her self-pity state of mind.

"Excellent! I can't wait. I'll call you from my hotel. Nice, little central place whose name I can't recall just now," he laughed.

She smiled at his high spirits and tried to erase their first sexual encounter from her mind.

*****

Chapter 37

Ioli had not been out and about in Athens in years, the last time being a long weekend with the girls during the festivities for the celebrations for the 25th of March; a double holiday in Greece. It was the anniversary of the uprising of the Greeks against their Ottoman oppressors, and it was also the day the Greek Orthodox Church celebrated the annunciation of Archangel Gabriel to the Virgin Mary that she was pregnant with the Son of God. Ioli and her group of girlfriends had come with two missions in mind. Shopping and meeting singer Saki Rouva backstage after enjoying his extravagant show at the nightclub where he performed. They had accomplished both tasks and left Athens satisfied.

She felt relaxed and enjoyed Michael's company though the economic crisis had surely changed her beloved megacity. There were many homeless lying around and others roaming the streets begging for spare change. The lay-off of municipality workers resulted in dirtier streets, though if one kept to the main tourist areas, it would be easy to not realize such a fact. One thing Troika could not take away was the city's vibe. Athens was unique and had much to offer. The Greeks had been through worse during their turbulent history and have always come out on top. Ioli always said that hope died last and she was reminded of this as she strolled with Michael, hand in hand, through Omonoia's square and saw a young, homeless couple sleeping in each other's arms as they made the rough bench their bed.

‘‘They could take away their home but not their love,’’ Michael commented and Ioli leaned in close and placed her lips on his neck.

Michael proved the sort of company Ioli enjoyed the most. He enjoyed good food, laughed often, never complained as she zig-zagged in and out small charming shops, and drank more than three coffees during their excursions.

“How often do you think of your case?” Michael asked over their third coffee at a little ten-table cafe with a stunning view of the Parthenon.

“Who said I am thinking of the case?”

“Your eyes,” he smiled and touched her hand.

“I feel guilty,” she admitted.

“Guilty? Why?”

“I feel like I am sitting here having the time of my life, carrying the knowledge that some poor person will be brutally murdered and there is nothing I can do about it. The public has no idea that Bill was not our killer and we have no idea who is or where he is going to strike next. We have failed. *I* have failed!”

“I think you are being too hard on yourself. You did your best and it is your chief's idea to keep things quiet about Bill. The next victim's blood is on his hands.”

“Can we change the subject?” she asked. She was in no mood of talking about blood.

"I'm sorry; I was just trying to be supportive."

"I know. You're a good boy," she laughed.

"Good enough to enjoy a positive answer to my inquiry if you are going to come stay the night with me at my hotel?" he said and anxiously tried to read her facial expressions. She looked down to the left and opened her mouth but did not respond.

"I don't mean to be pushy and all but we have been having such a great time the last two days and I am leaving tomorrow..."

"That's the thing, Michael," she replied. "You're leaving and the last thing I need at the moment is good-bye sex."

"Who said anything about goodbyes?"

"Let's not kid ourselves, Michael. How is this going to work?"

"I did not want to say anything because I was afraid of scaring you off, but..." he said and went silent.

"But?" she urged him to continue.

He leaned forward over the round table and covered her soft hands with his. He looked straight into her eyes and stared at her for a tender moment before saying, "I am in love with Greece. Always have been. You think if I met the right woman, I would not give it all up and move here?"

She was lost for words and took a second to gather her thoughts.

"Michael, you can't give up your job. I'm flattered, but you love teaching..."

"And who says I cannot teach here? There are many private schools that teach in English and who knows? Maybe my Greek will one day reach a sufficient level and I could teach at a Greek university."

"I can't believe we are having this conversation."

"If you believe it, it can happen. Come on. Live the moment and live it with me."

"Okay, no need to get dramatic. You men would say anything to get laid!"

"You *men*?" he laughed out loud and tilted back his head, reminding her of her partner that was somewhere far away across seas and oceans.

His laughter died down slowly and he wiped away his laughter's tears.

"Finished?" he asked, looking at her white coffee mug. She lifted up her mug and showed him the bottom as a reply.

"Great. Where to next?"

"What do you mean?" she asked.

"What do *you* mean?" he replied puzzled.

"Thought we were going back to your hotel, Mr. Johnson."

He jumped up from his chair and yelled "Taxi!" gaining stares from bystanders.

"You're mad!" she laughed as she got up and joined him on the sidewalk.

"You have no idea, Ms. Cara," he replied as he opened the taxi's back door.

"Your carriage awaits, my princess," he kneeled down and bowed.

"Yes, I can see that!" she replied to his previous statement and entered the taxi slightly embarrassed by the driver's disapproving look as he waited in the traffic for the mad American to get in the car.

The professor's hotel was not far. In fact, it was the ultra-luxurious King George Palace, located in the heart of Athens, just a ten-minute drive away. Michael surely did not have money problems. For Ioli, money was never a goal in life, however the professor's well being was a positive note as it would make it easier for him to move to Greece. She could not imagine herself ever leaving her sun-kissed homeland.

They held hands, sitting in the back of the cab, all the way to the hotel. Michael paid the man, adding a generous tip and together they exited the vehicle. Swiftly, they jogged up the marble steps and entered the hotel's vast and luxurious lobby. The suited to her attire, fifty-ish looking, slim lady with the wavy auburn hair smiled at them from behind the quartz reception.

"Suite 601, please," he said.

"Here you go, Mr. Johnson," she replied and gracefully passed him the electronic card.

They held hands as they waited for the elevator to come down and exchanged high-school guilty looks.

"601. Top floor huh? Suite?" Ioli remarked as she watched him press the red glowing button that ordered their golden cage up to the top floor.

"Rich family. Rich allowance," he honestly replied and quickly added, "I'm not spoilt though. I work and I do not spend much. Hotels are one of the few luxuries I offer myself. I have an issue with places being spotlessly clean and as you have realized, I enjoy eating. The more stars a hotel has, the longer the buffet!"

"Amen to that," she laughed and sealed her laughter with a passionate kiss on his half opened lips. She was going to try her best to make a better memory than their first time together.

The card slid through the metal grip and beeped open the expensive door. The maroon carpet fitted room was far more spacious and opulent than what she had pictured it to be. Everything was catered for to the finest detail. The curtains opened symmetrically, the same shape and color apples in the glass fruit holder, the many spotlights offering various ways of lighting the room, the paintings in color harmony with the expensive vases, the fresh flowers and the spotless surfaces. The balcony drew her out to enjoy the view. The bustling metropolis was in eyesight, but no noise found its way up to the tranquil 6th floor. She turned and looked back inside the room. Michael had kicked off his white sneakers and had sat down on the double bed. She loved the way he looked at her: a warm look with hints of desire. She felt him eating her up with his blue eyes and she felt special. She walked over to him and stood between his legs. His hands ran up her thighs and reached her waist. He pulled her on top of him and his hands continued under her shirt to caress her back. Their lips locked and the environment faded away. Hands moved around and clothes fell quickly to the floor. She felt his lips biting her neck softly and she closed her eyes in delight.

"Don't leave," she exhaled.

"Your wish is my command, my Athena," he replied.

The stimulation blocked the registration of the words, but when they reached her brain, she stopped in shock.

"What did you call me?"

He looked puzzled.

"Don't stop now, baby. Come to me."

"I am just going to freshen up and I'll be right with you," she replied in a flat voice and got up. She kneeled next to her jeans and her hands searched frantically.

"Looking for this?" he said in a playful tone.

She slowly stood up and saw her gun in his right hand as he stood on the bed, towering over her.

"Oh, don't worry. Guns are not part of my M.O. as you would say. Knives are more my style!" he said with a glow of thrilling joy painting his eyes.

Ioli gathered herself fast.

"So I was Athena all along?" she asked, not moving a muscle. She stood scared and naked opposite her enemy.

"Clever, single, against marriage, dynamic, carries weapons, beautiful, owl-like eyes. Oh, yes. You are a perfect Athena. Who would believe my luck when you said you had to come to Athens? Your sacred city!" he said overexcited as he waved the gun at her. He jumped off the bed and hissed orders at her.

"Open the bed side table's drawer and take out the handcuffs. Kneel down, put your arms behind your back and put them on."

She obeyed. She moved slow, trying to gain time to assess her situation. Should she try to attack him? He did imply he would not shoot. Where was his knife? Was there a way to call for help? She had not noticed anyone staying in the nearby suites.

"Hurry up, my goddess," he continued hissing out orders and interrupted her thoughts. She did as she was told. He kneeled down behind her and that was when she felt the cold blade touch her neck.

He pulled down his grey underpants, pressed his naked body upon hers and whispered, "let's have some fun first, right? That's why we came here after all."

He pushed her head hard down on the mattress and licked her face hard.

Ioli closed her eyes and that was when the loud noise of the door being kicked in was heard.

"Get off her, *now*!" I shouted.

"Costa?" Ioli cried out, not believing I was really there.

Michael pulled her up by the hair and placed her in front of him as a human shield.

"Don't do anything stupid, professor. There is no escape for you. The hotel is surrounded. It's over. Let her go."

"She's *mine*!" he howled while his eyes moved rapidly from side to side.

"Tell them to back off or I will cut open her pretty little throat right now!" he ordered as he fixed his stare at the door and the two men of the swat team.

I waved to the men to pull back and I stepped closer to the professor and Ioli.

"How did you find me?" he demanded to know.

I lowered my gun and replied "you were clever. I'll give you that. Very clever. But as I always say, it is the little things that matter. And they always add up and give you away."

"And what were my *little things* mighty, great detective?"

"Bill mentioned that the killer said that they looked alike. And indeed. Bill fit the description given to us by the shop owner in Cyprus. That got me thinking. Why would such a careful planner like the Olympus Killer give away his appearance so easily? Twice! Because it was not *his* appearance. That's why. You walked into that shop not caring because it was not truly you, my blue eyed, blond friend. Think about it. What could someone change so easily about his facial appearance? His hair with a wig and his eyes with a pair of colored lenses. When Bill said the killer was American, it just all fell into place. You and Bill are exactly the same build and height. After interrogating Bill, I went home and changed my sketch. It's funny how something so obvious can avoid the mind. I drew blond hair and blue eyes and guess who was staring back at me?"

"Me," he said proudly.

"Yes, you, my American, mythology-loving prick. You gave the performance of a lifetime. I remember you sitting there all scared on that beach in Cyprus with your swollen, red eyes and scratching your head awkwardly. Guess the wig was itching and you were not used to wearing eye contacts for so long next to the sea and with all the sand swirling around. You sat there as Ioli said that she thought the gods were twelve and you replied yes, they *are*! Not *were*, you said *are*. They are real to you, aren't they?"

"You said he was flying to the States," he yelled and pressed the knife tighter on Ioli's throat. Drops of blood ran down her neck.

"I did go. That was no lie. You had an alibi. You weren't even in Greece when the Blairs died right? Or so you told the police in Lemnos. I had my friend Jimmy check you out. Apparently, when Eric Blair was being slaughtered, you were at a fundraising gala in New York. You spoke at the event for everyone to see and hear. Had everything planned out didn't you?"

"You don't know the half of it, detective. Good luck getting a jury to convict me with such proof. And as for Athena here, it will be your word against mine. I will say you did it. You went mad after your daughter's gruesome death and came to Greece a maniac," he said and lifted up the knife, ready to stab.

Ioli followed the knife forward and hit back with all her strength, head butting the professor in the face. She ran forward and two shots were fired.

My bullet swirled through the room and hit the professor hard in the chest, pushing him down to the floor. The professor's bullet hit Ioli in the back and she fell forward into my arms. The swat team filled the room while Ioli laid in my arms, breathing heavily. Her blood oozing out quick.

"*No, not again*," I thought.

"I need a paramedic here," I yelled.

"Thank you," she said and swallowed hard. I looked down at her with watery eyes.

"Another case solved," she said, and smiled before coughing out blood and closing her eyes...

*****

Chapter 38

New York, three days earlier

The plane touched down at JFK airport and I was feeling disoriented in time. I had left Athens with the sun in my face and now thirteen hours later, the sun was still facing me. I took comfort in managing to sleep for the most part while in the air. I dreaded the fact that in a couple of days, I would be entering the '*metal prison bird*' once again for another double-digit hour flight with at least an hour stop in Heathrow, London. All thoughts of the flight were washed away as I walked out the airport's see-through doors to find Jimmy arguing with a cab driver about taking his parking space.

"Costa!" he shouted with his distinctive, cheerful tone and ignoring the red-faced driver who was cursing the feds and their rude ways. He rushed towards me and opened his big arms out wide and I walked into his brotherly hug.

"Hey, bro. Thanks for coming."

"Anytime, my man. You owe me one. If your mother knew you were here and that I kept it a secret, she would kill me and then call up Toula to apologize!"

I threw my head back and laughed. It always amazed me how good Jimmy made me feel. To be honest, he was really the only one I missed in America. The bond between men that grew up together was hard to explain and even harder to break.

“Here you go,” he said and passed me a bunch of printouts that he had scribbled on. I read through them as Jimmy drove through *my* city. New York would always be home. The professor taught at UCLA, but he was in New York in June, giving lectures about the outcome of the Trojan War and how it affected the Hellenic society of the time. Apparently, he stayed in the city after the series of lectures and on Wednesday, the 24th of July, the night Eric Blair was killed, he attended a formal gala hosted by the American Historian Society that took place at NYU. His flight to Athens was booked for Saturday, the 27th. However, as Jimmy found out after my request, the professor never boarded the plane. The only plane that he did board was the one from Athens to Cyprus on Monday the 29th. How the hell did he get to Athens? And how did he kill Eric Blair if he was at a gala on the other side of the planet?

My thoughts swirled through my mind as I gazed upon Meadow Lake. Jimmy turned at Corona Park and took the 495. Soon, we would be at New York University. I could only hope for answers.

“Did you read about the librarian?” he asked.

“Who?”

“Jesus, you are a slow reader. I already checked up on the gala. A librarian, Aliza Lowitz, was his date for the evening. We are meeting her at Elmer Holmes Bobst Library in half an hour. If she confirms she was with your professor, then that blows your theory out of the water.”

"You're the best, Jimmy."

"I know. Call my jerk of a boss and tell him that. I deserve a raise!"

"How's life going by the way?" I asked.

"Shit, but it's liveable. I miss you man," he answered frankly like he always did.

"I know. Who wouldn't?" I said and continued my apparently slow reading. Before I reached the end of his notes, Jimmy had parked his spotless, white Buick Enclave opposite the south facade of the twelve story library, along west 3rd street.

"I never could understand what fucking color this building is," Jimmy said as we stepped out of the car.

"It's a kind of reddish, pinkish, faded brown."

"Well, that's another mystery solved by the great detective Costa Papacosta!" he said and started to walk towards the building, beeping his car to lock.

We walked through the main entrance and looked up. The building had surely changed since the last time I was here. Tracy had been a law student here. She would spend hours in the library and time was never enough. I remember standing outside, by my old yet trustworthy banger of a car, smoking another cigarette as she had not finished studying. She would run out apologizing and always rewarded me with one of those passionate wild kisses that as we grow older, we forget to give.

Plexiglass barricades stood tall on each floor and work was undergoing on a fencing construct over the see-through barricades.

"Why are they ruining the place?" I complained.

"They can't seem to be able to stop students leaping to their deaths."

"I remember hearing about a couple of incidents quite a while back..."

"Well, there have been new attempts. One was successful. Somehow, he managed to climb over the barricades and fly to the ground."

I was ready to answer Jimmy with something along the lines of how it was a shame at such a young age to feel that life had nothing to offer you but I did not utter a single word. A very stylish forty-something-year-old woman with chestnut hair and large round brown eyes approached us.

She stood opposite us, took off her reading glasses and introduced herself.

"I am Aliza Lowitz. How do you do?" she asked, but did not wait to receive an answer. "I would prefer if we spoke outside. It is such a fine day, shame to lock ourselves up. I have made sandwiches."

"Guess we do stick out from the crowd. I am Costa Papacosta and this is..."

"Jimmy. Enchantée."

"I'm sure you are. Follow me, boys," she said, and cat-walked herself out the building, leaving us no option but to follow her to what she described her favorite spot on the grass.

"Sit down. It's quite clean, I can assure you. This is where I eat most of my lunches. Here. Hope you like pastrami," she said and passed us our sandwiches.

"Guess it can get stuffy in there with all those books," Jimmy said. Aliza gave him an empty look. She was a librarian. Books were never stuffy to her.

"I respect the books too much to dirty their place with food."

She was an honest lady and that was my favorite characteristic with potential witnesses.

"Aliza. Can I call you Aliza?" I asked.

"That is my name," she replied and bit down into her sandwich. She seemed to be enjoying our little picnic.

"Aliza, we are here to ask you a few questions regarding a history professor, a Michael Johnson?"

"Yes, I already know that. The enchanted fed guy next to you told me so over the phone," she said and took another substantial bite. With a wide smile, I asked her to confirm that she was with the professor on the night of the faculties' gala, the 24th of July. I passed her the photograph of the professor that I had downloaded and enlarged from UCLA's web page.

"Yes, that's him. And yes, we were together that night. He escorted me to the party."

"How well do you know Michael?" Jimmy asked.

"Not so well, but he seems like a pleasant guy. I have a special itch for history and we had met a few times before at various seminars. I participated in his lectures, providing him with all the books he would be needing. I guess to thank me, he asked me out."

"And you were with him the entire party? Afterwards?" I inquired.

"That is a bit of an offensive question," she said, not sounding offended at all.

"I don't mean it that way. I am just trying to form a time frame of his whereabouts," I said and she still did not ask why we were asking all these questions. Not once did she show any signs of wanting to know what this was all about.

"Time frame? Well, he was very punctual. I remember he picked me up at nine o'clock sharp; I was not ready. We went straight to the gala. It must have been past one o'clock when we parked outside my house. He did not stay the night." She stated the last sentence with slight regret.

"Didn't go as well as you wished? If you don't mind me asking that is," I said and smiled for an answer.

"To be completely honest, I thought it was leading somewhere, but the night of the gala, he was a bit... off. He never made a move, so neither did I."

"A bit *off*? Can you elaborate in what manner?" Jimmy asked.

"I know this may seem kind of strange to you, but for me, it mattered. He did not speak about history all night. I mean nothing at all. I had never been with him for more than ten minutes without him saying something related to the past."

"Do you know what hotel he was staying at?"

"The Ritz-Calton, Central Park," she said with admiration and a wide opening of the eyes.

We thanked her for her help, her company and of course, her delicious sandwiches.

"Thank you for adding some spice to my otherwise dull routine."

We started to turn, to walk away when I felt I could not leave without an answer.

"Aliza, can I ask you one last question? Why are you not interested in finding out why we are investigating him?"

She smiled. "I guess most do ask that first. Well, as he was with me, it means he was not where you think he was, not doing what you think he was. Right?"

"That is what we are trying to find out. Thanks again. Have a nice day."

"Weird chick," Jimmy whispered in my ear as we approached his car.

"Helpful chick though. Take us to the hotel."

"Aye, aye El Capitan!" he joked and sped to our destination.

I had no time to waste, so I let Jimmy do his whole FBI emergency performance and in a matter of minutes, we were sitting opposite the hotel's manager explaining that we had no warrant but it was really a matter of life and death.

"Serial killer you say?" the pale, fifty-year-old said, lowering his reading glasses to take a better look at us.

"You do realize I cannot give out information..."

"We are well aware of the circumstances, Mr. Roberts. However, we require no records or any testimonies. Just a simple yes or no to help us with our case. We only need to know if a Michael Johnson stayed here on the night of July, 24th."

He read my face for a second and without replying, turned to his computer's screen. A minute of typing and pressing enter later, he looked up. He took off his glasses and coughed.

"No."

I could not help but smile.

"Though his name does show up on a receipt."

"Meaning?" Jimmy asked.

"Meaning he paid for someone else to stay in the room."

"Who?" I asked.

"Gentlemen, you asked me for a yes or no. No, the man you mentioned did not stay at our hotel. You are placing me in a very discomforting position. I am not at liberty to reveal the names of our guests."

"Mr. Roberts, this man has slaughtered and beheaded a set of young twins. He has murdered innocent women and tortured them in ways I do not wish to describe."

"I am afraid I am going to have to ask you to go," he said.

"Mr. Roberts..."

"Wait, my phone," he said even though his phone made no sound or move. He got up and turned his computer's screen slightly towards us. He walked over to the window, apparently talking on the phone.

Room 317. July 22nd - July 25th. One guest. Alfred T. Lawrence. Billing: Michael D. Johnson.

"I am sorry about that," Mr. Roberts said, placing his phone back on the wooden office desk.

"No problem. We are thankful for your help. Have a good day, sir," I said and left the office satisfied. As the elevator doors opened, Jimmy dialled his secretary and asked for information about an Alfred T. Lawrence.

Either FBI secretaries were amazing or the FBI system was astonishing. Maybe both. All I know was that in the eight-minute drive along Broadway, the one minute along West 4th street, the one minute to park and the two minutes up to the 23rd floor of the Federal Plaza building, Jimmy's secretary had formed a list with all the Alfred T. Lawrence currently residing in the States. We easily cut down the number by using an age margin. Thirty to fifty years of age brought our Alfreds down to forty one. I flicked through their passport card photographs and you can imagine my shock when on the computer screen opposite me appeared the professor, the name Alfred Theodore Lawrence underneath it.

"Michael Johnson is an alias?" Jimmy asked.

"It says here, that he lives in Utah and works as a used car salesman. He is married with three children, a boy and two daughters. How can it be an alias? The professor has lectures every week at UCLA."

"Nothing is making sense. What are you doing?" Jimmy asked as I picked up the phone.

"I'm going to call him. It has a land line listed."

The second between every dial tone seemed to take forever. I was about to give up when a sweet, happy woman's voice was heard.

"Hello?"

"Hello. May I speak to Alfred, please?"

"Sure. Just a sec. Who may I say is calling?"

The question caught me off guard. I was not expecting him to be home.

"The FBI," Jimmy said and winked at me.

"You get more answers and quicker this way," he whispered in my ear.

"The FBI?" she asked and her tone changed. "What do you want with my husband? We run an honest business and..."

"Nothing to do with your business, ma'am. Just a couple of routine questions."

She did not reply. We faintly heard her order the kids out to the garden to play and her calling to her husband.

"Yes?" the man's voice was heard.

"Alfred T. Lawrence?"

"Yes, this is he. My wife said you were with the FBI?"

“Yes, sir. There seems to be a sort of mix up. Did you stay at the Ritz-Carlton in New York last July?”

He paused for a moment before he admitted that he had.

“What was the reason for your stay, sir?” I asked.

“Am I in trouble? What is this about?” he asked, stumbling on every other word.

“Do you know a Michael D. Johnson?”

“Yes, he is my twin brother.”

“Twin brother? Our records show that Michael Johnson has no siblings.”

“Yes, your records would show that. My biological mother gave me up at birth and kept only Michael. She was a seventeen year old girl, unmarried. I guess she thought it was for the best. Anyway, I did not even know about Michael’s existence until last year when he approached me at my work. You can imagine my shock when I saw myself walk into my office. Is he in trouble?”

“Not yet, sir. We are trying to clarify a few details about his whereabouts. So it was you that took the librarian to the ball?”

“Yes. I meant no harm. Michael said he had other engagements and needed my help. He offered me $5,000 and three nights at the Ritz. I would have been mad to turn him down. Things have been rough, with the economy down and all. And suddenly, a rich twin brother shows up out of the blue offering money.”

"Rich, you say?" I asked.

"Yes. You see, Michael ended up for adoption too, to a wealthy family in Los Angeles. He must have been eleven or twelve at the time."

"Why was he given for adoption at such an age?"

"Oh, it was tragic, he said. His... our mother Katie and her partner were shot to death by a burglar."

"Mr. Lawrence, thank you for all your help. May I request that if your brother gets in touch with you, tell him nothing about our conversation and call FBI agent Jimmy Papandreou on 2-1-2-3-8-4-1000."

"Yeah, sure," he said and hung up. I could not believe it. A twin brother. And all along Michael was in Greece.

"Jimmy, get your amazing secretary to check for Michael Johnson's flight to Greece. You search for the Johnson family that adopted him and I will look into his mother's death. And quick. I need to get back to Greece as soon as possible!"

*****

Chapter 39

This time Morpheus did not provide me with sleep. The hours of the flight to Heathrow were agonizing. All the puzzle pieces had fallen into place. Where there were once scattered incomprehensible fragments of events, now stood a clear picture. Katie Bishop gave birth to identical twin boys. One was given up for adoption to a family of farmers in Utah while the second one was named Michael after the father of the mother's partner, Alexandros Petride. When Michael was thirteen, a burglar broke into their apartment and apparently shot both adults dead. The only account of the night's events was that of Michael's. The boy was taken into custody and sent to an orphanage that dealt with children and teens with traumatizing pasts. The psychologist reports of that time spoke of a highly intelligent and cunning adolescent. The boy often got into fights with other children and the orphanage staff as he did not respond well to being touched. Psychologists suspected abuse. However Michael never opened up in any of his sessions. He only seemed to get along well with the orphanage's benefactor, Mrs. Rebecca Johnson, a wealthy philanthropist from Los Angeles who eventually adopted the smart and handsome teenager. The Johnson family raised him like one of their own and offered the intelligent youth the finest education. He grew up on the Johnson's ranch where without a doubt, he learned how the horses were given sedatives. The family spent most of their summers in Greece, cruising the Greek islands on their yacht. Young Michael had a talent for sailing and participated in many local races and events. The Johnson family was acquainted with the Blair family and Mrs. Rebecca organized many charity events with Eric Blair's mother. Undoubtedly, Michael heard about the Blair's divorce and their plans to travel to Greece. He had flown to Greece through Mexico on the 5th of June, having crossed the border by car and he was in Cyprus at the time of the Aphrodite murder. He was in Greece at the time of the twins' murder. He was in Lemnos at the time of the attack of the blacksmith. I was positive that Michael D. Johnson was The Olympus Killer.

I had called the police in Lemnos and had ordered them to not allow him to exit the island. I planned to tell Ioli myself about everything I had discovered and then go to Lemnos to arrest him.

The plane finally landed in rainy London and my phone searched for a network. Soon, multiple messages arrived in my inbox. One stood out amongst the rest.

Captain Papacosta, this is Lieutenant Andreas with the Lemnos Police. We informed the airport and port authorities of your request, only to be told that Michael Johnson has already left the island on a flight to Athens. We have notified central authorities and he will not be permitted to exit the country.

I immediately called Ioli. This was not the way I planned for her to find out, but I had to warn her.

The mobile number you have called is currently unavailable; please call again later...

“Fuck!” I yelled, causing many passersby to turn and give me disapproving looks. I honestly could not remember when the last time I cursed was. I even ducked slightly, expecting my mama’s hand to slap me on the back of my head. My nearly five-hour flight to Athens left in half an hour. I called headquarters and warned them of the situation and asked for backup to immediately go to my apartment.

As soon as the plane came to a horizontal position, I was out of my chair pacing up and down the plane’s corridor causing panic to my fellow flyers.

“I’m ok. I’m not a terrorist. I’m just agitated,” I informed the worried flight attendant. Lines of comforting words and three glasses of straight scotch later, I was back in my seat playing worst case scenarios in my mind’s home theatre. The not knowing was eating me up — so many advances in technology and still no signal on planes. Once again, I was out of my prison of a chair and banging on the culprit’s door, demanding to talk to the pilot. He was quite polite considering my menacing manner and he got in touch with Athens for me. Still no word of Ioli or Michael. The worst case scenario was underway.

Finally, the plane started to descend to Athens. I stepped off the plane and ran to the exit. My luggage of two trousers, a few shirts, three boxers and four pairs of black socks became even more unimportant to me and my brown, leather carrier bag was left to travel round and round until the police hauled it away to x-ray it.

A patrol car waited for me outside to deliver the fact that neither of them had been located. The car sped down the Attiki Odos highway and entered the grand city of Athens. Minutes before arriving at police headquarters, the car's silence was broken by an incoming message over the police radio.

"Patrol vehicle AE135, please come in."

"This is AE135, center control, please go ahead," the driver replied.

"Ioli Cara and Michael Johnson have been sighted by a taxi driver. They are together. He claims to have dropped them off at the King George Palace hotel. The swat team and all available vehicles have been dispatched to the location."

"Get me there, now!" I barked and closed my eyes in pain of regret. You always tell your partner everything and I had kept Ioli in the dark. If she came to any harm, it was in my hands.

I held my gun tightly between my hands and ran up to the hotel room door and exhaled in relief as I heard Ioli talking. The swat team rammed the door down and I leaped into the room.

Minutes later, I was leaving the room in fear and trepidation for Ioli's life. She was losing blood fast as the paramedics lifted her into the back of the ambulance. I jumped in and sat beside her, taking her cold hand into mine.

"Come on, Cara. You're a fighter. Don't you give up on me."

"Sir, you need to stay calm and sit back and let us do our job," the paramedic ordered.

"I am so sorry," I whispered in her ear, kissed her forehead and sat back as ordered.

*****

Chapter 40

Hospitals were such cold places. The lack of color and the lack of smiles combined with an overdose of death spread the chills through the narrow halls. I took refuge in a grey metal chair and my body's exhaustion finally got the best of me. Waves of drowsiness overcame me and I fell asleep. My sweet daughter, my companion in my dreams, waited for me once again.

"Is Ioli going to come and play with me, daddy?" she asked and laughed as she ran through the park.

"I hope not, baby. She still has work to do."

"When are *you* going to come to me, daddy? You still do want to come, right? Living is not worth it without me," she whispered as she twirled around me.

"Daddy catches bad guys, maybe one of them will send me to you one of these days," I smiled back to her.

"Captain Papacosta?"

"Yes, baby girl?"

"Captain Papacosta?" the doctor raised his voice yanking me out of my dreamland. The look on his face startled me.

"What time is it? Is the surgery over? How's Ioli? Talk to me, man. Don't just stand there!"

"The three hour surgery is over. She is alive..."

“Thank God! Sweet Mary, Mother of Christ...”

“*However*, she is still in a coma and on life support. The next few days will be critical. We can only hope and pray for the best. We have notified the family and...”

The rest of his words turned into low frequency noise. The words *coma* and *life support* were constantly repeated inside my mind.

The only highlight of the next day was meeting Ioli’s parents. Mr. Cara was an original Cretan. Tall, manly and proud, with a long, thick, well-maintained moustache. Mrs. Cara was the epitome of a Greek woman of her era. Though hard-working, she never looked tired and in her eyes, you witnessed Greece coming alive.

I would show up every day at lunch time with two chicken gyrous filled with extra tzatziki — her favorite. If Ioli woke up, I knew it would be for lunch or maybe even dinner.

I would say my “good day” to her parents and leave the food by her side. The next six hours I spent with my new friend: my grey, hallway chair. Then, it was down to Giorgo’s Grill House to order pork chops with fries for her dinner. I would say my “good evening” to her parents and replace the food trays.

On the fourth evening of replacing trays, Ioli’s mother asked me to stay. Her father Gianni was asleep on the uncomfortable-looking armchair under the oval window.

“You have trouble relaxing,” she said in a low voice. “Just like my daughter, always moving, always thinking. Sit down, my child.”

I mechanically pulled a plastic chair to my side and sat opposite her. She placed her hard-working, worn-in, wrinkled hands upon mine.

"You really care for her, don't you?"

"She is one of a kind. You have an amazing daughter, Mrs. Cara."

"On that we agree," she said with a warm, motherly, gentle smile that did not manage to change the sorrow in her eyes.

"I'm so sorry..."

"What are you sorry about?" she interrupted me.

"I should have protected her; I should have been there for her. This is all my fault. If only I had..."

"*If* was planted and it never grew, my grandma used to say. No need for *ifs*. Nothing comes from an *if*. Anyway, you can apologize to her when she wakes up. Do not apologize to me."

She read the look on my face and anger painted her next words. She leaned forward and spoke from behind her teeth.

"Now you listen here, boy. Don't you go looking sad on me. She *will* wake up, you hear me?"

I nodded in response, lost for words. She sat back into her armchair.

"Let me tell you a few short stories, Captain. When Ioli was born, doctors told me that due to my constant working during my pregnancy, as they so tactfully put it, she would have problems breathing right. Her lungs had not fully developed or something like that. I sat there, beside her incubator, thinking of a lifetime of things that my poor child would not be able to do. A month or so later, this old doctor walks up to me with these tests in his right hand, explaining to me that my baby was fine and her lungs had performed some sort of miraculous recovery. When Ioli was seven, she was out riding her bike with the neighborhood boys when a pickup truck came round the corner and knocked her flying off the bike and threw her to the ground. Once again, more foolish doctors advised me to not have high hopes as most likely she would have difficulties walking. Years of physiotherapy later and I had a teenage daughter wearing God knows how many inch high heels, capable of running in them!" she said and chuckled. She looked straight at me and continued. "I will never forget the day the barn of the Zampetaki family, next door to us, caught fire. Their youngest, a four year old boy, was in there playing. Ioli must have been seventeen at the time. Without any hesitation whatsoever, she ran into that barn searching for the screaming boy. You can imagine the shock on my face when the barn collapsed right before our eyes. Maria Zampetaki walked up to me to comfort each other over our loss, but I knew and I was right. She came out of those wooden, burnt, charcoal ruins, boy in arms with only a few hairs burnt at the edges. And you think a silly bullet is enough to take my Ioli out? No sad looks, Captain. You keep bringing in the food and my girl has a good appetite!"

I stood up and with tears in my eyes, I kissed her on the cheek.

"Now I know where Ioli gets everything good from. I'll see you tomorrow, Mrs. Cara. Food in hand, of course!"

I kept my promise and the next day, at lunch time, I walked into the small room with gyrous in my hand. I stroked her black hair and turned to leave when I heard her weak voice say, "those better fucking have extra tzatziki in them! Come in here, every day, busting open my nose with your cheap food from that shit hole grill house of yours!"

I had no reply. I just turned and smiled in relief.

"Child, watch your language!" a teary-eyed Gianni said.

"As if she ever listened to that before," Anna laughed and hugged her daughter.

"Is someone going to feed me or what? I'm starving. What do they put in these tubes? Liquid vegetables?"

*****

EPILOGUE

Ioli was not the only one to survive surgery that day. Michael pulled through too, though with a small 'gift'. Due to lung puncture and the infection that followed, he had to wheel around an oxygen tank for the rest of his life. He did not seem to mind. He did not speak a single word throughout his trial. He did not even move a facial muscle as the judge announced his sentence. Life without any chance of parole.

In the dark cell room numbered 17, Michael sat on the left bunk bed, face in hands and lost in his thoughts.

"Where are you now, *Alexander the Great*? Huh? To see your Gods *dead* by my hand! They think they have stopped me!" he whispered to himself and laughed out loud.

"Seven down and only a few to go! I will kill my demons! I will kill *ALL* the Gods!"

"Yo, psycho, keep it down. I don't want to listen to your crap!" yelled his cell mate, clearly annoyed by his behavior.

Michael lifted his head up slowly and looked straight at the man. He stared at him for a good whole minute and then asked calmly, "and what do you do for a living?"

The man stood there, taken aback by the odd question.

"Listen dude, I am a captain in the army and I have just killed my wife so watch it, will you? You don't want to piss me off," he threatened, but Michael heard nothing after the word army.

"*Army* you say! Well, won't you make a perfect *Ares*!"

The End...

About the author:

Luke Christodoulou is an author, a poet and an English teacher (MA Applied Linguistics - University of Birmingham). He is, also, a coffee-movie-book-Nutella lover. His books have been widely translated and are available in five languages (with more on the way).

His first book, THE OLYMPUS KILLER (#1 Bestseller - Thrillers), was released in April, 2014. The book was voted Book Of The Month for May on Goodreads (Psychological Thrillers). The book continued to be a fan favorite on Goodreads and was voted BOTM for June in the group Nothing Better Than Reading. In October, it was BOTM in the group Ebook Miner, proving it was one of the most talked-about thrillers of 2014.

The second stand-alone thriller from the series, THE CHURCH MURDERS, was released April, 2015 to widespread critical and fan acclaim. The Church Murders became a bestseller in its categories throughout the summer and was nominated as Book Of The Month in three different Goodreads groups.

DEATH OF A BRIDE was the third Greek Island Mystery to be released. Released in April, 2016 it followed in the footsteps of its successful predecessors. From its first week in release it hit the number one spot for books set in Greece.

MURDER ON DISPLAY came out in 2017 and enriched the series.

HOTEL MURDER, the fifth and 'final' book in the series, followed in early 2018.

Luke Christodoulou has also ventured into 'children's book land' and released 24 MODERNIZED AESOP FABLES, retelling old stories with new elements and settings. The book, also, features sections for parents, which include discussions, questions, games and activities.

He is currently working on his next project, a different kind of book which he is secretive about.

He resides in Limassol, Cyprus with his loving wife, his chatty daughter and his crazy newborn son.

Hobbies include travelling the Greek Islands discovering new food and possible murder sites for his stories. He, also, enjoys telling people that he 'kills people for a living'.

Find out more and keep in touch:

https://twitter.com/ @OlympusKiller

https://www.facebook.com/pages/Greek-Island-Mysteries/712190782134816

http://greekislandmysteries.webs.com/ (Subscribe and receive notice when the next book in the series is released)

Feel free to add me:

https://www.facebook.com/luke.christodoulouauthor

Note to readers:

First of all, thank you for choosing my book for your leisure.

If you enjoyed the book (and I hope you have), please help spread the word. You know the way! A review and a five star rating goes a long way (hint hint).

For any errors you may have noticed or questions about the story, let me know: christodoulouluke@gmail.com